# Feels Like

# Home

# Brooke Harris

1

# 1

Eva looked up at an almost cloudless sky. *Where was the snow even falling from?* It was as if even the weather was trying to sympathise. It was so cold, a couple of degrees above freezing at most. A thick blanket of snow covered the ground, glistening under the winter sun. The usually busy road that looped around the cemetery was deserted of cars and people. Branches of the large, old oak trees that lined the sidewalk bowed under the weight of snow scattered all over them. They were nature's guard of honour leading the way to the grave.

Eva stepped off the sidewalk. The slim, high heels of her black patent, knee-high boots were ridiculously impractical in this kind of weather. She stood in the middle of the road and looked back at her footprints; the only evidence that anyone had passed by that way in the last day or so. She closed her eyes, tilted her head toward the sky, and stuck out her tongue. The snowflakes melted as soon as they touched her tongue and she smiled. For the first time in eleven years, she smiled while thinking of her father.

*'Never eat yellow snow,'* he'd advised her one harsh Jersey winter. She couldn't have been more than four or five years old, but she remembered it as clearly as if it were yesterday. Her whole family had been out playing in the backyard. Their hands

were blue from the cold as they made a huge snowman and were distracted every so often by snowball fights. She could almost hear their laughter now. That was before her mother started spending half the day in bed with her head under the pillow. And before her father drank until he fell down in a pool of his own vomit. Before her sister cried herself to sleep every night. And before Eva knew what it was like to feel hollow inside.

Eva's eyes jolted open feeling a hand on her shoulder and she spun around.

'Hey. The driver said he's going to try to come around from the other side. The snow is too deep at the foot of the hill and the hearse is slipping. He said he'll be there in about fifteen minutes. We should get going,' Shelly said.

'Okay. Thanks, Shell.'

Shelly made her way back to the sidewalk, taking large steps and waddling like a little duckling learning how to walk. Eva followed, slipping equally as much. Catching up with Shelly, Eva linked her arm and gained some balance.

'Thank you for coming,' Eva said, staring at the ground as they walked. She couldn't bring herself to look at Shelly. She'd already glimpsed the sympathy in Shelly's eyes earlier. Sympathy she wasn't sure she deserved or wanted. She couldn't bear to see it again.

'What are you like? You don't have to thank me. This is what friends do. They stick by each other through the shitty times.'

'And this is a shitty time.' Eva nodded, still staring at the ground.

'The shittiest.'

'It's getting colder,' Eva said, shivering.

It wasn't. If anything, it was thawing a little. But Eva was looking for an excuse to change the conversation.

'I still wish you'd just come and stay with me. That hotel must be costing you a fortune,' Shelly said, pulling a face at Eva's lame-ass attempt to discuss the weather.

'HTK is paying,' Eva explained.

'Oh, wow. Well, that's nice of them.'

'Pam called shortly after we landed last week. Apparently, news travels fast. Mr. Thompson heard about what happened to Julian and the company wanted to offer their sympathies. Throwing money at me is the best way they know how. They're covering Melissa and my mom's room, too. It's good that we're all staying in the same place. Or it would be if...'

'Melissa still not talking to you, then?' Shelly said as Eva trailed off midsentence.

'Not really.' Eva shrugged.

Melissa had made it very clear from the moment she and Eva were reunited that she wasn't interested in rekindling their relationship. She was bitter and angry with Eva for abandoning her, and Eva understood; she had every right to be. But it didn't stop it from hurting. *Sometimes things are so badly broken they can never be repaired*, Eva thought. Maybe Eva's relationship with her sister was one of those things. Eva tried not to think about it. Especially not now.

'Must be nice to work for a company like that,' Shelly said interrupting Eva's wallowing.

Eva looked at Shelly for the first time, her face pinching like she might laugh. 'Erm, you work for Ignite Technologies. I don't think any boss lavishes his staff in quite the same way as your boss does.'

'Yeah, I know. But…' Shelly sighed. 'It's all very different now since… Well, you know, since everything that has happened with Julian.'

This time Eva didn't make an effort to change the subject. She just stopped talking. Her whole body was aching with sadness. It pulled her shoulders down and made her crouch like a little old woman; like if she stood up tall and straight, the weight of everything that had happened in the last few days might be too heavy and she would snap.

'We're here,' Shelly said suddenly, as if the large, wrought-iron cemetery gates weren't already confirmation. 'You going to be okay?'

Eva shrugged her shoulders again. 'I have to be.'

They had reached the open grave just moments before the hearse crept in through the opposite gate.

A thin, haggard lady stood too close to the edge of the freshly dug grave. A younger, slightly taller woman stood beside her, but far enough back that she didn't look like she might topple into the hole in the ground at any second.

'Your mum and sister,' Shelly said.

Eva nodded, and still linking Shelly's arm, she walked towards them.

'Mom, step back, please. You're too close to the edge there,' Eva said.

The lady turned around. Her pretty face appeared weather-beaten and her once warm blue eyes that Eva remembered so well were an icy grey and watering. 'Life with your father meant I was always too close to the edge, Evangeline. I don't want to change the habit of a lifetime now.'

Eva looked at her sister. But Melissa shook her head. 'Just leave her. I have her. I always have.'

Eva swallowed hard. Now was not the appropriate time for Melissa to take a dig, but she had done it nonetheless. Eva felt Shelly's grip tighten on her arm. Melissa's bitchy comment hadn't gone unnoticed by Shelly, either.

'This won't take more than half an hour. And then I'm taking you back with me. No arguments this time,' Shelly whispered.

7

The little old priest shuffled out from his little old car and took his place at the head of the grave as the pallbearers lowered a generic, pine coffin into the ground.

'Dearly beloved. We are gathered here today to say goodbye to our friend and loved one, Cameron Andrews.'

There were only four people at the graveside, but the priest spoke loudly and clearly as if addressing a whole congregation of mourners.

'I met Cameron just once, many years ago. He'd stumbled into my church here in Dun Laoghaire late one Saturday afternoon. He didn't waste any time in telling me that he'd mistaken the house of God for a pub and he even asked if Jesus served Guinness. But I saw past the jokes. And Cameron knew it. He swapped his Guinness for a cup of tea that afternoon and we talked for hours. He was a broken man in need of guidance. He told me how he had lost his way in life, made mistakes, and hurt the people he loved the most in this world. I told him that saying sorry wasn't enough; he would have to show it. I didn't see Cameron after that day and I always hoped he found his way home and back into the loving arms of his family.'

The priest paused and coughed hard and Eva thought he might cry. Her chest hurt. A priest, thousands of miles away from Cameron's home, had managed to get to know her father better in an afternoon than Eva had her whole life.

'I look at you all now, Samantha, Melissa, and Evangeline, dressed in black and standing here in the freezing cold saying good-bye. And I know, what I hope Cameron realised before his passing, is that although you're not saying it with words, your presence here today is showing that the love in your family was only ever scratched and never truly broken.'

Samantha bent forward and an animal-like wail burst out of her. Eva stood alert as her mother verged closer still to the edge of the grave. Melissa's arms crept around Samantha's waist and eased her gently back from the edge. Samantha shook herself free and dropped to her knees. She used the tips of her fingers to brush away the snow to reveal a small patch of green. She clasped her fist around the frosty grass and pulled up a clump as she stood up.

'You always loved Ireland, Cam. Even more than you loved me, I think. Rest in peace.'

Samantha opened her hand and blades of grass rained from her palm. They landed scattered across the top of the coffin. The bright green was a stark contrast to the dreary pine box cradled in the black-brown muck of the earth. Eva couldn't look away; her eyes were drawn to the chrome plaque now framed with grass.

**RIP**

**Cameron Andrews**

**Beloved Husband and Father.**

**Gone but not forgotten.**

'Remembered for all the wrong reasons,' Eva mumbled under her breath as she turned away.

'I heard that,' Melissa said, finally speaking.

Eva turned back around.

'If you can't say anything nice, then maybe you shouldn't be here,' Melissa added.

Dark black crescent -moons rested under Melissa's eyes, and she was far too thin. But her words carried the weight of a heavyweight boxer hitting Eva straight in the chest.

'Mel, that's not fair. I've as much right to say good-bye as you do,' Eva protested.

'You gave up the right to say anything when you ran away, Eva. Jesus Christ, do you know that at one point Mom thought you might have been dead? Dead, Eva. Can you imagine how hard that was?'

'I...I...I'm sorry,' Eva said.

'I know you are. But that doesn't change the past.'

'What do you want me to say?'

'Nothing,' Melissa snapped dryly. 'There's nothing you can say. But don't think that you can send your boyfriend to come be a knight in shining armour and suddenly we'll all be a happy family again. Life isn't that simple.'

'I didn't send Julian. I didn't even know he was coming,' Eva said, the weight of the day taking its toll on her voice as much as her body. She ached for the comfort of Julian's arms around her.

Melissa pulled a face and shrugged, but she wasn't convincing Eva of her indifference. The pain in her eyes couldn't be hidden with a shake of the shoulders. Melissa had already made it clear that her relationship with Eva was over. They were sisters in blood but nothing else. Melissa had promised to never forgive Eva for running out on her family. And the venom in Melissa's eyes every time she looked at her told Eva she wasn't bluffing.

'Oh, for fuck's sake. Would you get over yourself? Both of you,' Shelly said stepping forward. 'Julian risked his life to save yours. The least you could do is be grateful.'

'Okay, that's enough,' Samantha said loudly, her eyes barely open.

The three girls stood silently, like scolded schoolchildren.

'Thank you, Father O'Malley. We're very grateful for your time.' Samantha shook the priest's hand and slowly walked away, never looking back at the three girls or her husband's open grave.

Melissa followed immediately. Eva acknowledged and thanked the priest with little more than a head nod, and she and Shelly reluctantly walked after Melissa and Samantha.

11

'She has every right to be angry, Shell,' Eva whispered, out of Melissa and Samantha's earshot, as she and Shelly walked side-by-side with their heads bowed.

'And she has every right to get a grip, Eva. She'd still be stuck in that hellhole if it wasn't for you and Julian.'

Eva smiled. Shelly's loyalty always warmed her heart. 'You're sweet, Shell. But I think it'll take more than a fancy hotel room in a country Melissa doesn't know to fix things for us. She's pretty much homeless and unemployed now. And she sees that as Julian's and my fault.'

'And what about your mother? How are things with you two?'

'She's talking to me. That's a start. But I don't think I'm her favourite person right now, either. I know it's understandable. I expected it, to be honest. I just wasn't expecting it to feel quite *this* crappy.'

Shelly's expression wore a seriousness that Eva wasn't used to seeing. 'You know you're not the wicked witch in all of this, Eva. Your mother thinks she needs to forgive you, yeah? Well, she needs to earn your forgiveness, too. It's got to be a give and take thing on both your sides.'

'I left, Shell. I abandoned them.'

'Bollocks. You were a kid. Your mom should have protected you.'

Eva shook her head, sadly. 'She couldn't even protect herself.'

'Yeah, I get that,' Shelly replied, softly, 'but you can't beat yourself up because your parents sucked at being parents.'

'They…they didn't always.'

'Yeah. And you didn't always suck at being their kid. Just please don't blame yourself, Eva. I hate seeing you like this.' Shelly sighed. 'God, Eva. I wish there was something I could do.'

'You're here. That's something.' Eva smiled.

Shelly clasped Eva's hands in hers and gave a little squeeze. 'I'll always be here.'

'Thanks, Shell.'

'Well, except for now,' Shelly's said, her lips twisting to one side.

'What?'

'I'm going to leave you to it.' Shelly tilted her head towards a wonky wooden bench near the gate of the cemetery where Samantha and Melissa had just sat down. 'Just talk. It can't do any harm. I'll call you later.'

Eva took a deep breath and nodded. She watched as Shelly passed her mother and sister, silently raising her hand to say good-bye. Samantha returned the wave as Shelly rounded the gate and was gone. Eva brushed the last of the snow off the bench and sat beside Samantha.

13

## 2

Fresh snow began to fall, but Eva didn't notice the revived chill in the air. Her fingers were blue around the knuckles and her lips had gone a little numb, but she was warm inside. She sat contentedly and listened as her mother told stories of two little girls and the mischief they got up to as children. Eva could see the smile in Melissa's eyes and she knew her sister remembered some of the funny anecdotes Samantha shared, even if she wouldn't admit it.

'You were so headstrong as a little girl, Eva. Your father used to say that he pitied any man who would dare take you on,' Samantha said.

*People change, unfortunately.* 'Well, life is a lot easier when you're two, Mom. All you have to do is pee in your pants to make your point,' Eva sighed.

'Yes, I'd certainly like to think you have found better ways to argue than lack of bladder control,' Samantha replied with a wink and a big, toothy grin.

Samantha and Eva laughed, but Melissa was present in body only. Samantha stood up and stretched her arms over her head and back down by her sides.

'Damn arthritis,' Samantha said, taking exaggerated long strides to stretch out her legs.

Melissa leaned forward on the bench, watching Samantha with concern as she walked around in a large circle. Samantha returned to the bench after a few painfully silent minutes and sat between Eva and the bench end, forcing Eva to scoot over to sit right beside her sister. *Arthritis, my ass*, Eva thought, rolling her eyes at her mother's transparent attempt to push her daughters closer together. Melissa and Eva might have been side-by-side physically, but emotionally, there was a world of distance between them.

'You know, Mel. You used to take Eva to bed with you every Sunday morning and read stories. You'd be there for hours together,' Samantha continued.

Eva smiled, remembering the *Elves and the Shoemaker*, her favourite. Melissa used to talk in a funny, squeaky voice when she read the elves' part. The memory warmed Eva inside; she could almost feel the comfort of Melissa's arms around her as they lay tucked up in bed on a Sunday morning.

'Well, something had to drown out the sound of you and Dad arguing,' Melissa snapped, leaning over Eva to glare at Samantha.

Eva's heart sank. She'd never realised Melissa had gone to such lengths to protect her from the shit going on in their house. Two years is practically no gap at all when you're twenty-seven and twenty-nine. But rewind twenty years, and the weight of protecting her younger sister had fallen heavily on Melissa's shoulders. Eva had been too young to even notice.

Samantha turned sideways on the bench to face her daughters. 'I owe you both an apology, don't I?'

'No. No, you don't,' Eva assured. 'It's Dad who should have apologised. Years ago.'

'Your father wasn't a bad person, Eva,' Samantha said, sternly.

'What? Just misunderstood.' Eva's sarcasm left a bitter taste in her mouth.

'No. I was the misunderstood one. Depression is a cruel illness, Eva. Not everyone understands how hard it is.'

'Anyone would be depressed being married to that man,' Eva replied dryly.

'You were too young to understand, Eva. You both were,' Samantha said making an effort to include an ever-distant Melissa in the conversation.

'I understand depression, Mom. I know what it feels like to have no hope...'

'Well, I'm sorry that you understand that, Eva. I really wish you had no idea what it felt like to feel that way,' Samantha said, dabbing just under her eyes with the tips of her fingers.

Eva shrugged her shoulders. She didn't have a reply to something that profound.

'Your father understood, or at least he tried hard to. He was okay that I was broken. He just wasn't okay with the fact that he couldn't fix me.'

'So he thought he'd beat sense into you instead?' Eva groaned.

'He thought he could drink his problems away,' Samantha replied.

'That's ridiculous. Drinking made it all so much worse.' Eva rolled her eyes. This conversation was crazy. She couldn't believe that, after all these years, all her mother wanted to do was defend a man who had destroyed their lives.

'Was it stupid? Yes, of course,' Samantha admitted without hesitation. 'But he was only human, Eva. And we all make mistakes. We can see how bad it made everything now, in hindsight, but at the time, your father was blind to the damage he was causing.'

'Sorry, Mom. I'm not buying this,' Melissa interrupted, bristling. 'No matter how bad his drinking problem was, it was no excuse for domestic violence.'

It was the first sign of real emotion from Melissa that Eva had seen. It was good. Not good that Melissa was angry and bitter, but good that she could feel. Melissa had worn a frozen expression up to this point, and Eva wasn't sure if she was just as cold on the inside, too. Eva wanted to grab Melissa and hug her tight. But something stopped her and she wasn't sure what. Years of hiding her emotions, maybe. The distance that had grown between them. The damage that Eva had caused by running away. All of it, none of it. Just time. Years and years passing. Eva's family had grown to become strangers. You didn't grab strangers and hug them; even if you did have the same blood running through your veins.

'Drinking wasn't all to blame, you know,' Samantha continued. 'I pushed his buttons, too.'

'You can't blame yourself, Mom,' Eva said, snapping out of the daze she had fallen into. 'Dammit. Why do victims of abuse do that?'

'I don't blame myself, Evangeline. I blame both of us. We were never good for each other. Yes, we were crazy in love. But sometimes love isn't enough. We were two broken souls. We were a bad combination.'

Melissa snorted, exaggerating her intolerance for the conversation.

Eva's upper lip stiffened as she stared at her mother. 'Are we *still* talking about you and Dad?'

'I am,' Samantha replied quickly, 'but the look on your face tells me that you are not.'

Eva closed her eyes. Melissa snorted again and Eva's patience was wearing thin. She didn't want to be there.

'Do you love him, Eva? This Julian Harte,' Samantha said Julian's name as if it meant something terrible in a language Eva didn't understand.

Eva nodded.

'And does he love you?'

'Yes. He really does.'

Melissa snorted for a third time.

Eva spun around to face her sister. 'Oh, my God, will you stop doing that. It's infuriating.'

Melissa looked like she might fall off the bench.

'I get it. You're pissed off at me. You're pissed off at Mom. You're pissed off at the world. Fair enough. But stop fucking snorting all over me. Get a goddamn tissue if you need to but give me a break. I didn't drag you here. Julian did. And the words you're looking for, when you finally get that snot out of your throat, are thank you. You need to say thank you. And you can tell Julian yourself if he wakes up.' Eva paused to catch her breath. '*When* he wakes up...I...I...*when*, I mean when. You can tell him when he wakes up.'

Eva couldn't bring herself to admit that Julian might not wake up. Saying those words out loud made Julian's condition real. And she couldn't handle real. Not now. Maybe not ever.

Eva jumped, feeling her mother's hand suddenly on her shoulder. 'And his wife, Eva. What about her? She must be hurting, too.'

'I didn't even know he had a wife until a few days ago,' Eva said, beginning to unravel.

'You're in love with a married man who kept his wife a secret from you. That's a dangerous game he's playing.' Samantha frowned.

Eva's stomach churned at her mother's choice of words. *Games, games, fucking games.* 'It's…it's complicated.'

'I can see that. What I don't understand is why you wouldn't run a mile.'

Eva forced a painful size lump of air down her throat. 'Run? I'm good at running away, aren't I?'

Samantha dropped her head. 'That wasn't what I meant, sweetheart.'

'Yeah, I know. Sorry.'

Samantha took Eva's icy hands and wrapped her gloved fingers around them, squeezing gently. 'Julian Harte has given you back to me. Both of you. And I am grateful. I am. But he almost got you both killed the process. I can't help but worry that he is a dangerous man.'

'No!' Eva pulled her hands free. 'Julian saved us. He's not responsible for this mess. Nathan got us into trouble. Nathan. Not Julian.'

'That Shelly girl's boyfriend,' Melissa said joining the conversation.

20

'Sorta boyfriend. Yes.' Eva sighed. She wasn't painting the people in her life in a very positive light.

'Let me guess? It's complicated,' Samantha said gently, but it still came out patronising.

Eva grimaced, eyeing the gate. She couldn't wait to get the hell out of there.

'Oh, Evangeline. I'm in no position to judge. I'm your mother, but we barely know each other, and it's all my fault for not being strong enough to stand up to the man I love. I just don't want to see you make the same mistakes I did.'

'Julian would never hurt me, Mom.'

'Emotional bruises are just as bad, if not worse, than physical ones, Eva. I should know. I inflicted enough of those on your father over the years.' Samantha's voice was barely above a whisper.

'What? Because you sent him to prison for the terrible things he did?'

'I had no choice. If I hadn't, I honestly believe he would have drunk himself to death.'

'So, what? You saved him by putting him behind bars,' Eva said, caustically.

'I saved him the only way I knew how. By keeping us apart. The mistakes of the past were as much mine as they were his. Don't hate your father, Eva. Allow yourself to grieve for a man who loved you.'

Eva shook her head, saddened that her mother was attempting to defend the monster that was once her husband. She thought about telling Samantha about the damage Cameron had caused and how he had destroyed Julian's family, but she held her tongue. Samantha didn't need to bear the burden of that knowledge. *What good would it do now?*

'Mom, we should go,' Melissa said out of nowhere.

Samantha nodded and stood up. Eva's heart sank watching her mother rush to obey, as always.

'Maybe you could join us for lunch back at the hotel?' Samantha said, smiling at Eva.

Eva returned Samantha's smile, but Melissa cut across Eva before she had a chance to reply.

'I'm sure *she* is busy, Mom.' Melissa was clearly refusing to say Eva's name. That hurt even more than the hate in her eyes. 'And I'm not hungry, anyway,' Melissa finished.

Eva looked at Melissa's wafer-like body. Her coat fell from her shoulders like there was no body underneath. She was quite obviously famished and had been for years. If she didn't want to have lunch with Eva, that was fine, but Eva shook her head at Melissa's tantrum-like reasoning.

'Okay, no problem. We can just get coffee, then. What do you say, Eva? You're heading back that way anyway, aren't you? Can you spare an hour?' Samantha pleaded.

Melissa turned her back and walked away. But Samantha stayed put, smiling and waiting for an answer.

*Maybe Samantha wasn't quite the pushover I remembered after all,* Eva thought gladly.

'I'm really sorry. I can't. I've somewhere I need to be,' Eva said.

'The hospital?' Samantha asked, but it was less of a question and more of an accusation.

'Yes.'

'Can you wait another couple of hours? We fly back in just a few days. It would be nice to catch up some more. I'm so enjoying talking with my girls.'

The tears glistening in Samantha's eyes hurt Eva's heart. And despite Melissa's icy behaviour, Eva was enjoying catching up, too.

'We will spend more time together, I promise. I want that, too. I just really can't right now. I have to go. I need to be there when Julian wakes up.'

Samantha nodded her understanding as the tears escaped her eyes. 'Okay, sweetheart. Okay.'

Eva could see in Samantha's face what she wouldn't dare say out loud. Samantha didn't think Julian would make it. But she didn't know him. *Julian could fight anything,* Eva thought. Trying desperately to believe herself.

'I hope he wakes up soon,' Melissa said, half turning around. It was a throwaway comment, but there was no signature snort or roll of the eyes, and at that moment, Eva allowed herself to believe that Melissa truly meant it.

'Me, too.' Eva sighed, trying desperately not to fall apart completely. 'Me, too.'

# 3

Julian lifted his head all of about two inches off the pillow before letting it drop back down. *Sweet Jesus, moving hurt.* He cast one eye around the room. Creamy-grey ceiling tiles that were probably once white were spaced evenly overhead. The room was offensively bright and opening more than one eye at a time wasn't going to happen while his head hurt this much. He lifted his arms one at a time and sighed at the bruises. He had cannulas in each arm and one in his left hand. His arms were black and blue from just inside his elbows to his wrist. *Someone really sucked at their job*, he thought, unimpressed with his puncture wounds. His bare chest was dotted with sticky white circles with wires connected to a bedside monitor that irritatingly beeped every few seconds. A light, white cotton sheet had been tucked around him at just above his naked waist. A nurse sat at the end of his bed with a clipboard resting across her knee. She hadn't noticed he was awake yet. He closed his eye and thought about going back to sleep.

*Ugh.* He could feel her hovering over him, gauging him. Medically necessary as it might have been, it was irritating as shit.

'Julian, Julian, are you with us?' she asked with a distinctive country lit.

*What the hell hospital was he in?* It definitely wasn't Dublin.

'Julian. Open your eyes if you can hear me.'

Julian thought about it, but the searing pain in his temples argued against her request. He kept them firmly shut.

'You're in Limerick Hospital, Julian. We've been keeping you in an induced coma.'

*Coma? What the fuck?*

'For how long?' Julian said. Finally accepting the pain, he opened his eyes and attempted to sit up.

The nurse's hands were on his shoulders immediately, pushing him back. 'Shh, don't rush things. Just lie back. You're bound to be a little woozy.'

'How long?' he repeated, ignoring her request to lie down and instead sat completely upright. He thought he might fall over at one point, but he kept the position regardless.

'Almost a week now. There were some complications.'

'A week?' *Jesus.*

'You've been very ill.'

Julian raised both eyebrows and glanced around the room, taking in a better view now that he was sitting up. 'Yes. I got that,' he said with a sarcastic nod.

'How are you feeling?' She continued moving away slightly to sit on the end of his bed again.

Julian eyed her up and down. She was about his age and pretty-ish. Not his type. She was a peroxide blonde and painfully bubbly. Despite her efforts to be friendly and caring, Julian really hoped he wouldn't be stuck with her perched on the end of his bed for a twelve-hour shift.

'Do you have to stay here?' he asked dryly.

She smiled. 'Yes, you have me all to yourself. It's policy. Every patient in intensive care must have one on one care. I've been here with you all week.'

Julian groaned inwardly, suddenly glad he'd been unconscious for the duration of her company. She was professional and attentive. But right now, Julian really wanted her to be silent and elsewhere.

'When can I leave?'

The nurse laughed. Julian's eyes slammed shut of their own accord. He'd been awake for about five minutes. That was four minutes too long to still be there.

'Where are my clothes?' Julian said, opening his eyes again reluctantly.

The nurse shook her head and gentle concern replaced her bubbly repertoire. 'Julian, you don't need your clothes.'

Julian looked out the window near his bed. Outside was just a whitish-grey blur. The sky blended into the ground as it snowed heavily. It was definitely minus conditions out there.

'A toga is all a little too ancient Greece for me,' Julian said tugging on the corner of the sheet to make his point.

The nurse giggled like a giddy schoolgirl and flapped her hands about. 'You're so funny. I like it. That's just the spirit you need to get you through this.'

Julian's back teeth clenched, and he forced a smile. It wasn't her fault that she was irritating the hell out of him. He just wanted the hell out of there.

'Yeah. All very funny. So, my clothes, then?' Julian's tone was registering his dwindling tolerance.

'I don't think anything came up from the ER for you. Sometimes when we need to access the patient very quickly, their clothes, unfortunately, bear the brunt of that urgency. I'm sorry, but I think your stuff might have been damaged. I'm not sure you realise, Julian, but you were in a very bad way.'

Each breath in felt like someone was running a cheese grater over his lungs and he had the taste of blood in his mouth. It didn't take a genius to work out that he wasn't going to be running a marathon that weekend.

'Of course. No need to apologise for doing your job. My phone? It was in my jacket pocket. Is that here?'

'I can find out for you?'

'I would appreciate that,' Julian said, genuinely, also hoping that a little sweetness would speed her up a bit. Anthony was at least a two-hour drive away. The thought of waiting that long made Julian's head hurt more than ever.

'The doctor should be in to speak to you soon. Or would you rather wait for your wife?'

'My WHAT?' Julian bolted rigorously upright as if electricity surged through him. His spine cracked and clicked in response, but pain no longer registered.

He clasped the sheet around his waist and stood up, his fingers shaking. His legs were as wobbly as fuck, but he wasn't giving in and sitting back down. *Wife. What the fuck was Meghan playing at?* He'd never called her that. If she had a reason for exercising the title now, he'd damn well like to know what it was.

'Mr. Harte, please. You need to lie back down. Please.' The nurse was panicking as she tried desperately to steer Julian back into bed.

'Is my *wife* the only who's been here?' God, that word tasted weird in his mouth.

The nurse's hands were firm on his shoulders once again as she tried to steer him back to the bed. She looked nervous and stressed, and she kept eying the door like she might call in a team of medics at any moment. That was the last thing Julian needed. He would deal with the Meghan revelation later. For now, it was easiest to play along, despite how odd it felt.

'Yes. Mrs. Harte has been so worried. She's been at your bedside every day. Really, Mr. Harte. You need to lie down. Please.'

*Jesus.*

The nurse's hands on Julian's skin were vexing him even further. 'Stop,' he growled. He freed himself from her touch with one hand and reached behind him with the other hand to grab the edge of the bed before he collapsed.

'No one else has been here, then. No one?'

'There's a strict family only policy, Mr. Harte. But now that you're awake you can take visitors.'

'Well, that's just a fucking fabulous policy to have for a once upon a time orphan.'

'I...I...' the nurse stuttered uncomfortably.

Julian lowered himself back against the bed, not fully sitting but using the edge to support some of his weight. He pressed two fingers between his eyes and rubbed gently. My God, his head hurt. Julian knew he was being obnoxious. He gritted his teeth as he realised the nurse didn't deserve his distaste. He forced some composure. 'Has an American girl been here? Pretty, petite, kind of quiet.'

'Oh yes, she's been here all right. Causing all sorts of fuss. Don't worry. Your wife dealt with the situation. I don't think she'll be back to bother you again.'

*Wife, wife, wife.* The term rang in his ears like acid. Julian exhaled sharply, keeping his temper under control. *Fuck. Fuck. Fuck. MEGHAN!*

'My phone. I need it. Now.' Suddenly calling Anthony wasn't his priority. He just hoped he could remember Eva's American mobile number.

# 4

'Are you sure that you're okay? Do you want me to drive?' Shelly asked softly.

Eva was aware that she was speeding, but she was getting used to driving on the opposite side of the road now, and compared to the New Jersey Turnpike, the Irish motorways were a breeze.

'The roads are like glass, Eva. Take it handy, yeah. You're not going to be much good to Julian if you kill yourself in a car crash trying to get to him.'

Eva eased her foot back off the gas. 'Sorry, Shell. I just want to get back to the hospital. I feel like I've been gone for ages.'

'You've barely been in Dublin for twenty-four hours, Eva. If he wakes up while you're gone, I'm sure he'll understand.'

Eva's foot weighed down on the gas pedal again. 'But I don't want him to wake up without me.'

The back of the tidy blue hatchback rental skidded more than was comfortable and Eva's grip tightened instinctively on the wheel.

'Right. Pull over. I'm driving,' Shelly insisted. 'Your head's all over the place and, to be honest, your driving is scaring the shit out of me.'

'There's a garage just up here. I'll pull in there.' Eva pointed ahead.

Eva was as good as her word and the girls switched places after picking up some tar-like, takeaway coffee and a couple of bars of chocolate to keep them going while they skipped lunch.

'So all this rush. Do you think the hospital will let you in today?' Shelly asked as they set out on the road again.

Eva shrugged. 'Probably not. But I can wait downstairs again.'

Shelly groaned softly, but Eva ignored her disapproval.

'How did it go with your mother and sister after I left earlier?'

'Yeah. Fine, I suppose.' Eva rolled her shoulders again. 'Can we talk about something else?'

'Yeah, sure. Sorry.'

The rest of the journey passed mostly in silence. Eva drifted in and out of fitful sleep while Shelly drove so slowly even a cyclist could pass them.

'Are you going to confront Meghan today, then?' Shelly said out of nowhere, jolting Eva fully awake.

'What? No. Obviously not.' Eva rubbed her eyes. 'I haven't spoken to her all week. I'm not going to make a random scene today.'

'Well, I don't mind making a scene.'

'Shelly, no. Meghan says that she's Julian's wife and the stupid, goddamn hospital has chosen to believe that. That's fine. Julian can set the record straight when he wakes up.'

'He has a lot of records to set straight when he comes around,' Shelly grumbled.

Eva's neck cracked to one side. 'Shelly, just drop it. Yeah? All I give a shit about right now is he being okay. I can deal with the rest after.'

Eva's brain felt like scrambled eggs. She was still reeling from her father's funeral. And she was struggling to get her head around Shelly and Nathan's theory that Julian had been plotting revenge behind her back since before they even met. Eva wouldn't have put it past her father to destroy another family in addition to his own. But as much as Shelly and Nathan's story made sense, and much as it explained why Julian was so secretive initially, something just didn't sit right in her gut about it all. Meghan's revelation was just the icing on an already rotting cake. But none of it even came close to the stress of not knowing anything of substance about Julian's condition.

'Yeah. I know. Sorry, Eva. I know you've so much on your mind. It's just that Meghan melts my head. Even talking about her puts me in a pisser. Jesus, when I think about how we used to be kind of friends. I never knew she was such a bitch underneath.'

'Yeah, you did. But you were just as bad.' Eva laughed.

'What? Excuse me. I was always a delight,' Shelly replied, blowing a raspberry after.

'Ha. You were too cool for school. You all were. Julian's Fuck Buddy Bitches. God, when I started in the office, I was so intimidated that I hated going to pee in case I bumped into one of you in the bathroom.' Eva was still laughing, but part of the giggling was a cover-up for how angry she felt now thinking back on it all.

'Fuck Buddy Bitches? Haha, what a name!'

Eva's laughing came to a sudden end, as the ball, the game, her father, and the Da Lucas all paraded across her tired mind. 'What if Julian won't share his secrets? What if he feels he can't? I need to understand why he's done all that he has, you know?'

Shelly's laughing met just as sudden an end. 'Look, I'm not going to lie. You two have the most fucked-up relationship I've ever seen. EVER. But if Julian can do love, then he's in love with you. He's a different person since you came along. But you've a shitload of problems. Mainly his bitch of a maybe-

35

wife. The crap with your dad. And his…' Shelly started giggling again. 'And his….his…his fuck buddy bitches.'

Eva's phone vibrated across her knee. She glanced at the screen and at a number she didn't recognise.

'Aren't you going to answer that?' Shelly said.

'Yeah. Yeah, of course. It's…it's a new area code. Limerick. I think.'

'The hospital?' Shelly squeaked.

'I think so.' *Oh God, Oh God.*

'Oh Jesus, Eva. Pick up the phone. Pick up the phone.'

'What if it's...' *What if it's bad news?*

'Eva, pick it up. Pick it up now, or I will.'

'Hello. Evangeline speaking.' Eva's voice was calm, but her fingers were shaking so much she worried she might drop the phone before she heard the reply on the other end.

'Miss Andrews.'

'Julian. Oh, my God. You're awake.'

'Where are you?'

'I'm on the way...I'm…I'm…'

'We're half an hour away, max,' Shelly whispered, dropping her foot heavier against the accelerator.

'I'm thirty minutes away. I'll be there in thirty minutes.' Eva's words raced as much as her heart. 'Oh my God, I can't wait to see you.'

Julian sighed heavily on the other end of the phone.

'Julian…' Eva gasped, worried he'd hung up the phone. She wasn't ready; she needed his voice.

'I'm here.'

'Are you…are you okay?'

'I am now that I've heard your voice. See you soon, baby. Drive carefully.'

The line went dead, and Eva dropped the phone back onto her knees. 'He's awake, Shell. He's awake.'

Eva tossed her head back against the headrest and cried hysterically. A mix of relief and built-up fear burst out of her in the form of large, heaving sobs and heavy, salty tears. 'He's awake, Shell.'

'Yeah, honey, I got that,' Shelly said laughing through her own subtle tears.

'I thought…I thought…' Eva stuttered.

'I know. I know,' Shelly said softly. 'But it's okay. I told you it would be. I told you that Julian Harte doesn't do losing.'

'You were right.' Eva sat back up, beaming. 'Can we go a little faster?'

'Ice, Eva. The roads are still as slippery as fuck, you know.'

## 5

'Hi! Hi, I'm Evangeline Andrews. I'm Julian Harte's girlfriend. I'm here to see him.' Eva smiled at the middle-aged lady behind the reception desk just outside the ICU.

'Hello.' The receptionist smiled back brightly. 'Just bear with me a moment.' Her smile slowly faded as her eyes scanned the computer screen in front of her. 'Unfortunately, I don't have your name here.'

'Well, that's 'cause my boyfriend has been in a coma and hasn't been able to give it to you. But he's awake now. He called me. Just a few minutes ago, actually. He's awake.'

'Okay, Miss Andrews.'

'Eva. Evangeline Andrews. Mr. Harte is expecting me. Can you hurry please?' Eva looked at Shelly as panic gripped her.

'She's just checking the paperwork, Eva. She can't do anything without the hospital say so. Don't worry, it's all okay,' Shelly said, stepping forward a fraction to stand right beside Eva in front of the dated mahogany desk.

'Miss Andrews, I'm sorry, I just can't find any record of your name here…' the receptionist apologised.

'Well, I'm giving you my name now. Write it down if you need a record. I'm Julian's girlfriend, and I need to see him.'

Eva's heart did press-ups against her chest. She could see the doors leading into intensive care from where they were standing. It was killing her to be so close to Julian and still so far. She couldn't wait to see him, touch him, feel him, and tell him that she loved him. All the horrible questions that had tortured her over the last few days about Meghan and why Julian had never told her that he was married settled far into the back of her mind, pushed away by the excitement and relief that he was awake.

'Perhaps if you come back later?' the receptionist suggested.

'Please. You don't understand. I need to see him now. I know he's awake. He called me.'

Despite Eva's distress, she noticed the receptionist eye the tall, broad security guard nearby. Eva knew she was fighting a losing battle. She could either pull herself together or be pulled out of the door by a uniformed wrestler.

'Come on, Eva. Let's go over here for a moment,' Shelly said, taking Eva by the arm and leading her towards a long, rectangular window behind them.

Eva's fingers were shaking as she rummaged in her bag for her mobile. She held her phone to her ear and tapped her foot rigorously as if that would make Julian answer faster. It rang out. She redialed and it rang out again…and again…and again. 'He's not picking up.'

'Maybe he can't use his mobile on the ward. Give Anthony or Anne a call. See if they know anything.'

'Yeah, of course. Sorry, Shell. I'm not thinking straight.'

'I know.'

'I just really want to see him.'

'Yeah, of course, you do but don't get yourself into a state. He's not going anywhere. You'll see him soon.'

Eva froze as Meghan brushed past carrying a paper cup of steaming coffee and a croissant wrapped in a napkin. She didn't recognise Eva and Shelly, or if she did, she did a very good job of playing dumb.

'Good afternoon, Nancy,' Meghan said, stopping at the reception desk.

Eva rolled her eyes, unsurprised that Meghan made it her business to be on first name terms with the women behind the desk.

'Oh, Mrs. Harte, I'm so glad you're here,' the receptionist said softly.

*Mrs. Harte. Ouch!* Hearing Meghan officially bear that title hurt Eva more than she thought it would.

'I've been trying to get hold of you all morning,' the receptionist continued.

Even from the back, Eva could see Meghan tense.

'Is everything all right,' Meghan said, taking a step back.

'Absolutely. It's good news. Mr. Harte is conscious.'

'What?' Meghan slammed her coffee against the top of the desk, spilling some down the side of the white paper cup. 'Why did no one call me?'

'I've been trying to get hold of you all morning, Mrs. Harte, but your phone is going straight to voicemail.'

Meghan pulled her phone out of her skinny, blue jeans pocket. 'I don't have any missed calls.' Meghan turned her phone around and practically shoved the screen in Nancy's face.

'Oh, Mrs. Harte. I'm sorry. I've been trying to get you on your landline...on the number Mr. Harte gave us.'

Meghan snapped the yellow Post-it out of the receptionist's hand and crumpled it up and flung it back at her. 'That's not my number. You've been trying to call his bloody housekeeper.'

'I...I...I'm sorry, Mrs. Harte. I was only doing as I was asked. Mr. Harte's mobile is missing. But he insisted on making some personal calls from the hospital line. Maybe your phone was out of service,' the receptionist said, looking like she wanted to run away.

Eva's face brightened. Julian had called her. He'd called her and not Meghan. Wife or not, he didn't extend Meghan that consideration.

'I need to see him. RIGHT NOW,' Meghan snapped, furiously.

'Of course. I'll release the doors now,' the receptionist replied.

'My son is still in the canteen. He'll be up in a minute. Can you let him know I've gone in? Ask him to wait out here for me, please?' Meghan said as she walked away from the desk.

'Of course. No problem. He can sit with me.'

Meghan didn't reply; she just charged through the doors aggressively.

'Son?' Eva stuttered as soon as Meghan disappeared from view.

'Yeah, I heard that, too.' Shelly said, equally wide-eyed. 'I can't believe Meghan has a kid.'

'Julian's? Do you think he's Julian's son?'

'Oh Jesus, Eva. I don't know. No! No, I don't think so. I can't see Julian as a father.'

'I couldn't see him as a husband either, but what do you know, turns out he had wife all along.' Eva gasped.

'What are you going to do?'

Eva zipped up the khaki parka jacket that she'd borrowed from Shelly and tossed the fur lined hood over her head, looking like a snug Eskimo. Suddenly, she was colder than she'd been in a long time. 'I'm going to get the hell out of here. Can we go? Can we just get the hell out of here? Now. Please!'

# 6

'Is there anyone I can call for you, Mr. Harte?' the polite, young surgeon said running the tube of her stethoscope through her fingers.

Julian's forehead pinched as he watched her. She didn't realise she was doing it. Maybe it was a subconscious habit. She seemed like a sweet girl. Julian imagined delivering bad news must have been very hard for her. Maybe she was in the wrong profession.

'I'm still capable of making a phone call, Doctor.'

'Of course, Mr. Harte...I didn't mean any offense.'

Julian sighed. *Of course.* God, those words were so redundant.

'Is my wife waiting outside?'

'Yes. She's just in the corridor. Would you like me to fetch her for you?'

Julian shook his head. 'No. No, thank you.'

'I understand. I'm sure this must be very hard. Take all the time you need.' The doctor smiled, awkwardly, like she wanted to be friendly and understanding, but she wasn't sure if smiling was the appropriate gesture under the circumstances.

'Water?' she said, pouring some from the cooler near the door before waiting for Julian's reply.

'Water? Seriously? I'm thinking something a little stronger.' Julian smirked.

'I can check your chart, but I think you're not due pain meds for another couple of hours. Are you in pain?'

'I meant alcohol, Doctor. But, hell, I'll take the drugs if you're offering.'

The doctor laughed reluctantly. 'You're taking the news exceptionally well, Mr. Harte. Have one of the other doctors already spoken to you?'

'No. You're the first white coat to visit today, Dr. Simmons,' Julian said reading the name tag just above the doctor's left breast.

'Of course. I'm sorry…' The doctor looked confused, as she scanned the chart hanging on the end of the bed. 'I've just never seen anyone react so calmly to this kind of news before.'

'Would it change your diagnosis if I reacted differently?'

The doctor lowered her head, pressed her lips together, and her warm smile saddened around the edges. 'No, I'm afraid not.'

Julian closed his eyes and sighed roughly. He didn't reply. He didn't need to. He'd made his point quite clearly. Tears or a tantrum weren't his style. But his mind was racing. Work and Eva were his main concerns. He'd have a lot of tidying up to do. *Fuck!*

'I'll arrange for one of our counsellors to come by later this afternoon,' the doctor said softly.

'Can your counsellor offer an opposing diagnosis to yours?'

The doctor lowered her head once again. Julian shook his head. She was too soft for this kind of shit. She was struggling to control the twitching of her fingers.

'Unfortunately, the diagnosis is final, Mr. Harte.'

'Well then, I'd prefer if you didn't waste the counsellor's time or mine.'

'But you can discuss any concerns you may have.'

'You've just told me that I'm dying, Dr. Simmons. The only concern I have is that I would rather not.'

The doctor drank from the cup she was still holding, gasping as she drained the contents in one continuous gulp.

Julian wasn't intentionally making her nervous, but it didn't take a genius to work out that he had that effect on her. Her reaction was rather unsettling, especially given the circumstances. He'd try to be less intimidating. Less himself.

'We have options we can explore,' she said. Crumpling the cup and dropping it into the bin near the door, she slowly walked back towards Julian's bed. Stopping before she got too close.

'Explore?' Julian snarled, failing in his attempt to be less himself.

The doctor cleared her throat. 'Mr. Harte, I'm afraid your kidneys are failing. That is a fact.'

Julian liked her more when she got her head out of her ass and just spat the information out. None of this beat around the bush to protect his feelings shit. He just wanted to hear the bottom line.

'And the rest of the facts, Dr. Simmons? Whenever you're ready.'

'The stab wound was minor, Mr. Harte. You can probably see that yourself from how neatly the tear has been stitched.' The doctor edged closer and pointed towards Julian's fresh, red scar.

Julian instinctively gazed at his side where some blue, wire-like stuff weaved in and out of his skin, piecing him back together. 'But…' Julian said casting his attention back to the doctor.

'But…there were complications.'

'The delay getting to the hospital?' Julian didn't regret that complication; he'd take that risk again in a heartbeat if it meant getting Eva to safety.

'Yes, the time lapse wasn't ideal. But, like I said, the wound was minor. And if it was a simple stabbing then we wouldn't be having this conversation.'

'So, what exactly is causing my kidneys to freak out and decide to take early retirement, Dr. Simmons?'

'Well, initially we were confused by your blood's inability to clot.'

'I like my whiskey, Doctor, but I doubt even I drink enough to cause haemophilia,' Julian joked dryly.

'Actually, Mr. Harte, that was our first suspicion. Not that you like to drink, just that you might have had a clotting disorder.'

'Well, I don't. So, your other theory?'

'We sent some blood to the lab, of course,' the doctor said.

*Of course.* There were those bloody words again. Julian's jaw twitched and he settled his head back against the pillow. Clearly, he was getting the long version of this story.

'And…?' *Sweet Jesus.* He might die before he found out what in the hell was killing him.

'We discovered there was a blood thinning agent in your system. We've checked your records, and you're not on any medication. Unless you count the whiskey?' The doctor smiled gently, treading carefully with her joke.

Julian tossed an eyebrow and flicked her a smile. He liked her.

'So we can only suspect that you ingested something unknowingly.'

'I had a drink in the club earlier, I think…I can't really remember now. It's a bit blurry.' Julian gritted his teeth, pissed off with himself that he couldn't conjure up more than a hazy memory.

'Understandable, Mr. Harte. You've been through hell.'

'What are we talking here? Poison?' *Well played Da Luca, well played,* Julian thought venomously.

'We're not entirely certain yet. It's certainly nothing that's legal here in Ireland. I have a colleague in upstate New York who is looking into it on her end. Seeing what she can find over there.'

'So am I to gather that by, explore our options, what you really meant was figure out what in the hell is going on?'

'Not exactly. We know something thinned your blood, and yes, finding out what that was would help, but it's not our only problem.'

'I'm all ears.'

'We also found high levels of mercury in your system. As we suspected when we swabbed the stab wound, it was concentrated in that area.'

'Mercury,' Julian almost gagged on the word. *Fucking bastard.* Da Luca really knew what he was doing. 'The knife must have been tainted in the stuff.'

'Yes, I'd imagine so. We flushed saline through and you've had numerous blood transfusions, but I'm afraid by that stage a lot of the damage was done. Mercury is a heavy metal, Mr. Harte, and in high concentrations, it's detrimental to the kidneys. That, combined with the lack of good blood supply at the time, has cause irreversible damage.'

Julian pressed his fingertips against his eyes and exhaled. Maybe he liked the doctor better when she was tiptoeing around the facts, after all. Da Luca didn't get to win. Not this time. Julian's chest tightened and drawing breath stung his chest. Darkness clouded his vision and his body grew strangely heavy.

'Mr. Harte…Mr. Harte…Mr. Harte…'

Julian's eyes shot open again, and he woke to the doctor leaning over him slapping his face. She smelt of chocolate biscuits and lavender. Eva wore lavender scented perfume. He remembered the first time he'd gotten close enough to her to smell it. God, he missed her. He didn't need all these drips and wires and medicine feeding into his veins. He just needed her. He *needed* her.

'Mr. Harte, I know this is terrifying for you.'

'How long?' Julian cut across her, already formulating a plan to make damn sure he had the last laugh where the Da Luca family was concerned.

'Don't get ahead of yourself, Mr. Harte. There are a lot of options to consider.'

'Dialysis?' Julian snarled.

'Yes. And a transplant when a match is found.'

'You mean nab the kidney off some poor bastard with worse luck than me who happens to have kicked the bucket first.'

'We'd explore living donors first. You can lead a perfectly healthy life with one kidney so the only risk to the donor would be the surgery itself and...'

'I told the nurse earlier, I'm an orphan. You're not going to have a bunch of family members queuing up at the door to offer body parts.'

'We can test your son?'

'No.'

'I understand your concern. But the test is non-invasive, and if he was a match, he'd be a perfect candidate in a few years.'

'I said no.'

'Well, I'll just leave this leaflet here for you. It has some information on the recipient process. Just in case you change your mind.'

'I don't change my mind, Dr. Simmons. But you can leave the leaflet if it makes you feel better.'

The doctor smiled, sighed, and slowly began backing out the door. 'Will I ask your wife to come in now?'

'No, thank you. But would you please check if Miss Andrews has arrived yet?'

'Of course.'

## 7

'Eva, it's freezing. Can we either get in the car or go back inside,' Shelly grumbled.

It wasn't the first time Shelly had aired her frustration as she paced with Eva from one side of the hospital car park to the other. Eva didn't answer.

'Can we at least get something to eat? I spotted a sign for McDonald's when we turned off the motorway. It can't be far.'

'I'm not hungry,' Eva dismissed.

'Well, I'm starving. And it's making me cranky and giving me a headache.'

'Okay. You go, then.'

'What? And leave you here? Eh, no,' Shelly moaned.

They paced more in silence until Eva couldn't take it anymore.

'A son, Shelly, a fucking son. I thought a wife was bad, but this is blowing my mind. I don't really know Julian at all, do I?'

'Eva, you don't even know that the kid is his. Or that Meghan is really his wife. Just 'cause she says she is doesn't make it true.'

Shelly made a logical point, and Eva considered it for a moment, but deep down she knew. Even Meghan wasn't crazy enough to make up a story like that.

'Do you think he's Julian's kid, Shelly. Honestly. Do you?'

'I told you, Eva. I don't know.' Shelly's lips chattered in the cold. 'But I know someone who does know. But instead of being inside WHERE IT'S WARM, we're out here like a pair of tits freezing and starving.'

'What am I supposed to do? Walk in and say, hi so glad you're awake. I know you have a wife, and by the way, do you have a son, too?'

'Yes.'

Eva doubled over and laughed. Well, it was either laugh or start crying again and she'd cried so much lately that she was possibly dehydrated. 'If only it was that simple,' Eva mumbled. 'I want to see him so much it hurts, but I just can't think straight right now. God, why is everything with Julian always so complicated.'

'It's not complicated, Eva. This is simple. You just have to ask Julian. You might not like the answer, but the question is simple.' Shelly began walking back towards the main door of the hospital.

'Where are you going?' Eva called after her without moving.

'Inside. I'm fucking freezing. There's a vending machine in the lobby. I need something to eat.'

The snow was falling at its heaviest now, and despite how distracted Eva's mind was, the cold was really starting to become too much to bear. She scurried after Shelly, slipping and sliding all the way.

Shelly paused in the lobby and shook herself from head to toe. Snow sprayed off her fashionable, grey leather jacket like a shaggy dog shaking himself off after a bath. Dry-ish, Shelly picked up her pace and marched up the stairs. Eva tossed her shoulders back, held her head high, and dashed after her.

'What about your candy?' Eva called, looking back at the vending machine she knew Shelly had no intention of visiting.

'Hello again,' Shelly said sternly, reaching the reception desk outside ICU. She folded her arms across the desk and tilted her head to one side.

Shelly meant business. Eva knew they weren't leaving again without speaking to Julian. Her stomach flipped.

'Hello.' The receptionist smiled, quite obviously not recognising Shelly.

'Nancy, isn't it?'

'Yes.' Nancy's smile turned to a look of confusion.

'My friend, Eva and I…,' Shelly turned and pointed to Eva, who was still catching her breath after running up the stairs, '…took your advice to come back later, and well, here we are. Now, may my friend please see her boyfriend?'

'Oh, yes. Miss Anderson,' Nancy said, recognition brightening up her face.

'Andrews. Evangeline Andrews,' Eva growled, stepping forward. Nancy was really beginning to bug the shit out of Eva. Eva pulled herself up as tall as she could. Compared to the shit of the last few days, a little confrontation with an incompetent receptionist was a walk in the park.

Eva licked her dried-out lips and was about to argue her case when she was distracted by a little boy sitting in a lonely armchair by the window. He was engrossed in whatever he was playing on his iPad and didn't notice Eva watching him. She quickly pulled her stare away. She was afraid to watch him for too long. Afraid she might recognise a feature or mannerism.

'I'll release the doors for you now, Miss Andrews,' Nancy said.

'What?' Eva's attention immediately returned to the middle-aged lady behind the desk.

'Mr. Harte has been asking for you. There was nothing on the system earlier, but I have strict instructions to let you straight through now. My apologies for the delay. These damn computers are the bane of my existence sometimes.'

'Thanks. But I just need a minute.'

'Eva. She's opening the door. You can go straight through. What are you waiting for?' Shelly asked.

Eva tossed her head towards the little boy near the window.

Shelly's face fell and her whole body softened. 'Oh.'

Eva nodded.

'I'll…eh…I…I forgot I wanted to check out the vending machine. I'll just pop back down now,' Shelly stuttered.

'Thanks, Shell. I won't take long.'

Shelly pulled her into an awkward shrug. 'Take as long as you need, hun. You know where I am.' Shelly's heels clicked and she raced back down the stairs just as quickly as she had come up.

Eva shuffled over to the window, not really sure what in the hell she was doing. What if it wasn't him? What if she was just a lady in a hospital soliciting conversation with a young boy? *Jesus.* There was only one way to find out. Eva ignored the eyes of the receptionist and security guard burning into her back.

'Hi, there. Mind if I sit down?'

The spikey-haired, blond boy looked up from his iPad, for a moment, to check out who was talking to him.

'You want to sit on the floor?' he asked, turning his attention back to his screen before he finished his sentence.

Eva looked around. He was sitting in the only chair. His smart mouth answer told her that he was definitely Meghan's son.

'Yeah. You're right. I'll just stand.'

'Okay.'

'So...' Eva shuffled from one foot to the other. She didn't really know any kids so she wasn't sure what boys that age would want to talk about. 'What's your name?'

'I'm not allowed to talk to strangers.' He looked up from his iPad once more. His big, brown eyes meeting Eva's. *Brown. He had beautiful brown eyes. Just like Julian.*

'I understand. Did your mom and dad tell you that?'

'My mom told me.'

Eva's heart was racing with his deliberate exclusion of the word dad. 'What are you playing?' Eva said softly, trying a different approach.

'I'm not playing. I'm writing.'

'Oh, cool. You like to write stories?'

The little boy snorted as if Eva has just asked him if he liked to dress up as a princess and wear a fluffy pink tutu.

'Not stories. Coding. For computer stuff.'

He spun the screen around to show Eva his symbols and squiggles. *Wow.* Eva remembered a conversation she had with Mrs. Cartwright after the ball in Julian's mansion. Mrs. Cartwright had told her about how young Julian was when he created his first app. Maybe the apple didn't fall far from the tree. Once again, she looked at the little boy's big, brown eyes.

'That's really cool,' Eva said, impressed.

'Thanks. It's pretty easy once you get the hang of it,' he said, softening.

Eva liked him.

'It looks very complicated to me,' Eva admitted.

'Nah. It's just computer stuff. Easy peasy, really.'

'I used to work for a big company that does computer stuff.'

'Really? So did you not understand your job? Did they fire you?'

Eva laughed. 'I didn't do the computer stuff. My job was to let people know about all the cool new stuff our company was making.'

'Like advertising?' the boy said, flashing his teeth with a bright smile.

'Yeah, exactly.'

'So did you work for Ignite Technologies?'

*Jesus. Not much got past this kid,* Eva thought, unsurprised. 'Yes, that's where I used to work. Do you know it?'

'My mom works there,' he said, still smiling. 'Do you know her?'

Eva froze. She didn't know what to say. But he was a sweet little boy, despite being spawned by the devil, and it didn't feel right to lie to him. 'Yeah. I know your mom.'

'Eva.' Eva jumped hearing Meghan spit her name behind her.

'Meghan…hi,' Eva replied and spun around, trying not to look like someone had just shoved a lightning rod up her ass.

'Daniel. What have I told you about talking to strangers?' Meghan snapped, addressing her son with concern.

'She's not a stranger, Mom. She used to work with you. Until she got fired for not understanding her job.'

'Did she tell you that?' Meghan snarled, and Eva knew the aggression was directed at her, not the child.

'I told him that we worked together; I didn't say anything about getting fired,' Eva soured.

'What are you doing here, Eva? I thought I made it clear you weren't welcome.'

'No. You made it clear that you didn't want me here. That doesn't make me not welcome. That makes me a pain in your fucking ass.' Eva winced, instantly regretting cursing in front of the child and giving Meghan some high ground.

'Well, you've had a wasted journey. Julian doesn't want to see anyone.'

Eva couldn't hide the big toothy grin that swept across her whole face.

'What the fuc…' Meghan cut herself off midsentence, briefly throwing her gaze onto her son. 'What are you looking so pleased about?'

'Maybe it's just his *wife* he doesn't want to see,' Eva smirked.

'I don't want to discuss this in front of my son.'

'I don't want to discuss this at all,' Eva retaliated.

'Daniel, sweetheart, will you pop down to the canteen again and get me a diet Coke? I'm so thirsty.' Meghan bent down so her head was level with her son.

'Mommmmm,' the little boy protested without saying anything more than that one word.

'You can get yourself an ice cream, too.'

He put his iPad down straight away and was on his feet. Meghan passed him some money and he skipped away happily.

Eva followed his lead and left, heading in the opposite direction catching the receptionist's attention as she passed, letting her know to release the doors to ICU.

'I am not finished speaking to you,' Meghan growled.

'Okay, Meghan. That's fine. If you'd like to wait here, I'd be happy to discuss things further with you when I get back from visiting my boyfriend.'

Eva quickened her pace, praying that her wet boots wouldn't land her on her ass against the slick polished floor tiles. She put both her hands out in front of her pushing hard on the door and walked straight through. She stopped on the other side, leaned back against the wall, and inhaled as if she'd just come up from too long under water. She'd always dreamed of standing up to Meghan like that and now that she had, no matter how damn good it felt, it didn't stop her from shaking all over.

# 8

'Miss Andrews,' a voice almost whispered.

Eva peeled herself away from the wall and turned to face whoever was talking.

'I'm Doctor Simmons.' The doctor introduced herself and extended her hand.

Eva shook it, recognising the doctor straight away. She was the same pretty, young surgeon who had turned Eva away from the hospital the night Julian was admitted.

'Hello. I'm Eva Andrews. I'm Julian's girlfriend. Is he okay?'

The doctor didn't answer the question. 'Mr. Harte will be delighted you're here. He's been asking for you.'

Eva's shaking stopped and was replaced with giddy excitement. 'Is he okay?' she repeated.

'He's just been moved to his own room.'

'Oh wow, really? He's out of intensive care. That's a great sign, then, isn't it?'

'He's on the next floor down.'

Eva looked back through the doors she had just charged through. She suspected Meghan would still be out there. She really didn't want to have to walk back out and let Meghan think Julian had turned her away, too.

'Can we get downstairs from here?' Eva hoped that didn't sound as desperate out loud as it did in her head.

The doctor followed Eva's stare. 'I'm very sorry for asking you to leave the night Mr. Harte came in. I didn't know.'

'It's okay. I understand. I'm just relieved to be here now.'

'Is Mrs. Harte in the lobby?' the doctor asked.

'Yes.' Eva winced.

'Okay. We can take the staff stairs, if you'd like.'

Eva guessed the doctor must think she was some home-wrecking whore, going around fucking another women's husband, but Eva had spent most of her life being judged by people who didn't know her and she was becoming immune. She had too much on her mind to entertain that kind of thing now.

'This way.' The doctor walked around the corner and Eva quickly followed.

'Mr. Harte is quite the enigma,' the doctor said after a few moments of awkward silence.

Eva sighed.

'My goodness, I'm sorry. That came out all wrong. I just meant...'

'He can be quite intimidating, I know,' Eva said reassuringly. Eva knew exactly what the doctor meant. She was professional and well spoken, but she was also human and her attraction to Julian was glaringly obvious.

'Just in here,' the doctor said as they walked down a long, sterile corridor. There were closed doors on both sides and random medical machines dotted outside every second door. It was eerily silent and a shiver ran the length of Eva's spine. There was a different feel to this part of the hospital. Almost like if they turned the next corner, the grim reaper himself would be standing waiting to shake their hand. Suddenly, Eva missed the intensity of ICU.

The doctor stopped outside one of the last doors on the corridor and Eva's heart raced furiously. Her breath was so quick and uneasy - and amplified by the stillness of her surroundings.

'Are you ready?' the doctor asked, reaching for the handle.

'Very.' Eva gulped.

'Don't be alarmed when you see him. He's pale and a lot weaker than he'd dare admit.'

Eva smiled. *I'd be more alarmed if he admitted to feeling like shit,* she thought.

'Okay.' Eva nodded, holding her breath as the doctor slowly turned the handle.

Julian was sitting up on the bed. He wasn't leaning back against the pillows, but he looked like he needed to. He was pale, like he hadn't slept in a while. Half-healed cuts and bruises on his beautiful face were a reminder of Da Luca's thugs' handiwork. And for a moment, Eva's heart almost stopped as she remembered the fear she felt as she watched those scumbags use Julian as their own personal punch bag. But despite his battered body, he was beautiful as always and a tingle ran through Eva's body right to the tips of her fingers and toes as his big, dark brown eyes locked on hers.

'Welcome to the party, Miss Andrews,' Julian joked.

Eva rushed to him, trying to forget where they were. She needed to touch him, to hear him breathe, to feel his heart beat against her palm.

'Oh God, you scared the shit out of me,' she said pressing her lips against his as tears of relief streamed down her cheeks. 'Don't ever leave me like that again. Oh, God. Oh, God.'

'I'm sorry,' he whispered, reaching for her, his thumb stroking the nape of her neck. 'It's so good to see you.'

'It's so good to see you, too. I was so scared I might lose you. So scared.' Eva pressed her lips against his again, sighing deeply. Her breath meeting his. Her lips tasting him. Her hands cupping his face. She couldn't get close enough. She wanted every inch of his skin against hers.

Julian pulled back a little and Eva let go straight away, worried she might have hurt him.

'Thank you, Doctor Simmons,' Julian said turning his attention to the doorway.

The doctor nodded, taking the hint. 'Okay, Mr. Harte. I'll leave you both alone to catch up. One of the nurses will be in to see you in thirty minutes to do you obs again. And I'll be back shortly to discuss that thing we were talking about earlier. If you get a chance to read through that stuff in the meantime, that would be great.'

'We've only got thirty minutes,' Eva sighed as she walked over to close the door the doctor left open behind her.

'There's a lot we can do in thirty minutes, Miss Andrews.'

'Julian Harte. I'm shocked. Do you ever think about anything else?'

'I meant we could catch up on your news. But if you have something else in mind,' Julian teased.

'Very funny, Julian. I know exactly what you meant. And for someone so exhausted, there's one part of your body that appears to be wide awake.' Eva smirked and dropped her eyes to the bulge under the sheet.

'What can I say? You have powerful healing qualities, Evangeline.'

Eva rolled her eyes, playfully. *What happened to him calling her Eva? Just Eva.*

'Really?' She giggled.

'Yes, really. Now why don't you come over here and kiss me better some more?'

Eva placed her hands on Julian's chest and eased him back against the stacked pillows behind. She ran her tongue across his lips, leaned over the edge of the bed, pressed her mouth against his, and exhaled. Julian sucked her bottom lip into his mouth and dragged his teeth gently against it before releasing.

'That's delicious, baby, but I wasn't talking about kissing my lips.'

Eva stood up and looked into the eyes of the man she was head over heels in love with. She glanced at the door. They had time. She looked back at Julian with a coquettish smile.

She leaned in to kiss him again, getting close enough to feel his breath on her skin, but she didn't allow her lips to touch his. For once, she was in control and the adrenaline running through her was both empowering and addictive. She slipped her hand under the sheet, gasping as she discovered that Julian wasn't wearing boxers.

'Going for something casual, Mr. Harte.' She laughed, gently tugging on the end of his hospital gown.

'I'm trying something new.'

Eva grinned. She suspected that if Julian arrived in the office on a Monday morning wearing just his hospital gown and a pair of slippers, half the company would turn up on Tuesday sporting the same look.

'Ready to try something else new?' Eva whispered.

Julian rocked his hips, thrusting his rock hard erection towards Eva's waiting hand. 'Ready, baby.'

Eva clasped her fingers around him, watching as he tossed his head back against the pillows and groaned.

'I love you, Julian,' she said, tightening her grip and pumping her hand confidently up and down his shaft.

'I love you too, Eva,' Julian gasped, closing his eyes.

Eva moved closer, letting her lips lightly brush against his. She slipped her tongue into his mouth, exploring the warm softness of his mouth as she tasted him.

Julian kissed her back. Hard. He wanted her. She could taste his hunger. She could feel his cock swell in her hand, aching to release. She could feel him letting her take complete control.

She let go, and Julian's eyes shot open. 'You're fucking kidding me?'

Eva wrinkled her nose and tossed her head towards the door.

'The nurse isn't going to walk in, Eva,' Julian assured quickly.

Eva looked at her watch. They still had fifteen minutes. 'Okay.'

'Now, the doctor, on the other hand…'

Eva tossed her head back and laughed. 'Not helping, Julian.'

'Come on, baby. The risk only makes it more fun. Show me what you've got.'

Eva rolled her bottom lip between her finger and thumb, thinking. 'So you want to play, Mr. Harte?'

Julian's delicious smile made Eva's mind up. The risk was certainly worth taking.

'Okay. My game, my rules,' she smirked.

'Miss Andrews, I don't do blackmail.'

'This isn't blackmail, Mr. Harte.' Eva's hand reached below the sheet again and she cupped his balls, letting him know exactly how she intended to play. 'It's just a game, Julian. And you do play games, don't you?'

Julian's pulsing cock gave her the answer.

'Okay. My game is called Truth and Dare. Do you know it?' Eva asked confidently.

'I think you mean Truth or Dare.'

Eva's had dropped a little lower, her finger pressing against his ass. He clenched, but he didn't stop her.

'No. I mean Truth *and* Dare.'

Julian grabbed Eva suddenly and pulled her mouth on his so roughly that she nearly fell on top of him. He forced his tongue in and out of her mouth with such aggression that she was left with no doubt that he wished it was his cock. 'Let's play,' Julian said. 'I only have one rule.'

'No rules, Julian,' Eva interrupted. 'This is *my* game. Remember?'

'Okay, fine…if you want to get caught?'

Eva looked at the door again. 'Oh, for God's sake.' She sighed. 'Okay, Julian. What's your rule?'

'Slide that chair in front of the door.'

Eva laughed and dragged the chair waiting by Julian's bed to the back of the room and pushed it up against the door, making sure the back of the chair locked under the handle. 'I will allow that rule, Mr. Harte. But the rest are mine.'

'Deal.'

# 9

Eva took off her coat, dropping it onto the chair, and flung her bag on top. 'There,' she said, satisfied, walking back to Julian.

'Hot?' Julian's eyes were undressing her.

'Very. But it's about to get a whole lot hotter.'

'So, Miss Andrews, are you going to teach me *your* rules?' Julian moved over on the bed and made room for Eva to sit on the edge beside him.

'They're simple. I ask you a question and you must answer with the truth,' Eva explained, sitting in the space he'd made for her.

'I've never lied to you, Eva.'

'I know. So this should be easy for you, right?' Eva replied, very business-like.

Eva was enjoying the intrigue written all over Julian's face. She knew he was relishing the prospect of a challenge.

'And the dares, Miss Andrews?'

'I ask the truths, you create the dares. You get to dare me to do whatever you like,' Eva glanced at Julian's cock.

'Whatever I like?'

'Um-hum.'

'This sounds like my kind of game. But what if I don't answer your question?'

'That's your prerogative, Mr. Harte. But then you forfeit your dare. And I know you're not the kind of man to take a forfeit.'

Julian tossed an eyebrow. 'You know me well. Okay, I understand the rules. Let's play.'

There was a cheeky twinkle in Julian's eye, and Eva was certain that he was already thinking of a way to twist the rules. She'd be disappointed if he didn't at least try.

'Okay. Round one,' Eva said trying not to laugh. This reminded her so much of their first online conversation. Only this time the tables were turned. She could get used to being in the driver's seat.

Julian sat up, away from the pillows. He folded one arm across his chest and the other reached to stroke his chin between his finger and thumb. He had his business face on.

*Fuck! He was hot.*

Eva cleared her throat. If business was how he wanted to play it, then she was ready to bring it. 'So. First question, Mr. Harte. How do you feel?'

'I've been better.'

Eva's whole body sank and her business approach met a sudden death. 'Julian, no! That's not an answer, it's a sidestep. You have to answer properly or you don't get your dare.'

'Okay, okay. Don't get your knickers in a twist. Actually, speaking of knickers. I'm pretty close to naked here. We're not playing on a level pitch. Shouldn't you be naked, too?'

'Save it for your dare,' Eva said, pulling herself back up straight again. 'Now. Are you ready to take this seriously?'

'Absolutely.'

'Okay. So my question again. How do you feel?'

'I'm high. I'm on a cocktail of drugs but I'd prefer less morphine and a little more whiskey. I haven't eaten in a while, but I don't think I'm hungry. I pissed by myself for the first time a little over an hour ago. It was rather enjoyable. And I'd like to get the hell out of here.' Julian raised both eyebrows and tilted his head. 'How was that answer?'

Eva took a minute to process. She wasn't sure whether to laugh or cry. 'It was good. Thank you. Your turn.'

Julian smiled. 'Take off your cardigan.'

'Seriously, that's it? My cardigan?'

'That's it.'

Eva's eyes narrowed to comma-shaped slits. She knew that he was up to something.

'Your question again, Miss Andrews.'

'What was the first thing you thought about when you woke up?'

'Ouch.'

'Ouch? That's it?'

'That's it.'

Eva pressed her lips together and sighed sharply through her nose. She didn't like his overly short answers. 'Okay, who was the first...'

'Erm, my dare, remember?' Julian interrupted her.

'Oh, yeah. Sorry.'

'Take down your hair.'

Eva reached for the scrunchie holding her hair back in a loose ponytail. 'There,' she said, shaking her hair free and letting it fall around her face. 'I thought your dares would be a little more adventurous,' Eva joked, tossing Julian a provocative grin.

'I'm just getting warmed up,' he insisted.

Eva's grin switched to a concerned lip bite and her stomach somersaulted like an Olympic gold medallist. 'Okay. Another question. Who was the first person you called when you woke up.'

'You.'

Eva swallowed hard. She wanted to hear that answer, but it made her chest tighten and her heart race. She started this game so she could ask Julian all the questions burning a hole in her head. About Meghan and his son and her father's involvement in his family's deaths. But his last answer had thrown her. She didn't want to play anymore. She didn't want to trap him into telling her everything; she wanted him to tell her because he wanted to.

'Me,' Eva instinctively tapped her fingers against her chest as she stood up and turned to face Julian. 'Me and not Meghan?'

Julian shook his head. 'Not Meghan.'

Eva inhaled so sharply through her nose that it stung. Part of her wanted to finish the striptease, climb on top of him, and make love until they both came. But another part of her, the less consuming and more reasonable part of her, knew the next question was paramount. Maybe they'd never make love again after she heard the answer.

'Julian?'

Julian looked at her with a seriousness she hadn't seen in a while. Eva realised that he knew the next question. He'd been one step ahead of her the whole game. But even knowing the question that would inevitably come, he'd agreed to play. Maybe he didn't want secrets anymore, either. Maybe he was finally ready to let her in.

Eva glanced at her watch. The nurse would be there in ten minutes. She had ten minutes to have her world come crashing down around her and pull herself back together again before she'd be asked to leave the room. Ten minutes just wasn't enough. No amount of time would be enough.

Eva ran her hands through her hair, tossing it all over the place.

'Ask, Eva,' Julian said, his eyes burning into her. 'I know you need to ask me. I promised you the truth and the game's not over yet.'

'You called me first...' Eva paused, and she had to force herself hard to say the next part of the sentence, '...but why didn't you call your wife?'

'Because I knew she was already here.'

*Oh, my God. Oh, my God.* 'I thought you were going to tell me it was all made up. That Meghan was just bullshitting.'

Julian shook his head. 'No you didn't.'

Tears were pouring down Eva's cheeks and catching her breath was becoming uncomfortable. 'You're right. I didn't. But it's what I wanted to hear.'

'I told you, Eva. I've never lied to you. I'm not about to start now.'

'Are you serious? You have a wife. You've been living a huge lie.'

'I never told you that I wasn't married.'

'You never told me that you were!'

'It wasn't relevant.'

'I can't believe you're saying this. Do you hear yourself? You didn't think it was relevant? You know something like that is more than relevant. It's just the goddamn facts. I deserved to know. I deserved at least that much,' Eva spat.

'I told you before that I don't believe in marriage.'

'You believed it once though, didn't you? You believed in it enough to marry Meghan.'

'It's not like that,' Julian said, calmly.

'Well, what is it like, Julian? 'Cause I just don't understand. No wonder Meghan hates me. Christ, I'd hate me too if I was her.'

'Marriage is a contract. An agreement on paper between two people. I don't see it as anything more,' Julian explained.

Eva's head was pounding. Her flared temper was making it hard to concentrate on anything more. Was he actually attempting to put forward a reasonable explanation? Or was he just being Julian? Calm and charming and always coming out on top.

'How long have you been married?'

'Ten years.'

Eva's face dropped into her hands. 'Oh, my God. You were childhood sweethearts.'

'No. We were kids who needed a quick solution to a problem. Getting married was our answer.'

The image of the kid Eva met in the corridor filled her head.

'The little boy? Daniel?' Eva said resolved.

'Daniel. Yes. He's a great kid.'

Eva sat back down on the edge of the bed. She didn't want to be close to Julian at that moment, but she had no choice. She needed to sit before her legs crumpled beneath her completely. A mix of anger, shock, and elation that she finally knew some truth fizzled through her body until she thought her head might explode.

'Meghan was pregnant at seventeen, Eva. She had another year in state care. Another year living with a family who'd kick her out on her arse as soon as she turned eighteen and the state stopped paying them to keep her. She had no money and nowhere to go. She was terrified. I was older. I was almost twenty-two. I was making money. A lot of money. I'd abandoned Meghan once, the day I left the orphanage. I couldn't do that to her again. I had to protect her.'

'Did you love her?' Eva asked, her chest tightening to the point of pain.

'Yes.'

Eva gasped. *Fuck!* That hurt to hear.

'Do you...do you still love her now?' Eva asked afraid of the answer.

'Yes.'

Eva eyed the door. She wished the chair wasn't there. She'd storm out if she hadn't made it like Fort Knox in the room. She was already humiliated enough. Struggling with

77

furniture, while trying to make a dramatic exit, was not going to happen.

'So, you married a woman you loved because there was a baby on the way, and you're still trying to tell me that you don't believe in marriage. Fucking hell, Julian. You're an even bigger liar than I thought…and you know the part that's pissing me off the most?'

'What might that be?'

'That I was too stupid to notice. All the signs were there, but I was too busy falling in love with you to add them up.'

'Eva, I love Meghan. But I am not *in love* with her.'

'Is there a difference?' Eva snarled.

'Yes, Eva.' Julian caught Eva's hand and pulled her back to sit fully on the bed beside him. She didn't pull away, but she refused to turn around and look at him.

'I never thought I'd hear this kind of crap from you. I really thought you were the type of guy who always had your shit together. But, right now, you sound like one of those pathetic guys off a reality TV show desperate for ratings. You know, the ones where the poor misunderstood husband comes on with some bullshit story about how he loves his wife, but he's not in love with her and he has to screw every woman he comes in contact with just to feel alive. Fuck, Julian.' *Fuck, fuck, fuck.*

'Meghan is my friend, Eva. I've loved her since I was eight years old and she was just a baby. I will always be there for her. ALWAYS. I'm not a conventional husband. We don't do Sunday morning walks in the park. Or have date nights. We are married on paper only. It's a financial agreement. Nothing more.'

Eva wiped away the tears from her eyes with the sleeve of her blouse. 'I don't believe you're really that cold. I know you. I think I know you better than you know yourself. You didn't marry her just because she was pregnant. You could have given her money and been there for her as a friend. Tell me the real reason. There's more, isn't there?'

'Yes.' Julian was nodding.

He was giving up the answers so easily. He wasn't hiding anything anymore. But Eva could already guess what he was going to say next. She realised at that moment that she knew him inside out. She didn't need him to tell her stuff to let her in. She was already in. She'd been there for a while; she was just a bit slow to catch on.

'You felt you had to save her. I see that in you now,' Eva said. 'It's something deep inside you. You don't even know it's there. You couldn't save your parents, and that guilt is eating you alive. It never goes away. You're always trying to redeem yourself.' Eva sniffled and exhaled sharply through her rounded lips. 'It's your curse. I know it's why you saved me. But you saved Meghan first, didn't you? What did you have to save her from?'

'From making the biggest mistake of her life.'

'Her son?' Eva sighed, turning to look at Julian. 'Was she going to,' Eva licked her dried out lips before continuing. 'Was she going to have an abortion?'

Julian shook his head. 'No. It was too late for that. She was going to give him up. She was young and scared, and she couldn't afford a kid.'

'But you said you had money at that stage. Did she not want your help?'

'She needed more than just money. She needed a guarantee that I'd always be there. A contract.'

'A marriage cert,' Eva whispered. 'The ultimate binding contract.'

Eva was only partially surprised. Meghan was smart. Even at seventeen, Meghan knew how to get what she wanted.

'Exactly. I couldn't let Daniel grow up in care. I hated every day that I spent in that orphanage,' Julian admitted.

'But maybe someone would have adopted him?'

Julian shrugged. 'Maybe. But I don't do maybes. I want guarantees. Every kid needs their mother. I couldn't keep mine, but I could make damn sure that Daniel kept his. Meghan and I were married just a few weeks before Daniel was born.'

'Julian Harte. A married man. Wow.' Eva's voice softened as she came to a strange acceptance.

'In theory, yes, but nothing more.'

'And Meghan's okay with all this?'

Julian's eyes pinched, like that question irked him. 'Meghan has money and security. And a great ten-year-old who adores his mother. Meghan is okay with everything.'

'Including you fucking your way around the office,' Eva accosted.

Julian's jaw twitched and he stared at Eva boldly. 'Including that! It's not a real marriage, Eva. All the usual emotional bullshit that comes with that piece of paper is null and void in our case.'

'Why haven't you gotten a divorce over the years? When your circumstances changed? I mean, Meghan doesn't need your money now. You pay her a fortune in work.'

'Because we never needed to.' Julian tossed his shoulders casually.

'Do you need to now?'

'Mr. Harte…Mr. Harte…' The door rattled. 'Is everything okay in there, Mr. Harte?'

*Dammit, the nurse.* Eva raced to move the chair. 'Sorry, my bag is in the way. I'll move it now.'

# 10

Julian watched with mild amusement as a nurse wrestled with a SpongeBob helium balloon that was half the size of her body and tied it to the side of the bed.

'I wouldn't have taken you for a big cartoon fan,' she said, still fiddling with the string and the bed railing.

'People are full of surprises,' Julian replied.

'There's a card. Would you like me to read it for you?' the nurse asked.

Julian studied the brightly coloured balloon, designed to excite a child. He knew the balloon was from Sergeant Hammond. He didn't need to read the card to know it contained about four words. 'It's over. Thank you.' And it was over. The police had their suspects in custody, Eva had her family back, and Cameron was resting in peace. It was over for everyone…for everyone except Julian. For Julian, it was just getting started.

'My kidneys are fucked, but my eyes are perfectly fine. Thank you,' Julian said drawing his attention away from the balloon and back to the nurse.

'Has the doctor spoken to you about the dialysis process?' the nurse asked as she checked Julian's blood pressure, obviously missing Julian's sarcasm.

'Yes.'

'And did you understand okay or do you have any questions?'

Julian's back teeth clenched hard against each other. 'I got the gist.'

The nurse was his less-than-favourite person after instructing, instead of asking, Eva to leave the room.

The nurse looked appalled. 'It's a complicated process, Mr. Harte. I'm sure one of the doctors would be happy to discuss it with you in more detail. It's important you have a good understanding of how it will all work. It will affect your life massively, so don't be shy. Ask all the questions you need to.'

Julian cast his eyes onto the blood pressure monitor, certain his reading would be skewed high if the nurse continued.

'Has anyone found my phone and clothes yet?'

'I think someone gave them to your wife.'

Julian's nostrils flared. 'No. I didn't ask for them to be passed on to my wife. I asked for them to be given to me. There is something very important in my jacket pocket. I need it immediately. Please.'

The nurse tidied up her apparatus in silence, which Julian greatly appreciated and hurried out of the room, leaving the clunky trolley of equipment beside the bed. She returned less than five minutes later with a green plastic bag and left it at the end of the bed.

'Everything should be in here. There are no phones allowed on the ward. So, I'm sorry, but you'll have to switch it off.'

Julian's eyes growled. 'Thank you, Matron. I'll see you in another half an hour.'

She smiled and pulled her trolley of medical bits and pieces behind her as she walked away. Julian rubbed his eyes with his fingers, hoping that when he took his hands down, she'd be gone.

'I hope you don't mind me asking, Mr. Harte, but are you Mr. Julian Harte of Ignite Technologies?' she said, stopping in the doorway.

Julian pressed his chin against his chest and back up, offering a single nod to answer her question. He really didn't want to get into personal conversation.

'Oh, my God. I thought it was you. How exciting.'

Julian pressed his fingers against his eyes again. His head hurt.

'My son is just finishing a degree in computer science. He's sent CVs out to all the big companies. But working for Ignite Technology would be his dream job.'

Julian forced a reluctant smile. 'I'll make a call and see what I can do...'

'That would be fantastic,' she said, practically bouncing on the spot with excitement. 'Oh, but we have the no phones policy.'

Julian's smile brightened. *Oh, the irony.* 'That's unfortunate, Matron. Looks like my hands are tied. What a pity. If your son has your charming disposition, I'm sure he'd be a valuable asset to Ignite Technologies.'

'Oh, no. He'll be broken hearted to miss this opportunity. Maybe you could call in a few days when you've the strength to walk down the hall?'

'Or,' Julian was practically beaming. She'd clearly missed his sarcasm. Her naivety would work to his advantage. 'If you could get your hands on his CV, I'd happily look at it personally.'

'Oh, my God, really?'

'Really.'

'That's such good news, Mr. Harte. I'll bring it in to work with me tomorrow.'

Julian exaggerated a sigh. 'Oh no, that's a pity. I'm transferring to a Dublin hospital first thing in the morning. I'll be gone before your shift starts.'

'I don't see anything on your chart about that,' the nurse said, scooping up the notes hanging on the end of his bed and flicking through them.

'Ah, I'm pulling a few favours,' Julian lied.

The nurse looked like her whole world had just tumbled around her ankles.

'But I could look over the CV now, if you like?'

'But I don't have it.'

It was a long shot, but Julian was hoping email wasn't really her thing. 'You could nip home for it? I won't tell if you don't.'

'Oh, God no, I couldn't. I've to do your obs again in thirty minutes.'

Julian shook his head and sighed. 'Of course, I understand. It's a pity. Your son sounds like just the kind of guy we'd love to have on our team.'

'Okay, okay.' The nurse's fingers twitched. 'I live just a few miles away. I could make a dash for it.'

'Great.' Julian's grin was lighting up his whole face. 'I look forward to it.'

The matron hurried on her way.

Julian called after her, quickly getting her son's name out of her. If he was going to be gone when she got back, he'd at least have to get her kid a job when he was finished sending her on a decoy.

Julian waited until she closed the door to stand up. He was a little more stable than earlier; that was progress at least. He pulled his suit out of the green plastic bag and lay it on the bed. It still smelt of vodka. Dried blood on the back of the

86

jacket made it stiff, Julian gauged, noting how the dark navy material was masked in a murky brown coating. His shirt was unwearable. Aside from changing from a crisp white to a streaky red, brown, and somewhat pink, it had been cut into pieces with scissors. The doctors had obviously removed it in a hurry. His trousers were cut straight up the centre of the legs, looking more like Batman's cape than a pair of pants. He couldn't wear this. And he couldn't leave the hospital semi-naked. *Fuck it!* He searched in his jacket pocket for his phone and turned it on.

It beeped like crazy as hundreds of emails, texts, and missed calls flooded in. He quickly turned the volume down and made a call.

'Where are you?' he said before the person on the other end even had time to say hello.

'Oh. So you're talking to me now? I've been waiting out here for hours. I can't believe you let Eva in and not me.'

'I can't believe you're jealous.'

'I'm not jealous, I'm just pissed off. Have you any idea how it felt to shunned like that?'

'No. But Eva has. You had no right to stop her from visiting,' Julian scorned.

'I had every right. I'm your wife.'

'Meghan, STOP IT! If anyone has a right to be angry – it's me.' Julian raised his voice but quickly pulled himself together. He didn't have time for an argument or one of Meghan's tantrums. 'Meghan. I need to get out of here. I need your help.'

'What? Jesus, Julian. No! Have you any idea how sick you are?'

Julian rolled his eyes. Today was exhausting. 'You sound like the nurses in this place.'

'Well, good. At least some of us have sense. Is this Eva's idea?'

'What the fuck kind of question is that? No. Of course, it's not. She's waiting outside my room right now. She doesn't know I'm leaving.'

'Good. Well, at least that's something.'

Julian's pressed his lips together tightly; frustration laced his expression.

'You can't leave. Christ almighty, Julian. Stop being ridiculous,' Meghan said.

Julian was already seething with Meghan. Her questioning him was tipping his temper over the edge.

'Meghan. I'm leaving. With or without your help.' Julian was serious, and he imagined Meghan could guess as much.

'Okay, Okay. Give me a minute to think.'

Julian could hear Meghan's panic and he wondered if she knew more about his condition than he'd appreciate sharing. Perhaps, as his wife, the hospital had kept her up to date. He hadn't instructed them not to. It was an oversight on his part. He had been too preoccupied with thoughts of Eva. Haphazard irritated him, and he was furious with himself for making such an obvious mistake. Suddenly, making sure that Meghan didn't speak to Eva would have to become his first priority. Everything else would have to wait.

'I'll meet you in twenty minutes in the car park,' Julian said.

'The car park? Julian, it's snowing outside. Are you mad? I'll come up and get you.'

'No,' Julian raised his voice. 'I don't want to be seen leaving.'

'Julian, it's a hospital, not a prison.'

'Meghan, like you said, I'm sick. They're not going to be happy about me leaving. I don't have time for a lecture or any of that shit. I'll be in the car park in twenty minutes. I need you to be there too, okay?'

Julian hung up without waiting for an answer. He needed every second he could get. He had less than twenty minutes to completely break Eva's heart.

# 11

'Nice balloon,' Eva said gliding back into the room.

'Suits me, doesn't it?' Julian joked, standing leaning casually against the edge of the bed. Half for comfort, half for support.

'Have you read the card yet? Who's it from?'

'Why don't you read it for me?' Julian stretched out his arm and beckoned Eva closer. Eva looked at him with bright, innocent eyes. Eyes filled with hope and excitement for the future. Looking at her was killing him more than his failing kidneys. She chased some ribbon with her fingers and found the card tied at the end. She cleared her throat with a gentle cough and read. 'Julian. Thank you, man. We won. Take care of the girl; she deserves it. Hammond.'

Julian swallowed a lump of air.

'Melissa,' Eva said, smiling brightly.

'No.' Julian shook his head. 'Sergeant Hammond meant you. I love you,' he said reaching for Eva's hand and pulling her into him. His legs were slightly apart, and Eva stood between them. But she wasn't leaning against him as tightly as he'd like her to and he knew she was afraid of hurting him.

'I'm so sorry I couldn't be there for your father's funeral. I would have liked to say goodbye. I hate that you had to be there alone,' Julian apologised.

'I wasn't alone,' Eva said, stretching up on her tiptoes to kiss him. 'Shelly was there.'

'And your mother and sister?'

Eva sighed. 'Yeah, they were there, too.'

'What's wrong?' Julian wrapped his arms tighter around her back and pulled her closer.

'Nothing,' she said, shaking her head. 'My mom's great. It's just Melissa is a bit…'

'She's been through a lot, Eva.'

'Yeah. I know. I feel bad for even saying anything.'

'She just needs time.'

'We don't have time, really. Her and Mom want to get home as soon as possible.'

'What? No. I thought they'd stay a while.'

'Well, they are here a while. You've been out of it for a week, Julian. And there's nothing here for them really.'

'You're here.' Julian kissed the top of her head. 'But you shouldn't be.'

'What?' Eva pulled away from him. Standing back far enough to look him up and down.

'You should go back with them, Eva.'

Eva shook her head and took another step back. She looked like she was either going to completely lose her temper or break down crying. 'I'm staying with you. You asked me to come back to Dublin and I'm here. You can't just turn me away again. Not for a second time.'

'I asked you because I needed to make sure you were safe; away from the Da Luca family. But they're all locked up now, Eva. They won't ever hurt you or your family again. You can go home. That was always the plan. You belong in New Jersey.'

'I am home. This is home. You're home. Please don't push me away.'

'I'm not. Remember that day in the park, after the work ball? I asked you to choose. You quit. You walked away. And you did it because you were strong and you needed to repair the damage to your family. You haven't come this far to give up now.'

'I'm not giving up,' Eva insisted. 'I'm making a conscious decision. And I chose you.'

Julian took a deep breath and exhaled hard. 'You can't have me.'

Eva's bottom lip quivered and Julian had to look away. *Fuck, this was hard.* Guilt twisted in his gut.

'Is this because of Meghan? I understand, Julian. I've been thinking about it and I actually get it. I don't need you to divorce her or any of that. I know it's just a piece of paper. I understand that you did it all to protect Daniel. I think I love you even more for it. I don't need you to be anything that you're not. I just need you to love me the way I love you.'

'We can't always have what we want, Eva. This is one of those times.'

'You told me you never lied to me?'

'I never have.'

'Well, then why did you ask me to be yours? You begged me when you were lying on the ground after we landed. When I thought you were going to die,' Eva said and Julian could see she was holding back tears.

'Maybe it was the pain talking,' he suggested.

'No. It was you. You meant it. I could see it in you. You wanted us to be together. I'm not going to believe you've changed your mind suddenly. I don't want to argue but something has happened. Julian, just tell me. Whatever it is, we can work it out.'

'We can't.' Julian leaned back against the bed. His body was growing too heavy to hold up.

'We can. I promise.'

'You should never make promises you can't keep, Eva.'

'But I love you. Isn't that enough?'

'It's more than enough. And it's more than I deserve. I love you, too. So, so much. But this is a done deal, Eva. We can't be together. I'm so sorry. I hope you believe that.'

Large, fat salty tears ran down Eva's face. 'I'm so confused. It's like what you say and what you do are always contradicting themselves. When you touch me, I can feel how much you love me. But then you say such cold stuff and you push me to the side, like a business deal that's gone wrong. Why are you doing this to me?

'I'm not doing this, baby. It's out of my control.'

Julian wanted her close to him, but she kept her distance. He hated how much this was hurting her.

'Nothing is ever out of your control, Julian. You don't let it.'

Julian reached for her. Grabbing both her hands in his, he pulled her chest as close to him as was physically possible. She was shaking like a feather drifting in the breeze. He buried his face in her neck, nuzzling close. 'Fuck, baby. I wish that was true. But everyone loses at some point. It's my turn.'

'Do you really want me to leave?' Eva sobbed.

'No. I want to keep you. I want to bury myself in you and pretend like the rest of the world doesn't exist. But I'm no good for you. I'll only drag you down now. And you've already been through hell. You deserve the best. And that's not something I can give you.'

'I think I have a right to decide what's good for me and what's not. You're good for me, Julian. You're so good for me.'

'You don't get a say in this, Eva.'

'Why the hell not?'

'Because it's not something I can fix this time,' Julian shouted, infused with frustration.

'Is that what this is all about? You losing control?' Eva shouted back, clearly just as charged.

'Yes.'

'Then let me take control. I can lead with all the relationship stuff that you're scared of.'

'I'm not scared of being in a relationship with you, Eva.' Julian's whole body softened, as he resigned himself to what lay ahead.

'Well, you're doing a good impersonation of a chicken.'

'That's because I *am* scared. I'm scared of not being with you.'

'Then let me in, goddammit.'

Julian's lips were on hers before she finished the words in her mouth. Her taste, her smell, the warmth of her wet lips, her everything; he wanted every piece of her, and he couldn't get enough. She was more intoxicating than any drug they'd pumped into his veins over the last few days. She was the only drug he needed. She was his cure.

Julian scooped his hand around her waist; his other hand slowly crept up her spine until his fingers found their way to the back of her neck, caressing it softly. His thumb stroked an invisible line from just below her ear, down her slender neck all the way to the tip of her shoulder and back up. She tilted her neck in response, exhaling softly. It was a beautiful sound and it told him that she was just as addicted to him as he was to her.

Julian's tongue explored her mouth, kissing her passionately for the first time since New York. Her coffee and cinnamon flavoured lips were delicious and the warm softness of her tongue around his had him aching to come already. His cock throbbed hard and he needed to feel her wet pussy around him. A deep groan sounded in the back of his throat as she tilted her hips towards him, stroking her pubic bone against his granite erection.

She dropped to her knees between his legs and caught a fist full of the bottom of his hospital robe. She reached her hand up his chest, still clutching the robe, pushing it out of the way. She gasped as she revealed how much he wanted her. She slid her other hand between his legs, cupping his balls in her warm palm. Julian twisted his arms behind his back, grabbing onto the edge of the bed for support. Eva's tongue traced circles around the tip of his cock and his knees were buckling from the pleasure. Her mouth opened a fraction more and she slurped his rigid length all the way to the back of her throat.

Julian groaned deeply, the exquisite combination of softness and warmth made him want to release and spray his cum into her mouth. Keeping one hand behind him holding the bed, he reached for her hair with the other. He knotted his fingers through her silky, brown strands, his hand pumping back and forth as her mouth bobbed up and down on him, tipping him closer and closer to the edge. His breath quickened and the trembling in his knees grew stronger.

'Stop,' he said, panting.

Eva did as she was told. She stood up, drying her lips as she wiped a finger across them.

*Damn, she was so sexy and she wasn't even trying.* It only made him want her more.

'Lie down,' he said tilting his head towards the bed.

Eva pulled a face and shook her head.

'Okay.' Julian unbuttoned her jeans. 'We can do this standing up.' He pulled her knickers and jeans down to her ankles before she had time to protest and he laughed as she gasped in shock. Her cheeks reddening as her eyes darted around the room.

He lowered himself onto his hunkers, yielding a little to the stinging in his side. Eva was at his level in an instant, her arms around him, ready to help him back up. Her shocked glow replaced with a worried, half-smile.

Julian slid two fingers under her chin and tilted her head back until her eyes met his. 'You won't hurt me, baby. I promise. Now, stand back up.'

Eva didn't say a word. She kissed his forehead and then stood up in front of him, her pussy level with his mouth. He pushed his thumbs between her knees and slid his hands up her thigh until he could feel her warm and wet. He gently parted her and exhaled slowly as he stared at her beautiful clit, just waiting for him to touch it. His tongue circled her. Her delicate piercing was a cool contrast to the warmth of her skin. The feel of smooth, round metal mixed with the taste of her wet in his mouth and drove his cock crazy. He flicked her from back to front, just how he knew she liked it, and slipped two fingers inside her, curling them to the front until he found her spot. A little more pressure and she was there, bucking on his hand, her clit pulsing in his mouth and her wet streaming like silky rain against his lips.

He waited until she came down from her orgasm before he stood up and kissed her. She winced, tasting her wet from his mouth. She always made the same face when she tasted herself on him. It was cute, and he loved it. He needed to remember that look.

Julian spun her around and bent her over the bed. Pausing for a moment to enjoy her perky ass cocked in the air waiting for him. He watched her body pant and heave in the aftermath of the pleasure he'd given her. He ran his tongue down her spine and she shivered. This was the last time his lips would ever touch her skin; he needed to remember what perfect tasted like. This was their goodbye and he couldn't think of a more perfect way to say it. He pushed inside her without a word and she whimpered as she pushed back against him, sucking him in deep. Julian fanned his fingers against her hips, gripping her tightly and pumping her up and down until he couldn't hold it anymore. He called her name as a powerful release tremored through his whole body. 'I love you, Eva. I need you to always know that. I love you so much.'

## 12

### One week later

Loud, hard knocks shook the door insistently.

'Go away, Shelly,' Eva said knowing who was on the other side of the hotel room door without needing to check. Anyone else would have given up twenty minutes ago.

The knocking stopped for a moment and Eva stayed very still and craned her neck. She didn't even notice that she was holding her breath.

'I'm not leaving. I can stay knocking all night if I have to...' Shelly shouted back. 'Let me in.'

Eva sighed.

'Let me in, Eva. Please? I'm worried about you.'

Eva turned off the television. She'd been staring through it, not at it, anyway. She stood up and ran her hands through her hair, her fingers catching in clumps and knots halfway down. *Dammit, Shelly.*

Eva opened the door and an automatic hello gurgled around somewhere in the back of her throat. She left the door ajar and walked back to sit on the edge of the bed, closing her eyes as she heard the door close. Shelly was following, and Eva would be face to face with her best friend in a matter of seconds. Shelly was one of the last people Eva wanted to see. Well, she didn't want to see anyone, but someone who cared about her made trying not to fall apart almost impossible.

Shelly pushed some messy blankets and an empty box of tissues to the side and made some space beside Eva to sit down. Eva waited for Shelly's bubbly voice to fill the air, but they sat in silence. Shelly was obviously waiting for Eva to say something, but there really was nothing to say.

'Have you eaten?' Shelly said eventually.

Eva tossed her head towards the nearby dressing table. The answer was scattered on top in empty pizza boxes.

'Oh God, Eva. This isn't you.' Shelly stood up. 'Look at the state of this place. You can't stay locked away in here. You're not even answering the door to housekeeping – obviously.'

Eva glanced around. The hotel room had passed messy about three days ago and was heading towards completely disgusting. Sniffled-on tissues were balled up on the bed like snowballs. Coffee cup rings stained the bedside table looking like a dodgy homemade Ouija board. The windows badly needed opening to clear the smell of nights and nights of takeaway lingering in the air. Eva should probably have felt embarrassed, but she didn't have any room left for another emotion on top of everything she was already feeling.

'Have you heard anything?' Shelly asked, edging a little closer to Eva until they were side-by-side.

Eva shook her head. 'His phone goes straight to voicemail.'

'Have you left a message?'

'And say what?'

'Eh, start with where are you?'

'Julian made it very clear that we're not together, Shelly. Technically, I have no right to ask.'

'That's shite. Technically, you've more right to ask than anyone. He's the whole reason you're even in the country. You have a right to be pissed off.'

'I'm not pissed off. I'm just worried. I know something is going on. I'm scared of what it is.'

'I love Julian. You know I do. But I think right now he's being a coward,' Shelly groaned.

'Shelly, if you're trying to make me feel better, it's not working. Julian risked his life to save mine. And Nathan's. Remember? I think a coward is the last thing he is.' Even now, Eva couldn't help but defend Julian. It was like a natural instinct. She was so mad at him, but that emotion was reserved just for her; she didn't appreciate Shelly talking trash about him.

'Sorry, Eva. Jesus, I always say the wrong thing. I just want you to know that I'm on your side.'

'Shell, there are no sides. I know you're still worried about the shit Nathan dug up from Julian's past. But right now, I couldn't care less about what happened years ago.'

'Eva, I get that. I totally understand,' Shelly placated.

Eva doubted Shelly meant to sound patronising, but it was tiresome nonetheless.

'I tried visiting his house in Ballsbridge, but security stopped me at the gate like some criminal,' Eva said, trying to hide her growing frustration.

'Ah, come on. They must have recognised you,' Shelly questioned, unimpressed.

'They did. Yeah. That's exactly why they stopped me. Meghan must have told them that I'm some crazy stalker or something. I don't even know if Julian is there or not.'

Shelly put her arms around Eva and hugged her tight. 'Okay, two things. First, Meghan is a super bitch so I'm not surprised that she's pulling some shite like this. Second, someone has to know where he is. Have you tried Mrs. Cartwright again? Or Anthony?'

Eva broke away from Shelly, her voice as jumpy as her body. 'I've tried calling lots of times. Anne is just as worried as I am. She hasn't heard anything at all. She's at the mansion in the country, but he hasn't been there. I think she's afraid to leave in case he turns up while she's gone. And Anthony isn't picking up his phone. And the hospital won't divulge any information to anyone who isn't family. But I think that's just them covering their asses. He disappeared from the hospital as soon as I left, and the hospital is just as clueless about where he went as the rest of us.'

Shelly sighed. 'So, do you think Meghan knows?'

'Maybe. But I'm the last person she's going to talk to.'

'Did you decide about phoning the police?'

'Shelly, Julian isn't a missing person. He's a hiding person. There's a big difference. I just don't understand what he's hiding from. Running away isn't his style. He's acting like someone who's scared, and I know Julian Harte isn't scared of anything.'

'Do you think it's something to do with Meghan and his kid? Maybe now that you know about them, it's too messy and he's getting cold feet.'

'No, it has nothing to do with that. We talked about it all.'

'You did?'

'Yes, Shelly,' Eva snapped, not meaning to. It was the situation and not Shelly that was frustrating her.

'It's something bad. I can feel it.' Eva sighed. 'Whatever it is; he thinks this is how to protect me.'

'Eva, I don't know…it seems like a strange way to protect someone.'

'Everything Julian does seems like a strange way, but he always had good reason,' Eva defended.

'Maybe this time is different. He broke your heart. And maybe he's just laying low for a while?'

'And not contacting the office or his housekeeper. Not returning home? That's not laying low, that's disappearing. Maybe it has something to do with the Da Lucas. Maybe they're after him and he wants distance between us so I'm safe.'

'The Da Lucas are locked up. The story is dominating US news. They have the whole family because Mickey crumpled like a baby when they questioned him. You've seen the coverage. You know that. The Da Lucas are never going to hurt you again. Julian made sure of that,' Shelly said.

'Well, I don't fucking know why he's gone, do I? But he's not gone running off like a fucking twelve-year-old who's kissed a girl and now doesn't know what to say to her,' Eva snapped.

Shelly was driving Eva crazy. One minute she was defending Julian, the next she was calling him a runaway coward. Eva really wished that if Shelly didn't know what to say that she would say nothing at all. It was hard enough to get her head straight; Shelly talking shit in her ear was making it even harder.

'Eva. I'm sorry. I know this sucks for you. I just don't know what to say.'

Eva's body language was apologetic, but she didn't actually say the word sorry out loud. 'There's nothing to say. Yeah, it sucks for me. But it sucks for him even more. Whatever it is, it's so bad that he thinks the only way he can protect me is by leaving me.'

'Maybe he's doing it to force you to go back to New Jersey?'

'That's not going to happen. I've made that clear. I'm staying in Dublin. I never should have left in the first place.'

Shelly's whole face brightened, but Eva didn't acknowledge it. Now was not the time for a happy dance.

'Can I show you something?' Shelly asked, rooting in her bag.

'Yeah, okay,' Eva said, hoping she didn't sound as uninterested as she felt.

Shelly pulled out a folded newspaper article, and Eva reached for it reluctantly. She unfolded it and read the bold, black font across the top of the page. 'The National Informer. Nathan's paper,' Eva snarled. 'Is this his article?'

Shelly nodded.

Eva refolded the paper and passed it back to Shelly. 'I don't want to know.'

Shelly stood up and threw her hands in the air, refusing to take back the page. The paper tumbled to the ground between the two of them. 'Trust me, Eva. You want to read this.'

Eva's expression soured. 'Oh, you've got to be fucking kidding me. You two are back together, aren't you?'

Shelly smiled brightly. 'Yeah. Little bit. Now, will you please trust me? Just read it, Eva.'

'Oh, Shelly. What are you doing?'

'I know, I know. But I love him, Eva. I can't walk away. Tell me you wouldn't do the same if you were me?'

'I wouldn't do the same?'

'Really? But here you are obsessing over the biggest player of all time.'

Bile burned in the back of Eva's throat and she hated Shelly a little bit at that moment. Partially because Shelly had made a good point, but mainly, because that point was misguided and Eva was the only person who understood that.

Eva bent forward and picked up the paper. A mix of last night's pizza and too much wine swirled around her stomach and her body objected to leaning forward. She stood up, hoping she wouldn't be sick all over the hotel carpet.

'Billionaire Businessman Julian Harte acquires numerous properties in West Cork and County Clare with the intention of expanding his technologies company to a staff of over seven thousand in Ireland, growing Ignite Technologies into the biggest company in the country,' Eva read the first line out loud, becoming silent as she scanned the rest of the article. It was all facts and figures and a mention of some of the charities Julian donated to. There was nothing of substance in it and certainly nothing personal.

'I don't get it,' Eva said shaking her head. 'This is old news. The office announced the acquisition of those companies down the country months ago. Nathan would have known all of this ages ago. Where's the real story? About the Da Lucas.'

'He didn't write it, Eva.'

Eva's forehead pinched. 'But he knows everything, he has all the research. All the stuff you told me in the hospital…even the stuff about my dad. It's a huge scandal. It would make him one hell of a reporter. He'd be the hottest journalist in the country.'

'And it would make him one hell of a shit friend. He couldn't do that to you. He couldn't even do it to Julian. Nathan owes Julian his life. He knows that. He's not about to stab Julian in the back now.'

Eva rolled her eyes.

Shelly slapped her forehead with her hand. 'Shit, sorry, terrible choice of expression.'

'Did you have something to do with this, Shell? Did you ask Nathan not to write it? Oh God, that's not why you're back together, is it?'

Shelly laughed and snorted. 'Ha, no. Jesus. It's been a while since I had to sleep with a man to get what I wanted.'

Eva's stomach was already dodgy enough without a reminder from Shelly that she had slept with Julian in the past. Thinking about it now made her feel even more galled than she already did.

'Nathan's here, isn't he?' Eva said realising that Shelly's eyes were darting towards the door every so often.

'He just wanted to check that you were okay.'

'Is he waiting in the hall?'

'He's gone to get us some coffees. I told him to give us ten minutes.'

'Ten minutes? That's how long you thought it would take to get me on your side?' Eva knocked her shoulder gently against Shelly. She was half-joking, half-furious. And wholeheartedly exhausted. She didn't have the energy for any more confrontation.

Shelly looked at her watch. 'Well, it only took five.'

Eva laughed dryly. 'It's going to take a lot more than coffee, Shelly. Nathan better not have any more surprises up his sleeve.'

'No surprises. Just a suggestion.'

Eva stared at her friend blankly.

'Go see Meghan,' Shelly said.

'Not a chance. No fucking way. Nope, nah-ah, not happening.'

'Go see her, Eva, before you completely crack up.'

## 13

Eva checked and rechecked the address that Nathan had given her. He'd asked someone in his office to do a little digging to find out where Meghan lived. Shelly could have easily pulled up Meghan's address from the office files, but Eva knew it was Nathan's attempt at a peace offering and she'd accepted it reluctantly. *But did Nathan have to ask someone with illegible handwriting,* Eva decided, squinting to try to make the words on the page out. She wasn't sure if she should be knocking on number twenty-seven or number fifty-seven. And looking down the street at a row of pretty semi-detached two stories, Eva wasn't even sure if she was on the right road. This just didn't seem like the type of place Meghan would live. It was very suburban family and very not Meghan. Then again, Eva didn't think Meghan would turn out to be a mother to a gorgeous ten-year-old little boy or married to the man Eva loved. A mismatched house was the least of the surprises.

Eva gathered herself on the porch for a few minutes. She'd thought about calling or texting Meghan first, but she'd decided against it. Meghan might have warned her not to come or had time to conjure some sort of a story. No! This was definitely something that had to happen spontaneously.

Eva pressed the doorbell and waited, regretting not taking Shelly and Nathan up on their offer to go for a couple of glasses of dutch courage in the hotel bar before she left.

She didn't have to wait long. Meghan opened the door with a smile, looking a lot less surprised than Eva anticipated.

'Oh, so you've decided you want to talk to me now after all,' Meghan said. 'Come in.' Meghan turned her back and walked back inside.

Eva glanced back out onto the road and down the street. It was starting to get dark but children were still out on the green playing. Eva didn't spot Daniel, but she hoped he was out with his friends and not in the house with his mother.

'Close the door behind you,' Meghan shouted back from the kitchen. 'It's bloody freezing out there.'

Eva took a deep breath and pushed the door over. She followed Meghan into the kitchen. *Fuck, it felt weird*, she thought, hoping her apprehension wasn't written all over her face.

'Coffee?' Meghan said as Eva came through the door. 'Or are you a tea person?'

'Neither, thanks. I'm not staying long.'

'Okay,' Meghan said, putting the kettle back down on the shelf. 'C'mon. You look positively frozen. I've a fire lighting in here.' Meghan walked through pretty double doors of pine and frosted glass leading into a small, cosy living room.

112

Meghan sat at one end of the sofa in front of a fabulous roaring, open fire, and Eva sat at the other end. A music channel, with the volume turned down low, was playing on the television in the corner. It was all so normal. Like they'd been friends for years and Eva had just popped over for a catch-up.

'Is he here?' Eva said breaking a short silence.

'Who?' Meghan seemed instantly on guard.

'Daniel?' Eva replied.

'I don't think that's any of your business,' Meghan snarled.

'Sorry. I just…I have some questions and I don't think they're something you'd like him to hear.'

'Well, he's not in this room. So unless you plan on shouting your head off, I think we're good.'

*Fucking Meghan. Always had to pass a bitchy comment,* Eva thought, furious.

'I'll start with the obvious. Do you know where Julian is?'

'Yes.'

Eva hopped up off the couch. She hadn't anticipated that answer. 'Where? Oh, my God, where?'

'So you *are* doing the shouting thing, then,' Meghan said glaring through Eva.

Eva wanted to take the fuck ugly lavender and mint vase off the mantel and crack it over Meghan's head. But she held herself together, apologised, and sat back down.

'It looks like we've something in common,' Meghan said changing the subject.

Eva snorted. She had *nothing* in common with Meghan. This was getting her nowhere. Eva eyed the door. She wasn't going to sit through Meghan's nastiness, but she'd kick herself if she came all this way and didn't at least ask what Meghan meant. 'Really, Meghan. What is it you think we have in common?'

'We both love a man who doesn't love us back,' Meghan finished.

Eva swallowed hard. Hearing Meghan's confession hurt more than Eva imagined it would. She wasn't prepared. She'd never expected honesty from Meghan and she had no idea how in the hell to reply to a revelation that big.

'So you're in love with Julian Harte.' The words tumbled from Eva's mouth without her thinking, as if somehow knowing the information gave her some sort of subconscious power. It made them equals at the least. Their marriage might have been nothing more than a fancy contract to Julian, but it certainly seemed to mean a lot more to Meghan than just a piece of paper.

'I love Julian. But I am not in love with him. There's a big difference.'

Eva grunted, hearing Julian's words in Meghan's mouth. 'Gah. Was that line one of your wedding vows or something?'

'Excuse me?' Meghan mumbled.

An uncomfortable tightness eased in Eva's chest. It wasn't gone completely but at least she could breathe without it feeling like the air in her throat might choke her.

'Nothing,' Eva said dryly. Meghan couldn't have known that Julian used the exact same expression when describing their marriage. Maybe they were both more alike than Eva had realised before, or maybe they'd rehearsed what to say if the truth ever came out. Either way, it didn't really matter. There was a big difference. And that big difference was that Julian didn't just love Eva. He was in love with her.

'Eva, sit back down,' Meghan said with a softness in her voice.

Meghan was attempting to act casual, like they weren't both in hell. But she needn't have bothered. They were so far past the point of niceties. Their mutual hatred for one another was only matched by their mutual concern for Julian.

Eva was so tense that she felt like she was leaning back against broken glass as she lowered herself into a nearby armchair.

'I think we're going to need something a little stronger than coffee,' Meghan insisted.

'No. Thank you. As I said, I'm fine,' Eva reiterated.

'Well, I'm not.'

Meghan disappeared into the kitchen and returned a few moments later with a bottle of red wine, a bottle opener wedged under her arm, and two wine glasses dangling from her fingers. She set both glasses on the table and opened the wine skilfully. The label looked beyond fancy, and no doubt expensive. The way Meghan handled the bottle, the way she poured the first glass...Eva guessed she knew a lot about wine. Maybe Julian had taught her. Eva's face pinched as she wondered what else Julian had shared with his wife. *Ugh!* That word hurt her brain.

Meghan didn't fill the second glass. She put the bottle down on the table with a force that was unnecessarily excessive. Eva's eyes narrowed. *Was Meghan trying to intimidate her?*

'So, you think you know the boy?' Meghan said, after sitting down on the sofa, leaning on the arm closest to Eva and draining a large mouthful of wine.

'The boy?' Eva said, not sure why in the hell Meghan was bringing Daniel into it.

Meghan snorted and Eva rolled her eyes. Meghan's sweet disposition was dissolving as quickly as Eva had expected it to.

'You've only met the man, Eva. I've known the boy.'

*Oh. She was talking about Julian,* Eva thought, relieved. If Meghan was trying to turn this into a competition, she was a little late to the event. Meghan was Julian's wife. She'd already fucking won!

'So I didn't know him as a kid. So what?' Eva replied.

'So, then you don't really know him.'

'Meghan. That makes no fucking sense. So people only know the people they've grown up with? Yeah, right. I know Julian. I know him inside out! You're just freaking out because the boy wanted you, but the man wants me.' Eva couldn't believe she had said something so cheesy, but hell if it worked, she'd throw every cliché in the book at Meghan.

'So you think he's in love with you?' Meghan said. For someone sipping so much wine, her words were painfully dry.

Eva stood up again, not sure why, since it was a little dramatic. 'I don't think it, Meghan. I know he is.'

'Why? Because he told you?'

'Well, yes actually. Because he told me.'

'Eva, he was dying. He would have told you Mickey Mouse was his uncle if he thought that would save you.'

'Save me?' Eva snapped. She was furious, she wanted to storm away, but she wanted information out of Meghan far more.

'From yourself. Jesus, Eva. You're so helpless. You're afraid of your own shite. Why are you the only person who can't see that?'

'I'm not,' Eva argued tiredly.

'I'm not,' Meghan mimicked. 'Excellent comeback, Eva. Real conviction from you there.' Meghan snorted out a laugh and quickly raised her hand to her mouth as wine attempted to come back out.

It was Eva's turn to laugh. 'That's fucking disgusting, you know.'

Meghan exaggerated a gulp and tossed an eyebrow in Eva's direction. 'There, I knew you could do bitchy if you tried.'

'What can I say? You bring out the bitch in me.' Eva tossed her head to one side instinctively as she spoke.

'Whoa! You're on a roll. Don't stop now, girl.'

'Meghan. Fuck off. Why did you let me in? So you could be nasty as usual? Aren't there enough new girls in the office for you to pick on?'

'You know, if you were a bit more like this most of the time…I think I could like you.'

'You know, if I was a bit more like this most of the time…I think I could hate myself.'

Meghan smirked. 'I think I know what he sees in you.'

'This question is probably redundant, but I'll ask anyway. What does Julian see in me, Meghan?' Eva fully expected a sarcastic ass answer, but she was past caring. If Meghan wanted to play, she was definitely up for the challenge.

'You've got fire. It's just covered in a smokescreen of damage and scars,' Meghan said, oddly softly.

'Scars? What the fuck do you know about scars?' Eva could have kicked herself as soon as the words slipped out, remembering that Meghan spent her childhood in the same orphanage as Julian. 'Shit, sorry. That was out of line.'

'No. It wasn't. I've been hard on you. You've a right to find out why,' Meghan said.

'So why?'

Eva watched as Meghan eyed up the bottle of wine in front of them. Her glass was drained and she was reaching forward to fill it again. 'You sure you won't have some? It's good stuff.'

Eva already had a headache; wine was the last thing she wanted. But maybe Meghan needed the security blanket of girlfriends chatting over a couple of drinks. They were far from friends, and Eva knew Meghan would be far from just having a couple of drinks, but Eva decided to play along.

'Yeah, okay. Just a small one.'

Meghan filled both glasses close to overflowing and passed one to Eva.

'Thanks,' Eva said taking a glass and concentrating on not spilling.

'You haven't heard from him since he left the hospital, have you?' Meghan asked.

'No.' Eva thought about lying to sound less desperate, but if Meghan knew where Julian was, then she most likely also knew that he was also avoiding Eva. Maybe Meghan even knew why. Shit as it felt that Meghan had the upper hand, it was worth a little humiliation if Meghan could give her answers.

Meghan shook her head. 'That's not fair of him. I thought he might have called you or at least text.'

Eva squinted. Meghan actually sounded genuine. Concerned even. It was Oscar-worthy.

'Well, you'll be glad to know I haven't heard a single word. He decided we were over and that was that.'

'Over before you even began,' Meghan mumbled into her glass.

Eva's jaw twisted and she sighed with her mouth closed.

'Don't get pissy, Eva. That's not what I meant. I actually think Julian is the one in the wrong here. He's not even giving things a chance.'

'Meghan, where is he?' Tears laced Eva's words.

'I can't tell you. I want to, Eva. I know you probably don't believe that, but I do.'

'Okay, and you're not telling me because…'

'Why do you think?'

Eva dropped her head. She didn't *really* want the answer to her next question. 'Julian told you not to, didn't he?'

Meghan nodded, and the already shattered pieces of Eva's heart turned to dust.

'I want to tell you because Julian Harte never needs anyone. But right now he needs you,' Meghan said.

Eva's head was reaching her bursting point. She'd never had a migraine that bad before.

'You look like shit,' Meghan said, taking Eva's glass from her twitching fingers and putting it down on the floor.

'Thanks,' Eva snorted, unsurprised.

'I mean you don't look well. Are you okay?'

'Not really,' Eva admitted. 'Have you any aspirin?'

'Yeah, sure. Hang on.'

Meghan stood up weirdly awkward and Eva couldn't miss the rectangular paper that fell out of Meghan's back pocket onto the couch. Eva waited until she could hear Meghan opening and closing cupboards in the kitchen before she reached for the pale blue leaflet. She scanned it as quickly as she could, barely taking in every second word. She flicked right through to the back. She couldn't believe the words on the page. Suddenly, no amount of aspirin would be enough.

'Well, that was subtle,' Eva barked, charging into the kitchen.

Meghan turned around with some small white pills in her hand. 'Here.'

'You wanted me to find this,' Eva said waving the pamphlet that was now shaken out into just one large page that she couldn't figure out and didn't give a shit about folding back.

Meghan calmly filled a glass of water from the sink. She dropped the two, small white tablets onto the counter and slammed the half-full glass down beside them. 'Take those.'

Eva looked at the pills through squinted eyes. Her head felt like someone was attacking her brain with scissors, but she wouldn't give Meghan the satisfaction.

'Why did you want me to see this? This is about organ donation, for fuck's sake. Do they want Julian to be a donor or something? Oh ,God. Oh, my God.' Eva's hands were on her head, and she was spinning around on the spot. 'Oh, my God.'

'No.'

'No. Fucking no? That's all you're going to say? Just one word?'

'Will you keep your voice down. Jesus, Eva,' Meghan snapped, rushing to close the kitchen door leading into the hall.

'No. No, I fucking won't. You want me to shut up? Well, tell me what in the hell is going on. I don't care how much you hate me…fucking tell me.'

'I told you. I can't! I promised Julian and I owe him a lot more than a goddamn promise.'

'So, what? Julian has banned you from talking to me, and you're just going to do what he says?' Eva growled.

'Oh, don't you dare pull that card on me, little miss pathetic,' Meghan replied equally aggravated. 'You're the queen of being bossed around. Tell me, Eva…was it your idea to come here or did your friends give you an encouraging push? You know Nathan, the guy who almost got Julian killed. The guy who's been plotting against him for months so he could print shit in his shoddy newspaper. And yet you still judge me? Fuck you, Eva. Fuck. You.'

'So, what? You're using this shitty hospital jargon on this page to say what Julian won't let you say with words.' Eva's grip on the leaflet was so tight her fingers burned.

'Bingo, Einstein.'

Eva breathed heavily and took a moment to pull herself together.

'And why would you want to help me?'

'Don't flatter yourself. It's not *you* I want to help. But as much as I hate you doesn't even come close to how much I love Julian. And you're the only person who can make him see sense. I don't have any other choice. They're not asking Julian to be a donor, Eva. He's not dead…yet. So get your head out of your arse. Julian's not a donor. He's a recipient. He needs a new kidney. Or he would be a recipient, if he'd just fucking consider it.'

Eva didn't say anything. She was so far past words. She grabbed the pills off the counter, shoved them in her mouth, and washed them down with the water.

Meghan smiled.

'Thank you,' Eva said, her words stretching much further than appreciation for some over-the-counter medication.

## 14

'Is she gone?' Julian asked, leaning over the banister of the stairs on the landing. He was comfortable for the first time in days in loose, dark navy jeans and a white V-neck t-shirt. His hair was tossed and messy like he'd just woken up.

'Yes.' Meghan gargled and stormed back into the kitchen.

He sighed and made his way downstairs to follow her. 'You're not going to tell me you're actually pissed off, are you?'

'Yes, Julian. I'm pissed off.' Meghan flicked on the kettle. 'I think what you're doing to Eva is terrible.'

Julian pulled out a chair from the kitchen table and sat down, laughing. 'You've changed your tune. You were the one who had her banished from the hospital, remember?'

'I didn't know the whole story, did I? I thought she was in cahoots with Nathan.'

Julian rubbed his hands roughly up and down his face. 'Nathan Shields is a fool. He's a sorry ass excuse for a reporter. If he prints one word, I'll sue the arse off him for slander. He knows that he was in way over his head. He was scared shitless at Vertigo. I don't think he'll be rushing to do another undercover piece for a very long time.'

Meghan laughed. 'Well, he certainly wasn't expecting the Da Lucas to be such a colourful bunch, I suppose.'

Julian cocked an eyebrow. 'Colourful is one word for them.'

Meghan placed a cup of hot coffee on the table in front of Julian. 'Here. You look like you need this.'

'Thanks.' Julian wrapped his hands around the hot cup. 'I know that I'm asking a lot of you, Meghan. But I wouldn't ask if I didn't think you were the best person for the job.'

'I'm just worried I'll fuck up,' Meghan said walking back over to the countertop.

'No, you're not. You can do business acquisitions in your sleep. You're worried I'll be six feet under by the time the job is done and you get back from New York,' Julian said before raising the cup of coffee to his lips.

Meghan made another cup of coffee and carried it over to the table to sit beside him. 'Julian, don't talk like that, please. It scares me.'

'Meghan, I want everything the Da Lucas own in my name by the end of the week. I don't care how much it costs. I want to buy up their whole empire. Mickey Da Luca is going to know what it feels like to lose.'

'I know you're angry, Julian. But I wish you'd use your energy to get better, instead of this…this…revenge plot thing.'

'It's not revenge, Meghan. It's just good business. The state has frozen Da Luca's assets, understandably, since every dollar was blood and drug money. I'll get a good price on it all.

126

I'm hoping that buying out the lot won't be more complicated than necessary. I don't doubt there'll be some legal mumbo jumbo and some red tape that'll need cutting, but I know you can sort that shit with a click of your brilliant fingers.'

'And then what? You're going to go into the pimping business.'

Julian took a mouthful of coffee and pulled a face. 'Fuck. That's disgusting.'

Julian meant the coffee not Meghan's business suggestion, but he laughed knowing his remark could be taken both ways.

Meghan laughed in spite of the tension. 'Julian, seriously. What are you going to do with Da Luca's properties? Are you expanding Ignite Tech in the states? You already have an investment in HTK over there; won't this be a clash of interests?'

Julian smiled. Meghan was such a good businesswoman; he had every confidence she could teach Eva everything she would need to know. 'This has nothing to do with expansion. I fancy a new venture. The Andrews Charity. It has a nice ring to it, doesn't it?' Julian said, grinning.

'What?' Meghan's whole face scrunched.

'I'll make sure it's all official and signed on the dotted line in time. Everything will be in Eva's name. It'll all belong to her.

She can learn on the job. You can help, of course. In fact, I'm counting on you to.'

'Help with what? Julian, I'm not following.'

'The Andrews Charity will be a reform house for ex-prostitutes. Give them somewhere safe to live while they get their shit together. There'll be counsellors on site, and in time, Eva can look into education programmes and anything else relevant and beneficial.'

'Wow, I didn't see that coming,' Meghan said, putting down her coffee cup.

'Melissa Andrews is fucked in the head. She's going to need a hell of a lot of support. Eva needs to be there for her family. This gives her the perfect starting ground. Eva knows what it's like to live through hell. She's just like us, Meghan. But we changed. We became tough and guarded. She never changed. She's a marshmallow inside and out. She's a bloody good person and she's the best person for the job…she's the only person. She'll do a lot of good there.'

'There? As in back in America.'

'Yes.'

'But you're crazy about her. What are you doing? Why in the hell are you pushing her away? Now, of all times?' Meghan asked, almost whispering

'Because, if she finds out how sick I am, she won't go. She'll want to stay here and try to fix me.'

'Is that such a bad thing? She loves you. Why won't you let yourself be loved? Stop always punishing yourself.' Meghan's whispering quickly changed to close to shouting.

'I know she loves me. She'll put me first and I can't let her do that. She needs this time to repair the damage to her family. She needs to be with her mother and sister.'

'She needs to be with you. Jesus, Julian, you're dying.'

'Meghan…' Julian said her name like it left a bad taste in his mouth and his eyes pinched and darkened. 'Eva doesn't need to know that. Maybe not ever.'

'So you're just going to break her heart and let her think you don't care about her.'

'If that's the best way to make sure that she will be okay, then that's exactly what I'm going to do.'

'God, you have a fucked-up view on how to love someone, Julian.'

Julian tossed his shoulders.

'What are you afraid of, Julian? Are you afraid to be normal? Normal people get sick. If you just thought about the donor programme…'

Julian slammed his hand on the table, shaking the coffee cups. 'This isn't open for discussion, Meghan.'

'Okay, fine. Forget the Eva thing for a moment. I know you want to fix her family. And I understand how important

Cameron was to you. But what about me? I love you. Don't I get a say?'

'No.'

'Julian, that's not fair. It's too high a price. You don't owe the Andrews your life.'

'Actually, Meghan, I do. Now, will you help me?' Julian asked sombrely. 'Will you help me or not?'

'Of course, I'll help you. God, you know that without even asking. I'm just worried about you.'

'Well, don't be,' Julian said. 'It won't change anything and this will be fucking hard. You don't need distractions.'

'What about Eva?' Meghan asked.

'What about her?'

'You can't just keep shutting her out like this. Christ, Julian. She's not exactly my favourite person and even I wouldn't treat her like that.'

'She will know everything when the time is right.'

'And, in the meantime, you're afraid to let her in in case she sees you be what? Normal? Vulnerable? Needing her?'

'I don't need anyone.' Julian soured, the legs of her chair scratching noisily across the floor as he pushed out from under the table.

'Bollocks, Julian. You've just told me that you need me. You asked for my help. And every move you make tells me that you need her. Grow a pair, Julian, and tell her that. If you don't, I will,' Meghan growled.

'Eva knows I love her.'

'Why? Because you told her? Cop on, Julian. Maybe she thinks you lied. You have to show her. Is that so hard for you?'

'Yes.' Julian dropped his head. 'I love her, Meghan. I never believed in that bullshit. I never thought you could care about someone so much that the thought of ever hurting them tore you apart inside. But that's how I feel about Eva. I adore her. And I will do everything I possibly can to protect her from everything I possibly can.'

'You're going about this all wrong.' Meghan softened.

'I don't have any other choice. Everyone she's ever loved or trusted has left her. And now I'm leaving her, too. I need her to walk away from me; I need it to be her choice. I can't be responsible for fucking things up for her.'

'But you're not letting her walk away. You're pushing her. That's not giving her a choice. It's the exact opposite. And it's not fair,' Meghan argued gently.

'It's the only way I know how,' Julian said, honestly.

'Well, learn a new fucking way, Julian. Because if you love her as much as you say you do, then you owe it to her to explain everything and let her make an informed decision. And you owe it to yourself to LET HER IN.'

Julian didn't reply. He let Meghan have her rant. He knew it was her way of coping.

'You know, when Eva discovers what you've done, she'll blame herself,' Meghan said after a brief silence.

'Don't use Eva as leverage, Meghan.' Julian shook his head, unimpressed.

'I'm not. But it's true, she will. You won't get the treatment you need and you're going to fucking die. And why? All because you're hell-bent on repaying a debt from when you were a child. You were eight years old when Cameron saved you, Julian. You were just a little boy. He was a grown man. You don't have to spend the rest of your life trying to make it up to him.'

Julian could see Meghan physically shaking as she spoke. This was hurting her; he felt a knot of guilt in the pit of his stomach. None of this was supposed to happen. *Fuck the Da Lucas. Fuck them.* Julian's body was heavy and he needed sleep but pure hate fuelled him on.

'Cameron is gone, Meghan. He spent the last years of his life rotting in a prison cell because his head was so fucked up that he was a danger to himself and his family. He didn't have to risk his life to save me from the fire. But he did.' Julian paused and ran his hand roughly through his hair. 'I visited him in New York, just before he died, you know.'

Meghan's body language changed. Her feisty side paled for a moment and Julian knew she was prepared to listen now.

'Cameron was full of remorse,' Julian added.

'Well, rightly so. He messed his whole family up. Eva's a walking bloody disaster, and it's that man's fault. No good deed twenty years ago outweighs all that, Julian,' Meghan snarled.

'And I'm not saying it does. I'm saying Cameron wanted his family protected and that's my responsibility.'

'Why?' Meghan shouted, losing all composure.

'Because I damn well say so. Now, are you going to help me or not, Meghan? I'm tired.'

'And what if I say no? I can be just as obnoxious as you, you know.' Meghan stood up, flapping her arms.

'No, you can't.' Julian laughed standing up to tower over her.

'Okay fine, but I have conditions,' Meghan said, looking up at him with the saddest eyes Julian had seen in a long time.

'And they are…' Julian asked softening.

'You have to go to see Eva. You can't leave things like this.'

'Meghan!' Julian growled.

'I will help you, Julian. But promise me that you'll consider going back to the hospital. I'm begging you to just hear them out. I don't want to lose you. Please, just talk to Eva about it,' Meghan pleaded as the tears she'd done so well to hold in swelled in her eyes and trickled down her cheeks.

'No, Meghan. I've told you. That's not going to happen.' Julian shook his head and paced the floor.

'Okay, then I'm not going to New York,' Meghan barked, wiping her eyes with the sleeve of her blouse.

'That's blackmail, Meghan. I don't take kindly to that kind of shit, and you know it.'

'No. It's negotiation.' Meghan tossed her head to one side, confidently. 'You're the one who always taught me to fight for the best deal. Always push to win. Those were your exact words, weren't they?'

Julian gritted his back teeth. He recognised the expression, but he didn't appreciate having it used to his disadvantage.

'Your flight is booked for tonight. Do you need me to check in on Daniel?' Julian said sternly.

Julian knew that Meghan was well aware that although they were best friends, he was still her boss. He very rarely exercised his right as her employer to end a conversation about a work related topic by simply raising his hand to signal a stop. So when he did, Meghan knew not to push it any further.

Meghan sniffled. 'Daniel is staying with a friend from school. They do sleepovers all the time so he shouldn't suspect anything is weird. I'll give the mother your mobile number. There shouldn't be any problems, but just in case.'

'Okay.' Julian nodded. 'It should only take you a couple of days to sort out. The legal guys know to expect you. Any problems and you call me straight away, okay? This has to go smoothly.'

'Are you going to stay here while I'm gone?' Meghan gestured around the kitchen. 'You can, it's no problem…if you don't want to go back to your place.'

'No.'

Meghan's head sank into her shoulders. 'Are you going to tell me where you *are* going?'

'No.'

'Am I ever going to see you again?' Meghan's voice was breaking, and she was failing to keep her emotions under control.

Julian leaned over Meghan and kissed her on the forehead. 'Anthony will be here in half an hour. You should pack. I'll come to the airport with you to wave you off.'

Meghan left the room and Julian heard her feet pound painfully slow up the stairs.

He sat back down and exhaled until he was lightheaded. His elbows rested on the table and his hands cupping his face. His head hurt almost as much as his heart. He'd spent his whole adult life and most of his childhood as an emotionless prick. He'd broken women's hearts every day of his life. And for the most part, he really didn't give a shit. He'd convinced himself it was all just a big game and he'd always come out the winner. *Sex and love were two different things*, was his mantra. And for a long time, he believed in it. As long as he fucked his way around Dublin then love would never catch him, and if he never fell in love, he'd never feel pain like he did as a child again. Sex was his medicine and, once he never mixed it with emotion, he'd be cured. But he knew that just wasn't true.

Life wasn't a game, no matter how good he was at convincing everyone otherwise. And even if it was, there would always be someone who would break the rules. Eva broke every rule he had. He'd worked hard to set up the elaborate game for her; the ball, the masks, the one girl for the year, the test to be his plaything. She hadn't just passed, she'd turned the tables. He'd known from the very moment Eva walked into his office that he'd already lost and she'd already won. He loved her from that very second. She could have written in any rules she liked and he still would have played. The game was designed to help her find herself and make her stronger. And it did. But it also caused the one thing he never wanted to happen. He was head over heels in love with her. He had to see her. No matter how much he believed it was the wrong thing to do or how much he knew it would mess with both their heads. Meghan was right. He. Had. To. See. Eva.

# 15

Eva's phone vibrated in her coat pocket. It was begging for her attention non-stop for the last couple of hours, but she didn't want to talk to anyone. She'd gotten off the bus on a street she didn't know simply because she couldn't sit still any longer. It was getting dark and it was positively freezing. She eyed up a small, rundown, corner pub desperate for the heat of indoors.

Eva ordered a drink, found a dark, corner booth and slid behind the table. She chased the lemon around the glass with a swizzle stick and stared into space. She'd read the medical pamphlet from cover to cover a couple of times on the bus and now the words were written across her mind when she closed her eyes.

Eva opened her eyes after a long time, feeling a shadow leaning over her.

'Whoever he is, he's not worth your tears,' a tall, broad and slightly scruffy around the edges guy said. 'Can I get you another?' His eyes dropped to the glass Eva hadn't noticed she'd drained.

'You know what they say?' he asked.

Eva shook her head.

'There's plenty more fish in the sea. A beautiful girl like you won't have any problem going fishing. Whoever he is, get another drink in you and forget about him.'

'He's my boyfriend...or, kind of is, and I think he might be dying but he's too scared to tell me.'

'Oh sweet Jesus, love. I had no idea. The next one is on the house, okay.'

'Thanks.'

Eva didn't know why she had just told the barman her sob story. It wasn't like her. But sitting here, in a place she didn't know, drinking hot whiskey wasn't like her either. But maybe it was finally time she changed. Julian had saved her. Saved her whole family. Now he needed saving. She wasn't going to let his stubborn ass push her away. She had to figure this all out.

'Do you have Wi-Fi here?' Eva asked as the barman placed a fresh glass of hot whiskey in front of her.

'Yeah, of course. The password is booze.'

Eva sniggered. 'I like it. Very, um, apt. I might be here a while. Do you think I could switch to a white wine spritzer and keep them coming, please?'

'Absolutely. I'll set up a tab at the bar for you. Take all the time you need.'

Eva pulled her phone out of her pocket, smiling as she noticed her battery was almost at full charge, and settled herself comfortably against the back of the brown leather bench seat. She searched through endless Wikipedia articles about being a donor recipient, clicking from one link to the next. Devouring as much information as she could. She Googled the success rates and case studies; pros, cons, and aftereffects. She was drinking in the knowledge. The barman was as good as his word; keeping her supplied with delicious spritzers and minimal disruption to her reading.

Eva was finally drawn back into the moment by the flickering of the lights and someone shouting, 'Last orders.'

She pulled on her coat, threw her phone back into her pocket, and left some cash under an empty glass on the table, hoping she'd calculated correctly. She made her way back out to the street, trying to figure out where in the hell she was. It was late, dark, and cold. The last thing she wanted to do was ask someone for directions. It didn't look like the nicest part of the city and she didn't want to become a mugged tourist statistic. She hailed the first taxi that drove by and crossed her fingers that she had enough cash left to cover the fare.

Back at the hotel, she raced past reception. She didn't wait for the elevator but charged up the huge staircase in the centre of the lobby instead. She just wanted to get to her room, whip out her phone again, and continue reading up on all the articles she'd saved.

Eva came to a sudden stop outside her bedroom door, actually choking on a gulp of air. She coughed hard. 'Julian. Oh, my God. You're here. You're actually here.'

Before she knew it, her hand had flown of its own accord and slapped him across the face. 'That's for disappearing without a trace.'

Julian rubbed his red check and smiled deliciously. He didn't look surprised. Just amused. He'd obviously anticipated how she'd react. Eva didn't know which was more infuriating, that he was always second-guessing her, or that he always got it right.

'Fair enough. I deserved that,' Julian said, taking his hand down from his face.

Eva couldn't stay mad. The relief at seeing him was overwhelming. She didn't know what to do with her hands; they were on her face, her heart, back at her face again. Shaking. Finally, she wrapped them around his neck and held him tight.

'Can we go inside?' Julian whispered, his lips brushing against her ear.

'Yeah, sure.' Eva fidgeted in her bag for her key, peeved that her head was so fuzzy from the wine.

16

Eva slipped off her coat and dropped that along with her bag onto the messy bed. Julian was instantly behind her. He picked back up her coat, turned it upside down, and shook it. The pamphlet fell out of the inside pocket and onto the tossed white sheet. He dropped the coat and picked up the pamphlet all at the same time.

'Spying on me, Miss Andrews,' he accused.

Eva flopped down onto the edge of the bed. Her legs were weary. She'd forgotten to eat today and her stomach reminded her with angry growls. She was in no mood for one of Julian's interrogations. 'Meghan gave it to me actually. So, no. I wasn't spying on you.'

'So you were around in Meghan's for tea and scones, then?'

'Well no, obviously not. I went there to see if she knew where you were.'

'So you *were* spying on me.' Julian tilted his head.

'Jesus, Julian. I can ask Meghan if she's seen you if I like. You don't own her…or me for that matter. You made that very clear at the hospital when you dumped my ass and then disappeared without a trace.'

141

'I'm sorry.' Julian's eyes darkened. Maybe he was angry he'd had to apologise. But Eva felt she deserved it. She wasn't backing down.

'You fucked me, and then you practically kick me out the door. I went back to the hospital the next day only to discover you'd left. You didn't even give us a chance to talk things through. You're giving me such mixed signals; I feel like I'm losing my mind. I go from being so afraid I might lose you, to so relieved you're okay. For what? Just so you can have a change of heart and push me away. You're not playing fair, Julian.'

'Miss Andrews, you're the one who keeps mentioning games. If I didn't know better, I'd say you're the one attempting to win here.'

'Win what? You? Are you my prize, Julian? Well then, the game is flawed. It's FUCKING flawed. You give me everything; money, clothes, a great job. You've even given me back my family. But you won't give me the one thing I want. The only thing I want… I want you. So no Julian, there's no winner. The game sucks and I lose.'

'We've been over this,' Julian said calmly.

'No, we haven't. You've just told me that you don't want to be together. I didn't get a say.'

'I never said I didn't want to be with you. If you're going to quote me, I'd appreciate if you got it right. I said we couldn't be together.'

'It's the same FUCKING thing, Julian,' Eva shouted.

Julian's look was smouldering. Lust and aggression combined to make him irresistible to her. Her heart was racing and tiny beads of perspiration gathered on her palms. She wanted to slap him across his smug face again. Then pull his clothes off and fuck him until he shouted her name. Instead, she snatched the pamphlet out of his hand, tearing a corner in the process, and held it up. Waving it in frustration.

'Are you going to tell me what the hell is going on?' she said, trying and failing to keep her voice down.

'Do I need to?' Julian stepped away, creating a little distance between them. 'Clearly you've gone behind my back and figured it all out for yourself.'

'You didn't leave me any choice. You weren't going to tell me. You were saying good-bye at the hospital and I didn't even know. You just left me, and I didn't know if I'd ever see you again. Did you really expect me to just accept that? You had to know that I'd want answers. Anyone would.'

Julian didn't say anything, but he watched her with a burning intensity that sent a fire of desire racing across her skin.

'Why are you here, Julian? Is it just because you are angry with me for trying to find out the truth? Or have you changed your mind about us.'

'If you had questions, Eva, you should have come to me. Instead of hoping the internet would solve your problems.'

'How could I come to you? I had no idea where you were. And now who's spying on who? How do you know my internet search history? Do you have my phone tapped or something?' Eva knew that sounded a bit too CSI as soon as she said it.

Julian sighed. 'You were using your work phone. The server is monitored.'

Eva winced. *Dammit.* 'Fine. I'll use my personal phone from now on.'

'Okay.' Julian shrugged, exaggerating his indifference, and it was infuriating.

'While you're at it, would you please refrain from trying to extort information from my friends and staff,' Julian said.

'Anne doesn't know anything. And Anthony won't answer his phone,' Eva snapped, still angry at his shrugging.

'That's because their loyalties lie with me, Eva. I only work with people I can trust.'

'Have you told them not to speak to me?' Eva asked, her shock more obvious than she'd like.

'No. I didn't have to. They know me well enough to know when I don't want something discussed.'

'And I don't know you well. Is that what you're trying to say?'

'You're putting words in my mouth again, Miss Andrews. I'd much rather you put your pussy there.'

'Julian, stop it.' Eva threw her hands to the side. 'You can't change the subject with sex talk.'

Eva was lying to him and herself; her mind was instantly flooded with images of her straddling his face while he licked her good.

'They're your employees, Julian. They're going to do what you say. Their paycheck depends on it.' Eva copied Julian's shrugging.

Julian closed his eyes and his lips twitched. Eva regretted it as soon as she'd said it. She knew Anne Cartwright was much more to Julian than just his housekeeper. She was a mother figure to him. And Eva suspected Anthony was the nearest thing to a brother that Julian had ever known.

'I'm sorry,' Eva said reaching her hands out to pull him close to her.

Julian caught her wrist just before her fingers touched him and threw her arm back at her. He looked at her with burning eyes. 'Don't apologise for speaking the truth, Eva.

We've discussed this before. Apologising when you're not in the wrong makes you weak. Weakness is unattractive.'

Eva's pity for him was instantly wiped, replaced with exasperation at how cutting his remarks could be.

'You're right. They are my employees. But they don't respect me because I demand it. They respect me because I've earned it. You cannot just demand what you desire. You have to earn the right to it,' Julian explained dryly.

'What?' The wine was swishing around Eva's belly and her head was fuzzy. It was making it hard to concentrate. 'Are you talking about us?'

'I'm talking about all things,' Julian replied quickly.

'You're talking in fucking riddles. I shouldn't have to beg you for information. I'm your girlfriend. Or was. For all of five minutes until you went all bi-fucking-polar on me. I deserve to know what's going on.'

'Exactly. You *were* my girlfriend. You're now just my employee and my previous comment stands.'

'Okay.' Eva tried to hide her pain at his impassive remark. 'Then I quit. Consider this my notice.'

'Excuse me?' Julian's eyes widened.

Eva smiled. 'You heard me, Mr. Harte. I quit.'

'I expect the termination of the contract by either party, employer or employee, to be served in writing, Miss Andrews.

You know that.' Julian's stare was burning into her and she suspected he was undressing her in his mind.

'Well, my word was good enough for you the last time I quit, Julian. You're just bullshitting and playing the fancy big shot CEO now to piss me off.'

'Must I remind you, Miss Andrews, that you are currently contracted with HTK Associates. I am little more than a silent partner there. Your resignation must be rendered with Mr. Thompson, not me.'

'Bullshit. You own ninety-six percent of the holdings, Julian. I checked. That doesn't seem very silent to me.' Eva matched the intensity of his stare.

'Very thorough research. I admire that,' Julian praised. 'Someone with your cutting business sense must understand you have to resign IN FUCKING WRITING.'

Eva's fists clenched and her shoulders tensed. She raced to the bathroom, pulled a couple of sheets of toilet paper off the roll, hurried back into the bedroom, and grabbed a pen off the nightstand.

'Here,' she snarled, scribbling two words on the toilet paper and shoving the paper at Julian.

He took it and read it out loud with mild amusement. 'I quit.'

'There.' Eve tossed her head to one side. 'Now it's in fucking writing.'

147

'Much appreciated, Miss Andrews. And your choice of paper is very appropriate.'

Eva sighed, hopping mad. 'Why is that, Mr. Harte?'

'Because I plan to wipe my arse with it.'

'Nice, Julian. Very mature.' Eva groaned.

'You can't quit. You need your job. How are you going to survive in New York with no money? It's an expensive city,' Julian said cockily.

'I'm not going back to New York. I've told you. I'm staying in Dublin.'

'Eva, this is not open for negotiation,' Julian said, stepping forward.

'You're right. It's not. I am staying here and there's nothing you can do about it. I will type a proper letter of resignation and forward it to Mr. Thompson's office in the morning.'

'Eva, you're being irrational.' Julian moved closer.

'No. I'm being decisive,' Eva argued. 'This is my decision to make. I've done what you've told me before. I've gone back. I've met my mother and my sister, who incidentally hates me by the way, and now I'm doing what I want to do.'

'And throwing up your job and staying in this pissy wet country is what you want to do? You want to stay here?' Julian's eyes pinched.

'You're here,' Eva replied softly, looking into his eyes.

148

'But your mother and sister are there.'

'Mom and Melissa are grown women. I can visit them. There's not going to be a quick fix to our problem, Julian. It won't make a difference which side of the Atlantic I'm on.'

'Eva. I said no,' Julian growled with his lips barely parted.

'You're not listening to me. You can push me away all you like, but I'm not leaving. Even if we're not together, I'm staying here…because you're here.'

'And what if I'm not always here?' Julian said, finally sitting on the bed beside Eva.

Eva's gut twisted. Was he just messing with her words or did he really mean that? She looked at the pamphlet in her shaking fingers. Her body language, her tone, everything changed. There was no anger left in her. 'Julian, how sick are you? I'm begging you. Just tell me.'

'Very,' Julian answered without hesitation.

Eva's breath caught in her throat; like Julian had reached his hand into her chest and pulled the air out of her lungs.

'Okay. Thank you. Can we talk about it?' Eva asked, trying to stay calm on the outside, at least.

'No.'

'Are you going to die?'

Julian's nose scrunched. 'That's talking about it, Eva.'

'Please just answer the question,' Eva begged. 'Are you?'

'We all die at some point,' Julian simplified.

149

'That's not what I meant.'

'I know what you meant. I've told you this is not open for discussion but you just won't drop it. If you keep asking questions I don't want to answer, then I am going to give you answers you don't want to hear.'

'Who else have you told not to give me answers? The hospital? Taking pointers from your wife, I see.' That came out more bitchy than Eva intended and she regretted her tone.

'Stop calling her that.'

'Why?'

Julian was on his feet in front of Eva before the question had finished leaving her mouth. He shot her a don't-fuck-with-me look and spun her around to lean over the edge of the bed. 'Because the only woman I ever want to call my wife is you.'

Eva flipped herself back around, her stare meeting his. His eyes burned into her with an intensity that matched her own. She really regretted the last couple of glasses of wine now. 'Did you really just say that?'

'Yes.'

'You told me that you'd never marry me.'

'And at the time, I thought that,' Julian admitted. 'But things change. I've changed. Now I'm so fucking in love with you that I can't see straight.'

Eva pushed her hands against Julian's shoulders and shoved him away from leaning over. She stood up and paced the room with her hands on her head. 'So you love me enough to want to marry me, but not enough to tell me what is going on.'

'I won't tell you *because* I love you,' Julian said, watching her every step.

Eva swallowed hard. She was crying on the inside but no tears were falling. Her frustration and confusion were overwhelming them. 'That's not how stuff like that works, Julian.'

'It's how I work.'

'It doesn't matter anyway. This conversation is stupid,' Eva said, suddenly standing still. 'You're still married to Meghan.'

'I've told you. It's just documentation. It can be tidied up at any time.' Julian walked towards her.

'So you're going to divorce her?'

Julian pulled a folded white envelope out of his back jeans pocket and placed it on the nightstand next to them. Eva couldn't miss her name in bold capitals on the front.

'What is that?' Her eyes moved from watching Julian to staring at the envelope.

'It's for you. Anthony has been holding on to it for me,' Julian explained.

'What?'

'I asked him to give it to you when I was going into Vertigo. I asked him to give it to you in case…'

The tears that wouldn't fall before trickled down Eva's cheek now. 'In case you didn't make it back out?'

Julian nodded.

'Why now?' Eva asked, afraid of the answer.

'Because it's the right time. Don't read it now. Later. When I'm gone.'

Eva tried to hide the sting of disappointment. 'Can't you stay?'

Julian shook his head.

'Can't you stay even for a little while? We could order some room service. I'm starving.'

'I'm hungry, too,' Julian said.

'Okay great. I'll get the menu.'

'I don't think the hotel can offer anything to satisfy my appetite.' Julian's coquettish grin sent a tingle down Eva's spine.

'Oh. That kind of hungry.'

# 17

Eva walked back to the bed. Julian was still standing beside it. He didn't move. Eva stopped just in front of him and kicked off her shoes, instantly emphasising the height difference between them. She reached around his back, her elbows tucked close above his waist and her hands reached to clasp his shoulders. She felt his deep exhale as his breath danced across the top of her head that she tucked under his chin.

'I'm sorry, Eva. I tried to stay away from you, but I just fucking couldn't.'

'I'm glad you couldn't.'

'Knowing you were alone in this hotel room when I could have been here with you...it was all I could think about.'

'Shh...you're here now. We can talk about everything later.'

Julian caught the corner of the duvet and tossed it onto the ground behind them. His finger slid under Eva's chin and she tilted her head back, guided by his gentle touch until their eyes locked.

Julian leaned down and kissed her neck. His warm lips sent tingles of desire circling the nape of her neck. She'd never wanted him more. He caught the bottom of her sweater and she lifted her arms in response to let him tug it over her head.

His finger traced a line from her chin, down the centre of her chest, and stopped just between her breasts. He dropped to his knees and dragged the lacy, cream cotton of her bra between his teeth. He tugged at one cup and then the other.

'Let me see you,' he whispered.

Eva reached behind her back and unclasped her bra.

Julian groaned in appreciation. 'Fuck, Eva. The things your perfect tits do to me.'

He swirled his tongue around one nipple and then the other.

There was something so gentle about his touch; something so emotional in their connection. Eva had never felt so close to him before. Like they were the only two people in the world at that moment.

Julian slipped an arm around her back and he pressed the other between her breasts, easing her back onto the duvet on the ground behind them. Eva relaxed back against the softness and never took her eyes off him.

He unbuttoned her jeans, slid them and her underwear down her legs, and threw them to the side. He tapped her knees and she let her legs fall to either side, opening for him.

'You're soaking already,' Julian said, watching her.

'You have that effect on me.'

154

Eva's back arched and her hips drew up as he sucked her clit into his mouth.

'Ahhh,' she gasped taken by surprise at the intensity of the feeling. 'Julian…oh, my God, Julian.'

Her hands reached down, grabbing fistfuls of his hair. The tighter she gripped, the harder he sucked. One of Julian's hands made its way around to cup her ass, palming her cheek as his other hand rested on her belly.

She ground her hips, her body pleading with him to fuck her with his fingers. He lowered his hand from her belly, slowly moving down until he slipped two fingers inside her as he continued to kiss and suck her clit. A third finger followed, stretching her, massaging her walls.

'You're so fucking tight, baby.' Julian whispered, his breath rushing against her tingling clit.

'Ahh,' she gasped again, louder this time as he pushed a finger into her ass.

The sting took her breath away for a moment. She was so full and the pressure was mind blowing. She tried not scream but every time he curled his fingers to the front, just behind her pubic bone, teasing her spot, she lost control and his name passed her lips repeatedly.

She ground her hips as forcefully as she could, over and over, not able to get enough of him.

'Yeah, that's it,' Julian gasped. 'Fuck my face. I want to hear you come.'

'I'm going to,' Eva cried out as she reached her peak. 'I'm coming…I'm coming.'

Julian didn't give her time to recover. He was on his feet and pulled her up to stand in front of him.

'Hold on to this,' he said, bending her over the edge of the bed.

Without her noticing him unbutton his jeans, he slipped inside her, thrashing his hips against her. She struggled to keep her grip on the edge of the bed as she caught her hips and rammed them back and forth on his rock hard cock. He slapped her ass and finally released.

Breathless, Eva turned around to face him. She kissed him softly and scampered back onto the bed. She pulled out a crinkly t-shirt from under her pillow and slipped her head and arms though. Julian zipped his jeans back up and Eva tried to hide her need for him to take his clothes off and slip into bed beside her.

'Are you leaving?' she asked a little surprised with how suddenly making love had all ended.

Julian nodded.

'Are you going to disappear again?' Her voice was breaking. *Dammit.*

Julian shook his head.

'Julian, it's nearly one am. Why don't you just stay? I promise I won't ask any more questions – tonight.'

'I've some important stuff I need to sort out,' Julian explained.

'At one am?'

'It's not one am in the rest of the world, Eva.'

'Work stuff?'

'Read your letter, okay? And get some sleep.' Julian walked around to the head of the bed and kissed her softly on the forehead. 'I love you.'

'I love you, too.'

## 18

Eva was expecting the hangover from hell. But she woke up feeling surprisingly okay. Someone was knocking on the door and it took her a moment to get her bearings and remember where she was.

'Coming. Coming,' she called, grabbing the dressing gown from the back of the bathroom door as she passed.

'Good morning, Miss Andrews. Your breakfast.'

Eva looked at the trolley between the young waiter and herself. A full Irish fry, fresh fruit, orange juice. It smelt like heaven.

'I didn't order...' *Julian*. Eva sighed and rolled her eyes, standing to one side to open the door a little wider. 'Come in.'

Embarrassed she only had small change for a tip, she passed some coins into the waiter's hand and closed the door behind him.

She gulped down the orange juice, almost drinking the full glass in one go. She was thirstier than she thought and a headache was starting to kick in. She munched on some hot toast and sat on the edge of the bed. She picked up the white envelope with the slightly tattered edge and was about to open it when she was distracted by beeping from her phone. She had a few missed calls and texts, but she read the most recent one from Julian first.

**Meet me 4 dinner 2nite.**

She smiled brightly and put the envelope back down.

**OK Where?**

**It's a surprise.**
**Anthony will pick u up @7pm**

**But I don't know what 2 wear.**

**I left my credit card 4 u.**
**Go shopping...**
**C u l8r**

Eva devoured some delicious bacon, taking a moment to decide on her next text.

**R U going 2 answer my questions?**

She hit send with determination and Julian's reply came back almost immediately.

**I'll have all the answers u want.**
**And 1 question.**

Bubbles of excitement popped in Eva's belly like sparkling champagne. Was he really going to propose? She didn't even have to think about what her answer would be. But what about Meghan? She didn't want to be engaged to a man who still married to another woman. Marriage of convenience or not, Meghan was still the one parading around as Mrs. Harte and Eva was still the other woman.

**OK I love u**

**I love you 2**
**Read ur letter!**

*Oh my God, the letter.* She'd almost forgotten about it – again. She was surprised she'd fallen asleep last night without reading it first. She took the knife from beside her plate and slid it across the top of the envelope. Her fingers were shaking, but she didn't know why.

She slid out the pages from inside and unfolded them, shaking her head as she scanned the words. It was all legal jargon and complicated paragraphs. She might as well have been reading ancient Latin, until she got to one word she did understand. Nullity. She almost dropped the page.

She read and reread every word. Absorbing as much as she could, occasionally consulting the dictionary app on her phone. Julian said he didn't need a divorce from Meghan. And he was right. Eva held the paper to her chest almost hugging it. The fancy words decreed that Julian and Meghan's marriage was annulled just days after the date of their vows. Julian was telling the truth. Their marriage was null and void. And this piece of paper was proof.

Eva turned on the television and flicked through the channels, settling on an American news station covering the latest on the Da Luca's case. The family had hired some hotshot lawyer trying to make a name for himself, but the judge had denied bail. Eva smiled and tucked into the rest of her breakfast, listening to the report intently. There was no mention of Melissa or Julian. The station wasn't known for its discretion so if they had Julian's name, it would be splashed about like water at a pool party. Julian had obviously done a very good job at making damn sure his name stayed out of the papers. No one would ever know he was a hero. *Her hero.*

Eva glanced away from the screen at Julian's credit card. She thought about a day indulging in the most delectable boutiques Graton Street had to offer, but she slipped Julian's credit card into the desk drawer for safe keeping and turned her

161

attention to her own card with a scant limit. Something simple and paid for herself would do just as well. She wanted to take his breath away later, but on her terms. Maybe she'd splurge on some simple lingerie for underneath.

She grabbed a quick shower, threw on yesterday's clothes, and hoped she'd catch a bus without a long wait.

## 19

Eva looked into the shopping bag dangling from her finger. After two indecisive hours of shopping, she'd finally settled on a red bandage dress with lace three-quarter length sleeves. She hadn't tried it on, but she bought a size smaller than usual, vaguely remembering Shelly's concerns that she'd lost weight recently. She'd grabbed some black stilettos to go with it and a silver clutch. The only coat she had was Shelly's oversized parka. It definitely wouldn't match, but she didn't want to spend any more money. She was conscious of every penny, which reminded her that she needed to take a moment to email Pam about work.

She grabbed a takeaway coffee from a tiny corner cafe and leaned up against the outside wall of the cafe to give her attention to her phone. She hit send on brief but professionally worded resignation email and tried not to panic that she was now unemployed. She was certain HTK wouldn't pay for any further hotel accommodations once she was no longer an employee. She hoped Shelly's offer to stay with her for a while still stood.

Eva's phone vibrated in her hand and she was surprised to see her mother's name appear on the screen.

'Hello,' Eva answered.

'Hi, Eva. I wasn't sure I had the right number for you,' her mother said.

There was an awkwardness hanging over the line. Eva realised they hadn't spoken on the phone in more years than she could count.

'You do. This is me,' Eva said.

'Are you busy today?'

Eva looked at her shopping bag. She was hoping to take some time to chill in the bath back at the hotel and put a lot of effort into her hair and make-up before she met Julian later.

'No. Not really,' Eva lied. 'Is everything okay?'

'Can we meet?'

'Are you still in Dublin?' Eva's voice was an octave higher than usual. 'You told me you were going back to New Jersey. I thought I'd missed you.'

'We took a trip down the country. Did some sightseeing,' Samantha replied so quietly, it was almost apologetic.

*Sightseeing? What?* This conversation was too surreal. Eva tried to hide the sting of jealousy that her mother and sister had paraded around the country on some sort of overdue family vacation without her.

'I left you messages and voicemails, but I didn't get a reply. That's why I thought maybe I had the wrong number,' Samantha said.

Guilt thumped on Eva's chest. She'd been ignoring most of her calls, and she hadn't listened to any of her voicemails.

'I'm sorry. I've had a lot going on. I was going to call you. I thought you had gone home…I would have called you…' Eva trailed off, realising she was lying.

She wouldn't have called. Even if she'd known that Samantha and Melissa were still in the city. *Was there even anything left to say?*

'Where would you like to meet? I'm in the city now. Are you near?' Eva said.

'I'm in the hotel,' Samantha said. 'But I can meet you anywhere. Our flights are booked for this evening.'

'Let's say Haley's Bistro in an hour,' Eva suggested, surprisingly calm. 'It's nearby. Ask at the hotel receptionist for directions.'

'Okay, sweetheart. See you soon.'

Eva hung up and stared at the ground. Her last conversation with Julian ran through her head. He wanted to send her back to America to be with her family, yet she'd spent two weeks in the same hotel as them and the only conversation they'd had was crouched over her father's grave. They were so fucked up; they'd been under the same roof for two weeks and Eva hadn't even known. Eva was more certain now than ever that going back to New Jersey or New York was not an option.

## 20

Eva sat tapping her foot against the restaurant table as she waited. She waved to her mother as soon as she came through the door. Samantha looked like a little-lost child. Eva recognised her expression because she'd worn the very same one when she first came to Dublin. Alone in the city with a strangling metaphorical weight around her neck. Despite how daunted Samantha looked, Eva was glad to see her on her own. Eva really didn't fancy more cold shoulder from Melissa.

The conversation was broken and stilted as they sat with their heads down perusing the menus lying flat on the table. They chewed over the weather, gave the hotel room services a mention, but they avoided anything of real depth.

'Does your friend still want his story?' Samantha said oddly out of context.

'What?' *Where in the hell did that come from?*

Samantha picked up the menu resting in front of her on the table and held it close to her face but her eyes were peering out over the top. Eva lifted her own menu, ignored her mother's staring, and tried to choose something. She was actually really hungry despite her huge breakfast earlier.

The waiter appeared at their table wearing a bright smile, a crisp white shirt, and slightly too lose black bowtie. A bright, white towel draped over the arm he kept folded across his chest.

Eva took a quick look around. They were noticeably underdressed compared to the rest of the clientele. The restaurant was deceptive from the outside and Eva hadn't realised how exclusive it was. *And expensive*, she thought, glancing briefly at the wine list.

'Are you ready to order?' the waiter said, leaning across the table to pour some water.

'Yes?' Eva looked at Samantha, questioning. 'We're in a hurry,' Eva blurted.

Samantha's face fell and Eva realised how she had inadvertently let Samantha know she could only offer her a small window of her day. It wasn't how she'd meant it to appear, but Eva was conscious of the time, and she didn't want to be running late when Anthony came to pick her up later.

'What can you recommend that's quick and delicious?' Eva asked the waiter, but she was smiling at Samantha to try to ease the sting.

The waiter dropped his pertinacious swag and reverted to a thick Dublin accent. 'I'd go with the gourmet beef on a warm sesame bum with hand-cut potato strips.'

'Burger and fries,' Eva laughed.

'Exactly.' His smile grew more genuine and Eva liked him. 'Wine?' he added.

'Yes. I'd like a glass of house red please and…Mom?'

Samantha shook her head as if Eva had just asked her to sample rat poison.

*Shit!* Eva realised she had no memory of Samantha with a drink in hand – ever! *Of course.* With her father's issues, her mother was probably scared shitless of the stuff.

'Actually, you know what? Never mind, I'll just stick with my water…as I said, we don't have a lot of time,' Eva said.

'No problem. I'll let the chef know to put a rush on the order,' the waiter obliged.

'Thanks.'

Eva waited until they were halfway through their meal before she spoke again, partially because she was so hungry and partially because she wasn't entirely sure she wanted to know where her mother was going with all this.

'So….are you going to tell me?' Eva said, curiosity finally getting the better of her.

'It's good,' Samantha replied, between mouthfuls of delicious beef.

'Not the burger, Mom. The story. What can you tell Nathan that he doesn't already know?'

Samantha's chewing passed painfully slow as Eva waited with bated breath for her to gulp down the last bite.

'A lot. Your friend might be one of the worst reporters I know.'

Eva was surprised by how offensive that sounded, but she hid her distaste for her mother's comment. 'He actually knows more than you think. He could have written an article and shamed us all. But he didn't write anything out of respect for me, Mom. But that doesn't mean he couldn't.'

'Do Irish papers print complete nonsense, then?' Samantha snapped.

The waiter was back at their table clearing the plates and enquiring about dessert. 'Just the check please?' Eva dismissed, not meaning to sound so abrupt.

'The bill, of course.' He skulked away quickly.

'No. They don't print nonsense. Of course, they don't. What are you talking about?' Eva said, angrily.

'Good. I'd be disappointed if they did. So does he want the real story?' Samantha asked gently, dabbing the corners of her lips with her napkin.

'The real story?' *There's a real story?* 'I don't know if he'd be interested anymore.'

Eva did know. She knew Nathan would jump at the chance of an exclusive from Samantha. Eva just wasn't sure if she wanted to hear more. 'I can ask him, I suppose. Will I give him your email, then?' Eva said.

'Email?' Samantha sounded appalled. 'God, Eva. I'm barely able to use my phone to make a call. I don't know much about email. No. Ask him to meet us at the hotel in, what? Will we say an hour?'

'We won't have time.' Eva shook her head at her mother's confused sense of Irish geography. 'The hotel is heading back in the wrong direction. You'll need to head to the airport straight from here or you'll miss your flight. I'll come with you. I'll pass him your number and he can call you about the exclusive when you get home.'

'Eva, sweetheart,' Samantha said, standing up to put on her coat. 'This exclusive is for you.'

Eva blushed. She hadn't picked up on that. 'And what if I don't want to know?' Eva asked.

'You know what? You probably don't want to know. But you deserve to. And it's damn well time I told you,' Samantha replied.

'What about your flight?'

'I can book another one. It's no big deal.'

'Seriously? It's that important?' Eva said, surprised.

'Seriously.' Samantha's head bobbed up and down quickly.

Eva's face brightened with the thought of holding onto her mother for a little while longer. And she realised, no matter how preoccupied her head was with everything going on with Julian, deep down she really did want a chance of reconciliation with Samantha.

'Okay, I'll call Nathan now,' Eva said pulling her phone out of her bag.

## 21

Nathan was waiting in the lobby of the hotel. He looked slightly more haphazard than usual. His trousers were just a fraction too short, revealing his royal blue socks. One side of his shirt was hanging out over his trousers and he hadn't even taken the time to brush his hair and left it to impersonate a hedgehog sitting on his head. Eva sighed disappointedly. His appearance wasn't helping her argument with Samantha that Nathan was actually very professional and good at his job.

There were only a couple of days left until Christmas day and the lobby was bustling with eager shoppers checking in and out. A huge tree decorated in crimson and gold enraptured a large portion of the centre of the floor and festive spirit danced in the air. For a second, the delightful atmosphere enchanted Eva, but she quickly snapped out of it and made a beeline across the busy lobby towards Nathan, reaching him at almost the very same moment as Shelly appeared behind him. Shelly looked just as dishevelled as Nathan. Except her rosy cheeks and tossed hair just highlighted her natural beauty. Nathan's arms slipped around Shelly's waist and it didn't take a rocket scientist to work out their relationship was back on a very physical track and Eva's phone call had obviously interrupted their make-up sex.

Feeling almost like she should apologise for the interruption, Eva suggested they head to the bar. Melissa had replied with a one-word answer to Eva's text asking to meet in the hotel bar and Eva was conscious not to keep her sister waiting. One more hissy fit from Melissa and Eva was going to lose it completely.

There was only one free table in the corner, too small for them all to fit comfortably around but Shelly raced over to grab it nonetheless and looked back to beckon them all over. Eva looked around, but there was no sign of Melissa. Maybe she wouldn't come.

Melissa appeared at the main bar door just as they sat down. Eva stood back up and waved to let Melissa know where they were. Melissa made her way slowly to their table but she didn't wave back and her expression looked like it could turn a small child to stone.

They squeezed around the table, all sitting in silence and without any drinks. It was like the most awkward board meeting in the world. Eva wondered who would speak first. She wondered if she should start, since she was the only person there familiar with everyone else. But she just wasn't sure what to say. Hello felt desperately redundant and after fucking up earlier with the wine order in the restaurant, suggesting they grab a drink felt like an even worse idea.

'It's a pleasure to meet you, Mrs. Andrews,' Nathan said extending his hand from his side of the table to Samantha.

Samantha shook it. 'Yes. Indeed,' she said softly.

*Introductions. Jesus, of course.* Eva rolled her eyes; she should have started there.

'Mom, this is my friend and reporter with the *National Informer,* Nathan Shields. Nathan, this is my mother, Samantha Andrews. And my sister, Melissa,' Eva said turning to Melissa who, to Eva's surprise, held out her hand and shook Nathan's.

'How do you do?' Melissa said dryly.

'Can I get anyone a drink?' Nathan asked politely.

'I'll have a white wine please, love,' Shelly said.

'I'd appreciate a cup of tea, thank you,' Samantha added.

'I'd also like a white wine, thank you very much,' Melissa said.

Eva smiled brightly. Melissa was actually taking part in the conversation. She was being polite. And she was ordering alcohol in front of their mother. Maybe Eva had misread Samantha in the restaurant.

'I'd kill for a coffee,' Eva admitted.

'Did I even need to ask,' Nathan laughed, making fun of Eva's caffeine addiction.

'I'll just be a moment.' Nathan excused himself from the table and Shelly followed him, no doubt to help carry the drinks.

'They're a good couple,' Samantha said, watching them at the bar.

'Yeah. I'm glad they're back together,' Eva said.

'Had they split up?' Melissa asked

Eva could feel her whole body lighten inside at her sister's question; it was the first time they'd exchanged words about anything more than necessity and it felt so good.

'Yeah, Shelly was upset about some stuff.'

'Stuff to do with Julian?' Melissa suggested.

'Yeah. But more Nathan. He fucked up. I didn't even think she'd forgive him. But I'm glad she did.'

'Are you going to forgive Julian?' Melissa said, staring awkwardly at Eva.

'For what?' Eva snapped. Suddenly a lot less taken with this conversation.

'Do you want a list?' Melissa snapped back.

Eva's expression soured. 'You don't know Julian, Mel.'

'I know his type.'

Rage surged inside Eva's head and she could feel her face redden. She didn't even care if it was obvious. If Melissa meant Julian was anything like the sick bastards who frequented Da Luca's clubs then long lost sister or not, Eva would happily get up and walk away.

'Julian is one of a kind, Melissa,' Shelly said returning to the table and obviously catching the end of the conversation.

175

'I've known Julian for years, and I still don't even know his type. I think Eva is the only one who really knows him.'

Nathan and Shelly passed the drinks out and silence once again fell over them all.

'So, Mr. Shields. Do you have a pen? Shall we start?' Samantha asked before blowing gently into her cup of tea.

Nathan pulled a small black box out of his pocket and placed it in the centre of the table. 'Are you okay if I record this? It helps me get the emotion right in the story afterwards. You know, when I can listen back to it. I just don't get that connection with notes.'

Samantha winced.

'If you're uncomfortable….I do have a pen and paper.' Nathan fished in his inside jacket pocket.

Samantha placed her teacup back on its saucer. 'No,' she said pulling herself up to sit tall and straight. 'Getting the emotion right sounds very important. Will we start?'

Nathan pressed a small button on his black box and smiled. 'Interview with Mrs. Samantha Andrews. Friday, Dec 22rd,' he said calmly and impressively professional. 'In your own time, Mrs. Andrews.'

Shelly moved even closer to Eva until she was practically sitting on top of her. She grabbed Eva's hand and squeezed tightly. But her efforts to support Eva actually had the reverse effect and Eva was feeling decidedly nervous.

'My husband wasn't a bad man or a monster. I know you both remember him that way,' Samantha turned to her daughters, 'and that saddens me more than you'll ever know.'

'But he was a wife beater?' Nathan said accusatorily.

'Are you telling the story or am I, Mr. Shields?' Samantha said, turning her attention back to Nathan.

Eva smiled. Her mother had sass. It was really rather exciting to see.

'Apologies.' Nathan smiled. 'Please. Do go on.'

'Like I said, Cameron wasn't a bad man. But he messed up. Big time. And we all had to bear the consequences of that.'

Eva eyed up the bar, suddenly regretting her decision to order coffee. 'Whiskey on the rocks,' she said catching the attention of a lounge boy.

'Whiskey,' Shelly mouthed without any sound coming out.

Eva shrugged dismissively. 'If it works for Julian.'

'Make that two please,' Samantha called after the lounge boy.

Eva couldn't stop her jaw from dropping a little. It turned out Samantha wasn't someone she could read easily, and Eva loved that her mother had layers. She was more excited than ever to get to know every single one.

'Three,' Melissa piped in.

Eva's jaw found its way back up but only to form into a gentle smile.

'You know what? I think we're going to need a round. Five Jameson's please,' Nathan said.

An awkward silence descended until the waiter returned with a tray of burgundy filled tumblers. Nathan was the first to raise his glass and everyone quickly copied, the glasses clinking as they collided gently in the air.

'To Julian's good health,' Shelly said.

'To Julian's good health,' everyone mumbled.

Eva gulped down the fiery whiskey in one large mouthful. Shelly passed her glass and she knocked that back quickly, too.

*Julian's good health.* The words rang in her ears. Her mother was clearly about to share something huge, but Eva's head was already stuffed to bursting point with thoughts of Julian. *Were two whiskeys enough to make you feel sick?* Eva certainly felt on the verge.

'So, Cameron wasn't a monster,' Nathan said, drawing Eva back in.

'No. But sometimes I wish he had been. Things would have been very different if he'd had just a little more strength.' Samantha was soft spoken and genuine. 'Can we visit Dun Laoghaire?'

'What?' Eva's heart pinched hearing the familiarity of Julian's favourite place.

'Now?' Nathan asked, clearly taken aback.

'No. Not now, Mr. Shields,' Samantha giggled. 'But I would like to visit there before I leave. Tomorrow maybe? What do you say, Eva? Mel? Will you come with me?'

'Why do you want to go there, Mom?' Eva said, needing another drink.

'Your father never stopped talking about that place. I sometimes think he loved that port town more than he loved me.'

Eva swallowed hard. 'He told you about it?'

'Yes, Eva. Don't sound so surprised. He did more than just tell me. He wanted to show me. We were getting ready to move there. We were going to start a new life in Dublin.'

Eva's hands flew to her face. 'Oh, my God. When?'

'You were just a baby. Before you turned three.'

'Why?'

'Things were hard for us at home. Your father hated his job. And I hated being the nagging wife at home with a couple of kids tied to my apron strings forcing him out the door to a job that was draining every ounce of the man I loved out of him.'

'I thought Dad like his job driving the bus,' Melissa said, her eyes glossy and red.

'No, sweetheart, you girls liked taking a ride on his big bus, but he didn't bring you very often. He drove one of the toughest routes in Jersey. It was hard.'

'So what made you change your mind?' Eva asked. 'If things were that shit in New Jersey, why did you stay there?'

Samantha sucked in her bottom lip and looked at her daughters in turn, like what she was about to tell them might force them to hate her forever and she needed to remember this moment. The moment just before the reveal. 'Because hell found us and there was no escape.'

Nathan pressed the button on his little black box in the centre of the table. 'Mrs. Andrews, can I get you a glass of water or something? Would you like to step outside for some fresh air, maybe?'

'Hell found us?' Melissa repeated. 'What does that even mean?'

The colour was draining from Samantha's lips and Eva thought her mother might faint. 'Get that water, Nathan, yeah?' Eva said.

Nathan nodded and scurried to the bar.

'You okay, Mom?' Eva knew the answer even before she asked the question. 'Do you want to take your coat off? Are you too hot?'

'I'm fine. Just a little lightheaded.'

Nathan returned and Eva stood up and moved around the table to help Samantha lift the glass of iced tap water to her shaking lips.

'Hell, Mom?' Eva said when she felt Samantha steady herself.

'Your dad liked to gamble. Nothing crazy. He'd never mess with the grocery money or leave us too tight to pay a bill. But he liked to blow the little we did have leftover on chance.'

*A gambler and an alcoholic. Oh Christ,* Eva thought. It wasn't completely unexpected, but it was shit to hear.

'But he had a good head on his shoulders. He was clever. Much more clever than I was. I see that in you girls. You're very artsy, Mel. And, Eva, you're so analytical,' Samantha said, proudly.

Eva reached for a napkin from the shelf behind their table and passed it to Melissa. The tears were streaming down Melissa's face, but Eva was managing to hold it together. On the outside, at least.

'You might want to hit the record button again, Mr. Shields,' Samantha said. Her tears didn't fall, but they did glisten heartbreakingly in her tired eyes.

Nathan reached to the middle of the table in silence and Samantha waited until he sat up straight again to talk.

'My beautiful girls…' Samantha's voice cracked. 'My God, your father loved you. Maybe too much. Maybe that's what really broke him.'

'Well, he had a damn funny way of showing it,' Mel cried. Her whole body heaved under the weight of twenty years of pain.

'You think that you dragged those goddamn Da Lucas into our lives, Melissa. Well, I can't let you bear that burden.' Samantha's tears began to fall like a light summer mist. 'You didn't get mixed up with them of your own doing, Mel. They came looking for you. And Eva. If Julian hadn't arranged for you to take the job in his company in Dublin, they'd have found you, too. It was only a matter of time. I'm sure of it.'

'What? I don't understand. What would they want with us?' Eva said, her insides shaking but she wasn't sure why. Just the mention of their name scared the shit out of her.

'They wanted their debt repaid. Men like that don't lose,' Samantha explained.

*Men like that don't lose.* Julian didn't lose. *But he wasn't a man like that.* Eva hated knowing that Julian was coloured the same as the Da Lucas in the back of her mother's mind.

'You're not making sense, Mom. I…I…don't understand. Do you mean it was a trap? Me. The club. All of it?' Melissa's arms were flapping about like crazy, and she was shouting at the top of her voice.

182

'Shh. Melissa. Calm down,' Shelly said, gently patting Melissa on the back.

'Fuck you. FUCK YOU,' Melissa said jumping up and nearly dislocating Shelly's shoulder in the process.

Eva quickly glanced at Shelly, as if to say, *Are you okay?*

Shelly winced and nodded, nursing her arm.

Melissa was out of line, but Eva could understand. Shelly had been unintentionally patronising. *Maybe this interview was a bad idea.*

'Mel, sit back down,' Samantha ordered.

Melissa looked at her mother with a cloud of resentment in her eyes.

'Please,' Samantha added; her eyes were puffy and red now from keeping the floods of tears at bay.

'Mel. Please sit back down,' Eva pleaded softly, worried that if Melissa left, the moment would be over and Samantha might not ever open up like that again.

Melissa combed her fingers through her hair roughly and sat back down.

'A trap. A setup. A payment. Whatever you want to call it, the Da Lucas wanted their pound of flesh. Your flesh. You have Andrews blood in your veins. If the Da Lucas couldn't have your father, then you girls were the next best thing,' Samantha continued.

'Did Dad steal from them? Was that it? Did he take money to feed his addictions?' Eva asked, struggling to follow the confusing information.

Samantha's shoulders shook and her bottom lip dropped. Angry, painful sobs rippled through her body as she shook her head. 'Oh Christ, what have we done to you, my beautiful girls.'

'Mom, you're scaring me. What is it? What happened that we don't know? Just tell us. Please. Please just say?' Eva begged.

'I'll turn this off,' Nathan said, taking his black box from the centre of the table and shoving it back in his pocket.

Eva watched him. He didn't turn the tape recorder off. But she didn't say anything. Right now wasn't the time to discuss his gutter journalism tactics.

'Thank you, Mr. Shields, but off the record doesn't make this any easier to say.'

Eva's attention quickly flipped back to Samantha. Her eyes burned into her mother. Begging. Pleading. Hurting.

Samantha sucked some air through her nose and shot it back out her mouth before clearing her throat with a rough cough. 'Your dad had a good run in one of Da Luca's casinos. Real good. He made a lot of money over a couple of lucky weeks. Enough to build a better life for us. It was exciting.'

'But he lost it all?' Eva said sensing a pattern.

'Actually, no. He didn't, and that was the problem. The Da Lucas let your father play on as long he liked. They knew his luck would run out sooner or later. Everybody's does. And they count on that. That's how they get their money back. But your dad knew that, too. So when he had enough for us to start a fresh life, he stopped going to the club. He stopped gambling.'

'He wasn't addicted,' Eva said elatedly.

'No. He was just clever.'

'But we had nothing growing up. No money, I remember,' Eva said. Her brain hurt trying to piece all the information together.

'I told you. The Da Lucas don't lose,' Samantha reiterated.

'Did they take the money back? That's theft,' Eva said.

'God, Eva. If only theft was all they were guilty of.'

Eva looked at Melissa, understanding exactly what her mother meant.

'But your father had a plan,' Samantha said.

'Dun Laoghaire?' Eva smiled despite her aching heart.

'Mr. and Mrs. Harte were looking to expand their guesthouse business. They had their eye on a small, rundown hotel on the seafront. It was a fixer upper, but with the right investor, it could have been a little gold mine.'

'Oh, my God.' Eva's hand instinctively flew to cover her mouth. 'Dad was the investor. He was going into business with the Hartes. Oh, my God. Oh, my God.'

Eva glanced at Shelly and Nathan. They were both wide-eyed and very still. They were reeling from the revelation, too.

'That was the plan. Yes. But the Da Lucas…' Samantha coughed hard before reaching for some more water.

Eva pushed away from the table and stood up; the whiskey swirled around inside her belly like an acid whirlpool. She slapped her palm against the table shaking the empty glasses. Everything suddenly added up in her head and it was more than her mind could handle.

'The fire. It wasn't my dad, was it?' Eva looked at Nathan. 'It was them. It was the fucking Da Lucas.' Their name stung her lips as it passed. 'If they couldn't have their money, then no one could.'

'They took everything from us. The money went up in flames with house.' Samantha exhaled. She looked lighter now.

Eva noticed colour in her cheeks for the first time, like the confession had lifted a metaphorical weight off her shoulders.

'We lost money, Mom. Julian lost everything. He lost EVERYTHING,' Eva said.

She had to see him. She had to see him right now.

Samantha's face soured and her lips pressed together like a paper fan.

'There's more?' Eva said, reading the signs, praying she was wrong.

'I couldn't keep the boy, Eva. You have to understand,' Samantha cried. 'We were left with nothing. We could barely afford to feed you girls; I couldn't bring another mouth into the family. Please forgive me. I did what I thought was best.'

Eva's back teeth chattered uncontrollably, but she wasn't cold. If anything, she was burning up. Julian? No. Samantha couldn't mean Julian.

'When your father came back from Dublin, I expected to hear the investment was final. Our bags were packed and we were ready to go. I was so excited. But instead, I heard the money was gone, a family was dead, and he was standing on our doorstep with an eight-year-old boy clinging to his leg.'

'Oh, sweet Jesus. This can't be true. You turned Julian away? A child with nowhere to go and you turned him away?' Eva couldn't bear to look at her mother.

'Eva, sit back down,' Shelly said standing up beside Eva, catching her.

Eva could feel the blood drain into her feet, but she didn't do as Shelly asked.

'He wasn't an American citizen, Eva. I don't think we could have even kept him if we wanted to.' Samantha tried to defend herself.

'But you didn't want to, did you, Mom?'

'No. No, I didn't, Eva. Hate causes monsters to grow. Julian is full of hate. He can't help it. Knowing that's in him, I think I did the right thing.'

'Am I a monster, Mom?' Eva asked trembling.

'No, Eva. God, no.'

'But I am filled with hate…' Eva shook her head. 'Does Julian know about this? Does he know you're responsible for putting him in that orphanage he hated so much?'

'He was young, Eva. I doubt he remembers,' Samantha said.

Eva closed her eyes and all she could see was an image of her father's grave. God, how she wished her mother had told her sooner. It was too late now. She'd never get to tell her father that she understood. She even forgave him. But it was too late.

'Monsters hide in the darkness, Mom. You've been hiding for twenty years. I'm starting to understand why Dad drank.'

'Eva, take that back,' Melissa snorted. 'Too far, Eva. That was too far.'

Eva tossed her shoulders and pulled a face. 'I have to get out of here. I think I'm going to be sick.'

## 22

Eva burst through the doors, gulping in the fresh air like she had just spent too long underwater. Shelly was behind her in an instant but Eva took a step back and distanced herself, cutting across Shelly before she spoke. 'I need to be on my own, Shell. Okay…I just…'

'Are you okay? You don't look it.'

'Everything finally makes sense, you know. I have to go.'

'Go where?'

'To Julian.'

Shelly shook her head. 'Do you know where he is?'

Eva nodded. 'Yeah. I actually do. I've known all along. I just didn't realise. I was so busy waiting for him to come to me. But I should have gone to him. Go back inside, Shelly. Go back to Nathan. Tell him to finish the interview.'

Shelly shook her head. 'I'll come with you. You're in bits. You probably shouldn't be on your own.'

'No.' Eva raised her hand, wanting Shelly to stop. She didn't want her to come any closer. If Shelly tried to hug her or comfort her, she'd break down completely. She couldn't afford to fall apart now because she just needed to get the hell out of there.

Eva watched Shelly reluctantly walk away. She waited until Shelly was back inside before she pulled her phone out of her bag and dialled a number she knew by heart.

'Hello.'

'Anthony, hi. It's Eva.'

'Miss Andrews. Is everything all right? I'm not due to pick you up for another hour and forty minutes.'

'I know. But I'd like if you could come get me now instead.'

'Will Mr. Harte be expecting you early?'

'No, Anthony. He won't. And I'd really appreciate if you didn't tell him.'

'Oh, Miss Andr-...'

'C'mon Anthony, it's the least you owe me after ignoring my calls all week.'

'Eva, I was under strict instructions.'

'I know, I know. But please, Anthony? Just do this.'

Eva heard Anthony swallow hard.

'Okay. I'll be there in ten minutes,' he promised.

Eva imagined the employee in Anthony was warning him not to dare defy his boss. But the friend inside him was telling him to hurry and pick Eva up.

Less than half an hour later, Anthony announced they were there. Eva looked out the back window of the limo. She wasn't sure what she'd been expecting, but this wasn't it. She didn't know Dun Laoghaire well. She'd only been there once before with Julian and she'd spent most of that time miles out on the Irish Sea. Where they were now was beautiful. A narrow road wound back behind them. They were at the top of a steep hill. Eva remembered Julian pointing up the hill from the pier when they were here last. But she never imagined it would actually take her breath away once she was on top. Eva stepped out of the car and stood looking out to sea. Even on a dull, cloudy day, the views were spectacular. The heaviest of last week's snow had melted and there was just a gathering of slush in the corners of the road.

'This is it,' Anthony said, stepping out of the car to stand beside Eva.

Eva nodded as she turned around to take in the wrought iron gate behind her that was falling off its hinges.

'I better wait out here,' Anthony said.

'Thank you, Anthony.'

Anthony smiled and tossed his head toward the gates. 'Go on.'

Eva cursed the gates as they squeaked loudly as if to announce her arrival. She only opened one side enough to squeeze through the gap, and as soon as she let go, it snapped back closed behind her. She jumped, like a character out of a low budget horror movie.

The grass was overgrown but certainly not twenty years long. Someone was maintaining the grounds. Albeit not as often as it needed, but it wasn't gone to complete rack and ruin like she'd expected. The windows were all boarded up, completely free from glass. Any broken glass due to the fire damage had been cleared away. Black, soot-like stains ran around each window frame, like someone had coloured around the windows in a giant, black permanent marker.

Eva studied every inch of the old building. From the slates on the roof to the red brick stonework of the walls. Her heart pinched when she thought about Julian growing up here. About how this was the last place Julian saw his family alive.

Grass grew up through the tarmac driveway and Eva followed it to the front door. She knocked on the blue timber door. The sunlight and lack of care had caused the blue paint to fade and chip. But Eva could still see how quaint and inviting this guesthouse once was.

No one answered. She knocked again. And again and again and again. Nothing. She stared back at the road where Anthony stood leaning up against the car door. She twisted her arm behind her and signalled that she's going around the back of the house. She thought Anthony nodded, but it was hard to see in the distance as daylight changed to dusk.

Eva stopped abruptly as she rounded the corner of the house. There was an old metal swing set in the backyard, and

Julian was sitting on the swing rocking back and forth. As soon as he saw her, he lowered his chin against his chest and closed his eyes.

*Ah shit, he's angry*, Eva thought. But she didn't regret her decision to go there.

'You found me,' Julian said, looking back up.

Eva made her way to him. He let the swing come to a stop. Eva stood in the gap between his legs and draped her arms over his shoulders.

'This should have been the first place I looked,' she said, regretting the wasted time when she didn't think of there sooner.

'Well, you're here now.'

'Are you angry?'

Julian wrapped his arms around Eva's waist and dropped his head against her chest. 'No.'

'You're freezing,' Eva said feeling Julian shiver slightly.

'I've been out here a while.'

'Since last night?' Eva asked worriedly.

Julian didn't reply.

'You'll get sick sitting out here in the freezing cold like this.' Eva bit her lip immediately regretting her choice of words. *Sick, sick. God, that was a stupid thing to say.* 'I thought you had work stuff you needed to do?' Eva added, quickly trying to change the subject.

Julian took his phone out of his jacket pocket like a prop and held it up. 'I close most of my deals from up here. It's got great reception,' he joked. 'And it's quiet. I like quiet.'

Eva lowered her hands from around his neck and rubbed them together . 'Can we go inside? I'm so cold.'

Julian shook his head.

'Please, Julian. I'm just absolutely freezing. My feet actually hurt they're so cold.'

'Did Anthony drive you up here?' Julian asked walking towards the front of the house.

'Yeah, but don't be pissed off with him. I literally forced him to.'

'I'm not mad, Eva. I'd be more upset if he'd denied your request.'

'But you told him not to take my calls.'

'But he still ignored me.' Julian smiled. 'And I knew he would.'

'Did you want me to find you up here?' Eva squinted.

'Maybe.'

Eva relaxed. She would take that a yes. When Julian meant no it was resounding and there was no questioning. A maybe was as near to a yes as she'd get out of him.

'C'mon,' she said catching up with him and taking him by the hand. 'Let's go inside.'

'No, Eva,' Julian growled, pulling his hand away from her.

Eva jumped. 'I'm sorry…I just…,' Julian had startled her. Their poignant surroundings had her on edge more than she realised. But she quickly pulled herself together. 'I'm sorry. Do you not want me to see inside?'

'No,' Julian said, '*I* don't want to see inside.'

'Oh God, Julian. You haven't been inside in all these years, have you?'

Julian closed his eyes and shook his head.

'Do you just come and sit here?' Eva looked back at the swing set.

'Yeah. It helps me think.'

Eva reached for his hand again, and he grabbed hold with an intense tightness. She trod tread delicately with her next question. She was conscious of freaking him out. She imagined this must be insanely difficult for him. If she ever had to revisit her childhood home, she'd probably lose her mind. But it was the opposite for Julian. He wasn't hiding from horrible memories inside. He was hiding from great ones. So great that seeing everything again, missing his family so much, was more than his head could handle. It was more than anyone could.

'Do you want to go inside?' Eva asked softly.

Julian shrugged.

'I could go in with you, if you like.' Julian turned towards the house and dropped his head. Eva guessed he was searching for some old memories of what the inside used to be like. She stood beside him, sharing the silence. The cold didn't bother her anymore. She couldn't take away his pain, but maybe she could let him know she understood it.

'Let's go,' Julian suddenly began marching towards the car.

'Dinner,' she said with slight dread. The thoughts of eating again made her want to vomit.

'We have reservations,' Julian said as if they weren't just standing looking into the window of his past.

'I'm not dressed for dinner.' Eva pointed at her jeans and coat. She'd stormed out of the bar in such a hurry; she'd left the bag with her new dress inside behind her.

'Anthony, would you let someone in Brown Thomas know to have something classy and simple ready for us in twenty minutes. An entire outfit, including shoes, please,' Julian said as soon as they reached the limo. 'The same size as the stuff I ordered before. We'll make a pit stop at the store on the way to the restaurant.'

Anthony nodded. 'No problem, Mr. Harte.'

'Will you be okay changing in the car?' Julian turned to Eva.

'The same size as the stuff you bought before,' Eva repeated.

Julian's wicked grin set her heart racing. 'The stuff I bought you, Eva. I don't usually go around purchasing ladies clothes, you know.'

Eva blushed remembering she'd left Julian's credit card in her hotel room. She needed to give it back to him. 'I have a dress. I went shopping today. I just left it back at the hotel.'

'Okay, fine. We'll pick it up on the way. We have time.'

Eva sat into the backseat, deflated. She'd been so looking forward to dinner earlier, but now she just wanted to stay here, at the house from Julian's childhood, and talk. She desperately wanted to bring up what her mother had told her, but over dinner just didn't seem appropriate. Here was the perfect place. Eva's heart sank into the pit of her stomach as she glanced out the back window as they drove away.

Julian's phone rang and Eva was glad the call consumed his attention. She needed some time to get her head together without him watching her.

'That was quicker than I anticipated,' he said into the phone.

He turned his wrist and checked his watch. 'Less than twenty-four hours. I told you, you were a damn good businesswoman. Scan the paperwork and send it straight to me.'

Eva could hear a woman's voice on the other end, but she didn't know what she was saying and she tried not to eavesdrop, which was surprisingly difficult to avoid in the confined space of the backseat.

'Call into the HTK office. I'll let them know you're coming and make hard copies there. Leave some on file there and bring at least two copies of everything back with you,' Julian continued.

Eva's eyes widened hearing her office initials mentioned. If Julian called Pam, she'd almost certainly mention Eva's resignation email. Julian would be furious that she had quit and it would definitely spark an argument. She couldn't talk to him about his childhood then. She'd have to bring it up now. *Dammit.* Awkward and rushed was the last way she wanted to approach it.

'Thank you, I really appreciate all your help with this,' Julian said into the phone, drawing Eva's attention back to his voice. 'Book your return flight for whenever you're ready and I'll have Anthony pick you up. I told you I'd still be in one piece when you got home.'

*What paperwork?* Eva thought, her mind racing. *Did he mean a will?* Maybe things were happening faster than she'd anticipated. She'd have to up her game. No more treading lightly in case she irritated him. She was going in all guns blazing and to hell with whether or not he lost his temper. Some things were more important than being fucking polite.

## 23

'Anthony, can we pull over please?' Eva said loudly as Julian slipped his phone back into his jacket pocket.

'Mr. Harte?' Anthony called back, obviously double-checking with his boss before he did anything.

'Pull over if Eva needs to. Thank you, Anthony,' Julian replied. 'What's wrong, Eva? Are you okay?'

'No. Not really.'

Eva reached into her pocket and pulled out the envelope Julian had given her, the letter stuffed back inside. So was the medical pamphlet. She also had Nathan's voice recorder in her pocket, but she left that where it was. She had unashamedly taken it out of his jacket pocket while the commotion of her dramatic exit at the pub had distracted him. She slid over in the seat to create some space between herself and Julian and placed the envelope in the space between them.

The business card peeking out of the top of the open envelope immediately drew Julian's attention. 'How long have you had this?' he growled. Picking up the glossy paper, he ran his fingers over Doctor Simmons' name embossed on the paper.

'Does it matter?'

'Answer the question, Eva.'

'No,' Eva barked. 'How about you answer some of mine for a change.'

'Meghan gave this to you, didn't she?' Julian said staring out the window.

'I had to hear you're dying from your wife. Meghan, who fucking hates me, had more consideration for how this all might make me feel than you. You'd tell her you need a transplant but you wouldn't tell me. I asked you how sick you were and you still didn't tell me.'

'Don't try to play mind games here, Eva. You won't win. If Meghan gave you this,' Julian waved the business card in the air, 'then you've either already spoken to Doctor Simmons about my condition, or you didn't have to because you already knew the answer to your own question. It was a waste of your breath and my time.'

'I asked you because I wanted to give you a chance to tell me yourself. I didn't want to have to drag it out of you.'

'Like you're going to right now.'

'You're leaving me no choice. You weren't going to tell me, were you?'

'Possibly not.'

'Jesus, Julian. Jesus. But you told her. Was that who you were talking to on the phone? Meghan? Are you making plans for what will happen to Daniel if you die? Is that why you had to tell her how sick you are?'

'The hospital told her, actually. You know, being my wife and all that.'

'Ex-wife,' Eva spat.

Julian looked back at Eva. 'You read the annulment papers.'

'Yes.'

Eva knew her one-word answer pissed him off. She'd come to learn his jaw twitched to the left for the briefest of seconds when she was piquing him.

'I answer the questions you ask, Evangeline. You asked about Meghan, I've shown you the annulment details. You didn't ask if I was dying.'

'What?' Eva threw her hands to the side. 'That doesn't even make sense. Am I supposed to start every conversation with, 'Hello, Julian. Are you dying today?' You're not playing fair.'

'Who's playing? Really Eva, this obsession with games you have is getting out of hand.'

If that was Julian's idea of a joke, Eva didn't appreciate it, and she threw him a look that said as much.

'Right now, I don't care if you were or are married to half of Ignite Tech. I don't even care that you hid being married from me, for fuck-knows-why. Probably one of your power trip reasons.' Eva swallowed hard and tried to calm down.

That was a blatant lie. She was doing the one thing she accused Julian of and it felt disgusting to be such a hypocrite. And she knew before the words even finished coming out of her mouth that he'd see straight through her thinly veiled bullshit. Of course, she cared. She cared deeply about his past with Meghan. But it paled in comparison to how much she cared about losing him. She had cleared her throat before she continued. 'I just care that you're really ill and you're giving up the fight. What the hell?'

'Eva, you're out of line,' Julian snarled.

'Oh, Julian. Don't you dare talk to me about lines. You've been out of line since the day I walked into your office and you damn well know it.'

Julian didn't reply. Eva knew she was getting to him. She intended to push this as far as she had to.

The car pulled off the main road and came to a stop on the hard shoulder. Eva opened the door and got out. Julian slid across the backseat and leaned out the door. 'Eva, get back in. You're being ridiculous.'

'I need some fresh air.'

'Well, the hard shoulder isn't the place to get it. Get back in the car. What you're doing is stupid and dangerous.'

'No. What you're doing is stupid and dangerous. Are you going to get the treatment?'

'Dialysis?'

'Yes. To start. And then the transplant. You're going to die if you don't.'

'I do know that. But thank you for the fine diagnosis, Doctor Andrews.'

'And you have the nerve to call me stupid.' Eva was shouting. Her arms were waving frantically in the air, and to any passers-by, she must have looked like she was completely out of her mind. She was. She was worried to the point of losing control, and she didn't give a shit if she flapped about like a chicken with a firecracker up its ass.

'Maybe I will go back to America, after all,' she said, turning around and bending down so she was looking into the backseat of the car. Glaring at Julian.

'Good. Now you're making sense.'

'Because it's easier to get my hands on a gun there.'

Julian was out of the car and standing beside her before she could draw her breath. 'Don't you dare say shit like that.'

His hands were firm on her shoulders. He wasn't hurting her, but he was cementing her to the spot. She couldn't get back in the car now even if she wanted to.

'Why? It's not like you're going to be here to stop me. If you let yourself die for no fucking reason, NO FUCKING REASON, JULIAN, then you might as well take that gun, jam it against my head and pull the trigger. Because my life would be over, too.'

205

'You wouldn't do it,' Julian said, his whole face pinched in temper.

Julian's grip on her relaxed and she pulled away from him. She slammed the door of the car shut and pounded her fist against the window, so hard she thought the glass might break. 'Commit suicide? No. You're right. I wouldn't do it. And do you know why? Because I'm not FUCKING INSANE. I want to live. I'm young and I want to experience lots more shit. Why don't you? What the fuck is your problem, Julian? Why do you always have to be so alone in every decision you make?'

Julian's shoulders rounded and his face softened. Eva was expecting him to be furious, but he wasn't. He was so far the opposite; he looked like he might cry.

'My father was only a little older than I am now when he died. He wanted to experience life. He was a good man. A great man. He fucking deserved to live, Eva. My family didn't deserve what happened to them.'

'I know, Julian. I know it sucks. But what you're doing now has nothing to do with the past.'

'It has everything to do with it,' Julian shouted.

His anger and bitterness flashed in his dark brown eyes like smouldering embers. But Eva wasn't going to back down. She needed him raw and out of control.

'I shouldn't have gotten to live when they didn't. Why me? Why did I get a second chance at life when they all died? It's not fair.'

Eva's frustrations fizzled completely and all she wanted to do was wrap her arms around Julian, there on the side of the road, and kiss him better. She could hear eight-year-old Julian coming through. His fears, his heartbreak, his uncertainty.

'It's not fair. It's so not fair. But you refusing treatment won't bring them back, Julian. They're gone and you're still here.'

'Maybe I shouldn't be. Karma is a bitch, Eva. It catches everyone in the end.'

'Karma? Julian what have you ever done to deserve this?'

'My whole family is dead because of me.'

Eva's heart burned, like the fire Julian was talking about was literally ripping through her chest. Julian wasn't just carrying twenty years of missing his family under his skin. He was burdening twenty years of guilt. But she didn't know if it was guilt that he couldn't save his family or guilt that he was responsible. *Christ.* Either pain was unimaginable.

'Julian, why do you hate the Da Lucas so much?' Eva said gently. 'Tell me. Please. I need to hear you say it.'

'How could I not. Look at what they did to your family.'

*Do you know what they did to yours?* Eva thought. Her mind was racing. So many realisations and answers were streaming into her brain like her head had just received one massive download and she had to make room and file all of the information before the system crashed.

Eva wasn't sure if Julian would remember meeting her as a child in her home in New Jersey, and if he did, maybe he wouldn't want to admit it. If he knew she'd unscrambled the reasons behind all his games, it would change everything. It would make them equals. She deserved that, but Eva understood now that Julian deserved that even more. She took a deep breath and asked a hard question. 'How old was I when we first met?'

Julian's nostrils flared and his pain etched into his forehead in angry lines. 'Eva, get back in the car. I'm warning you.'

Eva shook her head. 'How old, Julian?'

'You're three and half years younger than me, Eva. Work it out.'

'So you're admitting that we did meet as kids. You remember my dad bringing you to New Jersey,' Eva asked forcing herself to stay calm.

'Yes. And you know that or you wouldn't be asking this bullshit. Did your mother tell you? I thought she might.'

'Yes. And I can only apologise for what she did.'

'She put her family first, Eva. She deserves to be commended. There is nothing to apologise for.'

'She turned you away. She forced you to go to that horrible orphanage that you hated so much.'

'She had no choice. Your family hadn't the price of their supper. They couldn't have an extra mouth to feed. Your father's heart was bigger than his head. He wasn't thinking sensibly. If anyone is owed an apology, it's Samantha. I burned down the house, Eva. I caused it all. The Da Lucas money went up in flames and it was all my fault.'

Eva's hands shook as her fingers raced to trace the lines of Julian's contorted face. So much pain was written in his eyes. It was as crippling as it was misguided. 'Oh God, Julian. No. No, no, no. No, baby. How can you think that?'

Julian caught Eva's wrists, pulled her hands away from his face, and dropped them down to her sides. 'Don't. I don't need your sympathy, Eva. I don't deserve it.'

'Julian, it wasn't Da Luca's money. My father had won it fair and square.'

Julian shook his head. 'Eva, it was gambling debts. Your father was an addict.'

Eva reached into her pocket and pulled out Nathan's voice recorder. She stretched out her arm and opened her hand. The little black box sat on her palm. 'Take it.'

Julian's eyes pinched.

'Please, Julian. Trust me. You want to take this.'

'Did your reporter friend give you that?' Julian asked as if the sentence was all one word.

Eva couldn't miss the sourness in Julian's tone. She closed her hand around the box, worried that Julian would strike out and knock it to the ground. She couldn't blame Julian for his distaste of Nathan anymore. Nathan wasn't particular in her good books, either. But maybe the information recorded on the device could save Julian. Really save him. Save him after more than twenty years.

Julian took the box from Eva, looking less than impressed. Eva sat back in the car and slid across the seat to make room for Julian to follow.

'Sorry about that, Anthony,' Eva said surprisingly composed – considering. 'If you could just drop me at my hotel, Anthony. I'd really appreciate that.'

'Certainly, Miss Andrews. I hadn't forgotten about your dress,' Anthony assured.

'No, Anthony. I think we will give dinner a miss tonight. I think Julian needs to go straight home.'

'Evangeline,' Julian said.

Eva knew that, by the way that Julian sounded out her name, he was inquiring why in the hell she was giving his driver instructions.

'Julian, I know you. And you are going to want to be alone when you listen to that tape.'

Julian held up the voice recorder and spun it around between his fingers. 'What exactly is on this?'

'Just listen to it. Okay. Promise me?'

Julian didn't reply.

'I'm just a phone call away when you do.'

## 24

Julian stood outside the worse-for-wear blue front door and took a deep breath. Too deep. The cold night air bit into his lungs with an icy sting. He'd waited a generous ten minutes after dropping Eva back at her hotel before he asked Anthony to turn the car around and drive back to Dun Laoghaire. It had been a spur-of-the-moment decision. Julian didn't do spur of the moment, and it disturbed him. But he knew the only place he wanted to hear what was on the tape was back in the familiarity of his childhood home. He could guess what he was going to hear, and it set his heart racing with a mix of anticipation and confusion.

He lined his shoulder up with the front door and knocked his full body weight on the door. It shook on its hinges, but it didn't move. Julian's whole upper body ached. His health was failing. He knew it. Despite how much he tried to ignore the strengthening signs, time was running out. A couple of weeks ago, he was bench pressing one hundred in the gym every morning before work; he would have made short work of charging through the door. But now, he had the failing strength of an old man.

Julian felt a hand on his shoulder, and he turned around to find Anthony behind him, smiling.

'I think you'll have better luck with this,' Anthony said, holding up a crowbar.

'Where in the hell did you get that?'

Anthony tossed his head towards the garden shed. 'Will I give it a go, Mr. Harte? You don't want to ruin your suit.'

Julian nodded slowly. Anthony's discretion was as commendable as it was appreciated. 'Thank you, Anthony, but I think we both know I have bigger concerns than scuffing my suit.'

'Does Miss Andrews know you're poorly?' Anthony asked gently.

'Yes. Do you?'

Anthony slipped the crowbar between the door and its frame and began forcing a gap between the two. He didn't look at Julian as he spoke. 'I know you're more shook than you'd like anyone to know. You haven't asked me to drive you to the hospital at any stage. So either there is nothing they can do or you're being a stubborn bastard.'

Anthony grunted as he pressed all his weight against the crowbar and with a loud snap, the lock broke and the door was free. He turned around to look at Julian. 'And I apologise in advance if this is out of line, Mr. Harte. But I know you, and that leaves me very certain the problem is the latter.'

'You do know me,' Julian said, leaving it at that.

'Have you told, Anne?' Anthony asked.

Julian's expression softened. 'No. And I'd appreciate if you didn't say anything.'

Julian knew by Anthony's sudden change in body language that he considered himself warned.

'She loves you like a mother loves a son,' Anthony added.

'Exactly. And that's why I don't need her freaking out with worry. I'll speak to her when the time is right.'

'And when might that be? To organise your funeral.'

'Anthony don't,' Julian warned. 'I've had this from Meghan and Eva already. I don't need it from you.'

'Everyone is worried about you.'

'An-thony,' Julian scowled.

'Mr. Harte.' Anthony walked back towards the car obediently.

'I won't be long,' Julian called after Anthony.

'Take all the time you need. I'll wait in the car.'

Julian's hand shook as he pressed his palm flat against the door and pushed gently. The door creaked and grunted, objecting to moving after all these years. Julian pushed a little harder and the door gave in, leaving him peering into the house before he had time to draw a breath.

His feet had stepped into the hall before his head did, and it took his mind quite a while to catch up with his body as he walked deeper into the room. A thick layer of black dust covered everything. The ground, the walls, the sideboard and mirror, even the ceiling had a coating. Julian pulled the sleeve of his suit jacket over his hand and used it to wipe the mirror clean. He stepped in front of the mirror and looked. It was too dark to see much. Light probably wouldn't have made much difference because as soon as he reached the familiar spot standing in front of the mirror, Julian closed his eyes. He could see a reflection clearly in his mind. As clear as if he really was looking into that old mirror. It was of an eight-year-old him getting ready for school. His mother had just brushed his messy chestnut hair that always stood up like an antenna in the mornings. She'd left the brush out of her hand on top of the sideboard and turned back to him. She kissed him on the top of the head, told him that she loved him, and to be careful on the winding road as he walked to school. He could see the pride in her eyes, and he knew how much she loved him. That was the last time his mother would ever help him get ready for school. The fire started less than twelve hours later.

Julian kicked some of the soot away with the side of his shoe and revealed a patch of the black and white checked tiles underneath. He gasped remembering how the hall floor always reminded him of a draughts board and how he had tried and failed to play a couple of times with stones he'd dragged in from the garden. He took his phone out of his pocket and tapped into the torch app. It wasn't as bright as he'd like it to be, but it was light enough to make sure he wouldn't break his

215

neck walking into something. Sticky cobwebs draped from one wall to another like elaborate Halloween decorations and the smell of twenty-three years without light or fresh air stagnated all around.

Julian walked deeper into the old house towards the back where the kitchen was. Everything was exactly as he'd remembered it. Clear away the soot and dirt, and it was just like coming downstairs on a Sunday morning to delicious scones or pancakes. But the smell of his mother's home baking that was synonymous with the kitchen was replaced now with the stench of a filthy ashtray.

Julian rushed back into the hall, slamming the kitchen door behind him and the walls around him shook and coughed up a cloud of sooty ash. His heart told him not to, but his stubborn head cast his eyes to where the stairs once were. The only remains of the solid pine staircase were a few charred timbers scattered on the ground. Julian's hands rushed to cover his ears as the sound of his mother's screaming rang in his head as clear as if she was calling to him now. His eyes slammed shut and the memories rushing through his brain paralysed him.

'Red, orange, red…red…'

He remembered the flames swirling on the landing. She'd shouted at him to get out as she rushed upstairs straight into the blaze trying to make her way to the baby's room.

'Red, orange, black…black…'

Julian's mother called out to his father between angry, gritty coughs. But his father didn't answer. Julian knew now that he must have passed out from the smoke. He was already gone.

Black, black...blackness all around. The cloud of darkness was racing down the stairs. It was coming to get him. Julian screamed and shouted. Begging his mother to answer him. But she'd gone quiet. The only noises coming from upstairs were crackling flames and timber as the fire consumed it. The baby wasn't crying, his mother wasn't shouting, and his father was silent.

Julian opened his eyes and took one last look upstairs. His lungs tightened like all the air was being sucked out of the room and his lungs were desperate to refill. He charged back through the front door and raced halfway down the driveway before he came to a sudden stop, bent forward with his hands just above his knees, struggling to catch his breath.

He hit the ground in what felt like slow motion. His legs gave way first then his shoulder collided with the cold tarmac, and then his weary head. His eyes stayed open just long enough to see Anthony rush out of the limo and race towards him. Black, black...blackness all around.

## 25

Eva read over and over the email on her phone. She was trying to decide if she was mad or relieved.

_____

**From:** Pamelawinters@HTK&associates.com
**To:** Eva135@mymail.com
**Subject:** Resignation
**Date:** Sun 6ᵗʰ Jan 21.16

Dear Eva,

Happy New Year! It was great to hear from you, but I have to admit, I'd prefer if you'd chosen a different way to start the year. You totally shocked me with your resignation. DON'T LEAVE ME LOL.

Mr. Thompson has suggested that under the current, exceptional circumstance, maybe a sabbatical would be an alternative to leaving us. Mr. Thompson is happy to offer six months' paid personal leave. How do you feel about that?

He's also asked me to pass on his very best wishes to Mr. Harte.

Have a think about it, Eva. I'd personally hate to see you go. And I know Mr. Thompson would be very disappointed, too.

Hope to hear from you soon,
Pam xx

---

**From:** Eva135@mymail.com
**To:** Pamelawinters@HTK&associates.com
**Subject:** Resignation
**Date:** Sun 6th Jan 23.39

Dear Pam,

Thanks for getting back to me, especially over the weekend. Mr. Thompson is working you too hard.

I thought you could only apply for sabbatical after two years with the company? But if that has changed, I'd be happy to apply. HTK is very kind. I appreciate the gesture. Please pass on my thanks to Mr. Thompson. And I will pass your best on to Julian. After I have a word with him about his interfering.

Eva x

---

**From:** Pamelawinters@HTK&associates.com
**To:** Eva135@mymail.com
**Subject:** Resignation
**Date:** Sun 6<sup>th</sup> Jan 23.42

Dear Eva,

Why do I get the feeling you're going to get me in trouble here lol. It was actually the strangest thing. An email from Mr. Harte came through, literally minutes before yours, highlighting a long paragraph from company policy, explaining that the two-year probation period before an employee is entitled to apply for sabbatical can be waived in exceptional circumstances. It didn't make any sense until I read your email.

Anyway, glad you've decided to go with this option. I'd miss you too much if you quit.

I'll get all the paperwork sorted out and on its way to you ASAP. I'll send it with the other files. There's a mountain of paperwork here so it's probably best to send it all to you snail mail. I don't have an address for you in Dublin. I can send it care of Ignite Technologies, if that makes it all easier? I'll be sending copies there anyway for Julian's lawyers in Ireland to look over. It's all very exciting. I'm sure you must be over the moon about it all. Congratulations, Eva. You're the best lady for the job. You'll make a fabulous head of the charity.

Give me a call soon. I'd love to chat.

Pam xx

**From:** Eva135@mymail.com
**To:** Pamelawinters@HTK&associates.com
**Subject:** Resignation
**Date:** Sun 6th Jan 23.48

Mountain of paperwork? Charity? Pam, what in the hell is Julian up to?

Eva x

Eva paced the floor, glancing at the screen of her phone every few seconds, waiting for Pam's reply. She waited and waited. Nothing. She dialled Pam's office line, but it rang out. She called her personal mobile, but it went straight through to voicemail. She couldn't believe Pam was ignoring her. So Pam had put her foot in it and obviously spilled the beans on some deal Julian wanted to be kept hush, hush, but ignoring Eva now was just rude. She imagined Pam was frantically trying to initiate damage limitation. Eva quickly typed out another email.

**From:** Eva135@mymail.com
**To:** Pamelawinters@HTK&associates.com
**Subject:** Resignation
**Date:** Sun 6th Jan 23.55

Pam.

I won't say anything to Julian. Stop freaking out and answer my call.

Eva x

Eva's phone vibrated in her hand. She was expecting to see Pam's number flash on the screen, but it was Anthony. Eva's mind hurried to the tape recorder she'd given Julian. He must have listened to it. Maybe Anthony was calling to come pick her up. Maybe Julian was ready to talk. Tiny bubbles popped in her tummy like someone had shaken a can of soda and opened it inside her.

'Hey,' Eva said trying to sound as breezy as possible.

'Hi, Miss Andrews. Did I wake you?'

'No. Not at all. Is everything okay, Anthony? You sound funny.'

'Can you be ready in ten minutes if I come pick you up?'

*Ready for what?* Anthony was usually so clear and concise, but his voice was so twitchy he sounded like someone was standing behind him using a Taser on him.

'Has Julian asked you to call me?'

'Eva, I'd prefer not to discuss this over the phone. I don't want to upset you. Can you be in reception in ten minutes, please?'

'Upset me? Okay now you're freaking me out. Where's Julian?'

'He's in the hospital. He's had a turn for the worse.'

222

*Was this it?* Anthony's words ripped through Eva like a sharp knife. And it took her a moment to get her breath back enough to be able to speak into the phone. 'I'm on the way down to reception now. I'll be waiting there. Hurry. Please.'

Eva thumped her fist against the elevator, but it was taking forever. She raced down the stairs instead, almost breaking her neck as she fidgeted with her phone as she ran.

'Hello.'

'Hi, Meghan,' Eva was panting and close to out of breath as she rounded the turn on the stairway at the third floor.

'Eva?'

'Where are you?' Eva panted.

'Excuse me?'

'Meghan. It's important.'

'I don't think that's any of your business, Eva,' Meghan said sternly.

'It's Julian. He's back in hospital.'

Meghan gasped and Eva could tell straight away that she was freaking out a little bit.

'I'm in New York on business. I'm just about to leave my hotel for the airport to come home,' Meghan stuttered.

Eva rolled her eyes, unsurprised that whatever Pam was talking about obviously had something to do with Meghan, too. It was work stuff and Meghan was Julian's most senior employee. It must have been what Julian was discussing on the phone in the car. It made good business sense that Meghan would have her hand in whatever the deal was. Eva knew better and wanted to be more professional than to let it hurt, but it stung nonetheless. But only for the briefest of seconds before Eva was pulled back into the panic and fear of the moment.

'Okay,' Eva said, sounding far calmer than she actually was. 'Call me when you land.'

Eva was about to hang up when Meghan called her name.

'Is he going to make it?' Meghan said, her voice noticeably breaking.

'I don't know.'

'Eva, please, you have to take Daniel to see him. I don't want anything to happen and Daniel not get a chance to say goodbye. Please.'

Eva swallowed hard. She didn't want any delay getting to the hospital, and she didn't know the child. How would he feel with a strange lady suddenly dropping all this on him? But she knew she had no choice. She had to do the right thing by the boy. The right thing by Julian. Julian never got the chance to say good-bye to his family. She couldn't deprive his son of his chance. 'Okay. Text me the address of where to pick him up.'

'Thank you, Eva. Thank you.'

'I'm doing it for Julian and his son, Meghan.'

'I know. But I'm still grateful. I'll call you the second I land. Bye.'

## 26

Daniel lay stretched out on the backseat of the car. His ankles reached the door on his side and his head rested on Eva's knee. He was tall for his age, or at least Eva thought he was. She'd never really measured up a ten-year-old before. He looked so innocent and sweet in his dinosaur flannel pyjamas. His coat covered him like a blanket, and he slept soundly as they drove.

'I'll wait in the car with him if you want to go inside on your own first?' Anthony suggested as they reached the hospital car park.

Eva nodded and smile as she opened the door and slid her legs out of the car. She was past words.

She stopped walking halfway across the car park, rushing to the curb to throw up in a lavender bush. Her stomach was in bits the last few days. Every time she stood up too quickly or walked a little too fast, her tummy objected and wanted to be sick. She'd never had problems with her stomach before; the stress must really be getting to her. She rummaged in her bag for some tissue, wiped her mouth, and stood up. She felt faint, and she was certain she smelt like vomit, but she marched towards and through the main hospital door and straight to reception without hesitation.

'I'm looking for Julian Harte, please?' Eva said through the glass around the reception desk.

'Mrs…?

'Harte,' Eva replied without some much as blinking. But her heart was racing like fuck.

225

'Straight through these doors,' the receptionist's arm stretched to one side, 'and around to your left. Will you fill these in when you get a chance, please?'

The receptionist slid a clipboard with a page and pen attached through a gap in the glass. Eva grabbed the clipboard and hurried through the doors to Accident and Emergency. The place was thronged. Patients were spilling out in the hall, lying on trolleys. Some looked like they'd had a few sherries too many and others looked like they might not live to see tomorrow. There was an overwhelming smell of piss, poorly diluted by the antibacterial cleaner. Eva's stomach heaved again and she scanned the corridor, desperate to locate a bin. The moment passed and she caught her breath again. This was becoming ridiculous.

Someone passed by in dark blue scrubs and Eva gently tapped his arm. The doctor turned around.

'I'm looking for Julian Harte,' Eva stuttered.

'Mrs. Harte?' the doctor said.

'Yes.' Eva smiled, becoming quite accustomed to the false identity.

'Follow me, please. We've been expecting you.'

The doctor exchanged some words with a porter who took over the leading and walked towards an elevator. Eva followed. There was no talking. They went up three floors and navigated more corridors and turns. It was like a maze and Eva wondered how in the hell she would remember her way back out. They finally stopped outside double doors and Eva read the overhead sign. *Renal Unit.*

Eva took a deep breath as the porter pulled the curtain back on a small cubicle at the end of the corridor. But her

226

breath quickly escaped and her head shook when she saw Julian sitting in an armchair, his phone in one hand and a cup of coffee in the other. A machine that looked like the hospital had taken a computer straight off the set of *Star Wars* was behind him and some very uncomfortable looking tubes stretched from the arm Julian held his phone in up behind him and into the machine. *So this is what dialysis looks like,* Eva thought, surprised that it was all so calm and peaceful. Not at all like in the movies. *Julian was getting treatment. Thank fuck.*

Eva didn't notice the porter leave as she stood with her arms folded and her foot tapping the ground.

'Miss Andrews,' Julian said, looking up at her smiling.

'It's Mrs Harte, actually.' Eva sniggered.

'Oh.' Julian pulled a face. 'Seems all the women in my life have taken to borrowing my name lately.'

'Sorry. I wasn't sure if they'd have let me in otherwise, and I didn't want a repeat of last time.'

'I like it. You should keep it. It suits you,' Julian said, and Eva suspected he was only half joking. God, she did not want to talk about that now.

'You're getting treatment, Julian,' Eva said, elated.

'Observant as ever, Evangeline.'

'Oh, don't pull that smartass shit with me, mister. You're in serious trouble. I nearly had a heart attack when Anthony called me. I didn't know what kind of state I was going to find you in.'

'You have my number, Eva. You could have called *me* to find out.'

227

Eva blushed. That made sense. But she was too panicked at the time to even think about it. She'd just assumed he'd be too sick to answer.

'So what kind of picture did Anthony paint you?'

'I thought you were half dead. Fully dead even…'

Julian laughed. It was very annoying.

'You really need to stop listening to other people and trust what you know. Trust me.'

'What I know? All I know is you're really sick, and up until ten minutes ago, I thought you were refusing treatment.'

'Yes. You did. But you didn't actually ask me what I was doing. You just added up all the clues and came to your own verdict. A completely wrong verdict, I might add.'

'Well, you certainly don't ever make it easy. You're almost impossible to figure out. I asked you about all this and you never told me that you were going to have dialysis.'

'No. You asked Meghan, and then told me what you knew. I just didn't correct you. There's a difference.'

'What? That's ridiculous. Why didn't you set me straight? I've been out of my mind with worry. Is this another one of your tests? 'Oh, will stupid Eva ever figure it out?' It's driving me crazy.' Eva's voice had a flippant tone, but she was quite serious.

Julian put his coffee cup down on the low table beside him and pulled a face. 'Christ, that stuff tastes like horse piss.'

'Julian,' Eva said, demanding his attention.

Julian's chestnut eyes meet Eva's and it was almost impossible to stay angry.

'It's not a test, Eva. Look at me; I'm hooked up to a machine that's washing my blood, for God's sake. Do I look like I have time for games?'

'Well, what then, Julian?' Eva shrugged.

'Habit. I've never trusted anyone. Ever. I've always dug deep to find out exactly what I need to know. Everyone has layers and you have to get past so many layers of bullshit to get to the real person underneath. But you're different. I could see the real you straight away.'

Eva smiled. 'Is that a compliment?'

'Yes and no. You're beautiful and intelligent but you let other people shape your opinion way too much.'

'What are you talking about? From the day we met, you've been shaping me.'

Julian shook his head. 'Never. I've been in love with you since the day you walked into my office...'

Eva cut across him. 'But you pushed me away...'

'No. I pushed you. Pushed you to breaking point because you needed to snap. You snapped, Eva, and now you're putting yourself back together. You can leave out the piece where the past is hurting you. And you can decide if you want to put in the piece that is me in your life.'

'That sounds a lot like a test to me.'

'Call it what you want.' Julian stroked his chin with his fingers.

'I will,' Eva grumbled.

'So? What's your decision?'

'On what?

'On the last piece?' Julian smiled and his nose twitched. *Oh, my God, was he nervous?*

229

'I don't think I would be here if I didn't want you. I would have walked when your game dragged me up on the stage at the ball, or when the Da Lucas tried to kill me, or when I found out the bitch from hell is your ex-wife.'

'When you put it like that, I'm one hell of catch.' Julian winked.

Eva laughed. 'Okay, first things first. How long are you going to be hooked up to that thing?' Eva pointed to the machine behind Julian.

'Three to four hours, I think. Maybe the first time takes longer…I don't know.'

'Does it hurt?'

Julian shook his head. 'It's a pain in the hole, does that count?'

'Right. We're going to need some decent coffee. I can smell that horrible stuff from here.' Eva tossed her head towards Julian's cup on the table. 'It's gross. I'll see what I can do. And when I get back, we have a lot to talk about.'

Julian suddenly looked like he was in pain.

'I have a lot of questions and now that I know you're, erm, tied up for a few hours, I'm asking them.'

## 27

Eva looked at her watch. It was almost one am. Where in the hell was she supposed to get decent coffee at this hour? She opened the passenger door of the limo and sat in.

Anthony's face had worry scribbled all over it. Eva looked into the back to check that Daniel was still asleep before she started talking.

'Panic's over, Anthony. Julian is okay. He's started dialysis.'

'At this hour of the night?' Anthony squawked.

'Shh,' Eva said, flicking her head towards Daniel.

'Sorry, sorry. But that's odd.'

'It's Julian we're talking about. Odd is normal.'

'True,' Anthony beamed, brightly.

'Okay, I have a couple of favours to ask. I'm sorry; I know you must be exhausted and this is way outside working hours,' Eva apologised.

'I'm here as Julian's friend now, so don't worry about any of that, Miss Andrews.'

'Well, then you're here as my friend, too…and, please, call me Eva.'

'Eva,' Anthony said with a nod.

'Okay, first…where in the hell can I get some good coffee?'

'Not a problem,' Anthony laughed, 'I'll sort that. And second?'

'Can you take Daniel back to my hotel room and stay with him?' Eva passed Anthony a key. 'I'm not sure what time

Meghan is due to land but someone needs to watch him in the meantime.'

'Absolutely.'

'And one last thing. Would you let Meghan know that Julian is okay? I think I completely freaked her out.'

'Eva, you're a sweetheart. It's probably not my place to say this, but I don't recognise Mr. Harte since you walked into his life. I only realise now that I'd never actually seen him happy before. You make him happy.' Anthony paused and shook his head. 'Apologies, that was way out of line.'

'Not at all, Anthony. We're friends now; don't forget. Friends don't have lines.'

***

Julian smiled as Eva walked back into the room, carrying two takeaway coffees. A small paper bag swung from her finger and he could smell pastries of some sort. He was starving.

'Hey, you. I was beginning to think you'd gotten lost trying to find your way out of this place,' Julian joked.

Eva laughed. 'Well, actually, I nearly did. You Irish aren't big fans of street signs are you? Sorry I was so long. We had to circle around trying to find somewhere open to get coffee. It's only from a gas station so probably not very good, but definitely better than that hospital crap.'

'It's fine. Thank you.' Julian reached for a cup and enjoyed the warmth of the paper cup in his hand. 'So c'mon. Are we going to fill all night with small talk or are you going to ask some questions?'

For once, Julian hoped she dug deep. All the secrets were exhausting. He had some heavy shit to share with her, and he needed her wanting the answers. He wasn't going to tell her anything she wasn't ready to hear. But he had a feeling that she was finally ready to hear it all.

Eva slipped off her jacket and sat in the armchair next to him. Her leg brushing his as she got comfortable. Her skinny jeans clung to every inch of her, leaving his imagination running wild. Christ, he ached to touch her.

'Okay, shoot,' Julian said, taking a gulp of coffee.

'I'm starting with important stuff.'

'Start with whatever you like.'

'Did you listen to the tape?' Eva asked, looking into his eyes.

'I didn't have to.'

Julian watched with mild amusement as Eva's face fell. 'I didn't have to because I already knew what it was going to say,' he said. 'I think I've known for years. Certainly all my adult life, but it was only ever in the back of my head. When I was eight, I was certain I had started the fire. And that had always stuck with me. Even though I now know it would be physically impossible for a blaze to take hold of the house that fast without an illegal acceleratant of some sort used, I still can't shake that feeling of guilt that I had when I was a child. I know the truth, Eva. And I love you for wanting to share it with me. But I will always feel like it was my fault. Even if I didn't start it.' Julian exhaled deeply through his mouth. 'I didn't stop it, and in my mind, that's just as bad.'

'Is there anything I can say to make you feel different? I wish I could make it stop hurting you.' Eva stretched her arm out and placed her hand just above his knee.

Julian looked into her beautiful green eyes. He ached to rip her clothes of and feel her bare skin against his. He wanted to feel her pussy tight around his cock. He needed to bury himself deep inside her. Because when he was close to her, that close, then nothing else in the world existed. Not even the past.

'Did you go into the house tonight?' Eva said, dragging her teeth across her bottom lip.

'I've been back there many times over the years,' Julian said. 'I've even thought about pumping some money into the old place and restoring it to its former glory. It was beautiful, back then. But I never had the balls to go inside. I was always so shit scared of what I'd see inside. But something about you being there with me tonight changed that.'

Eva's face brightened, and Julian could see she was proud of him. He hadn't felt anyone be proud of him in a very long time. Every achievement, every million made or company acquired, the growth of his business to an empire—it was always missing something. He'd never really known what. Not until that very moment. It was missing someone to be proud of him. God, it felt so good to see the pride in her face. *Christ!* If he didn't fuck her soon, he was going to explode.

'Was it how you remembered?' Eva said, her voice pulling him back into the moment.

Eva was shifting on her chair and Julian knew she was tiptoeing around the questions, but she didn't need to. He wanted to talk about it. Talk about it with her. Only her. Thinking about it didn't hurt like it usually did. It actually felt good to remember. He'd been so haunted by the memories of his family when he should have been clinging to them because they were all he had left.

'Yes. It was exactly how I remember. It was…surreal.'

Eva stood up. Julian tilted his head back to look up at her face and he reached up to wrap his free arm around her waist.

'Thank you,' he whispered.

'It's all going to be okay, baby,' Eva whispered. 'It's all going to be okay.'

Julian sucked some air through his teeth and dropped his head and his hands. He felt Eva jump.

'What is it? Are you in pain?' she asked, her eyes racing all over him.

'Eva, sit back down,' Julian ordered, keeping his voice as level as possible. This was going to be hard enough without letting her see that he was actually scared.

Eva did as he asked and her eyes burned into him with worry.

'I'm sick, Eva.'

'I know, baby,' Eva said as her hands rushed to his knees and she ran her fingers up and down his calves. 'But you've started the dialysis now. It'll be okay.'

'This is a stopping gap. And I know you know that. That's why I need everything in order. All the legal shit, you know. I need to know that you're okay.'

Eva's eyes widened. Julian knew that she understood. It hurt to see her take in the gravity of what he was saying.

'Julian, no.' Eva shook her head. 'Is this why you want me to go back to New York?' she asked.

'I might not always be here. I want you to be happy.'

'But I'm only happy with you.'

Julian exhaled sharply. He needed to approach this differently. She was becoming too emotional.

235

'Eva, will you marry me?'

Eva's eyes almost burst out of her head, and despite the intensity of the moment, Julian wanted to laugh. That was the ugliest face he'd ever seen her make and all he could think about was how much it made him want to kiss her.

'What happened to Mr. I-won't-wear-a-monkey-suit-and-march-up-the-aisle?'

'I still won't. I've explained before that marriage is just a contract. A piece of paper.'

Eva sat back down and Julian watched as the excitement of seconds before drained from her face. She was a mess of emotions and mixed-up facial expressions. He could understand that her head must have been all over the place. He was throwing a lot at her. But he knew she could keep up, even if it hurt like hell.

Julian hated that he was upsetting her. But she needed to understand that everything he was doing, every decision he made, from the very first day she walked into his office, was always for her. For her protection. And now that the shit had hit the fan and things were spiralling out of his control, it would be a hell of a lot easier to leave everything to her if they were married.

Eva was already named as the main benefactor in his will. He'd had his lawyers draw up a new will before he went into Vertigo. But there would be red tape and legal bollocks to sieve through once he died. She'd lose half the inheritance in tax. But not if they were married. He wanted her to have it all. Everything! Including his name.

'A contract? Just some legal mumbo jumbo to get some tax credits, right?' Eva said.

'That's a crass way of looking at it but, yes, that's what it boils down to.'

'So not two people who are madly in love and want to spend the rest of their life together?'

'A piece of paper has nothing to do with being in love, Eva. It's all financial.'

'So, is this just about money for you?' Eva was shaking her head.

'It's about making sure you're okay. I don't need a piece of paper to show you that I'm in love with you. And if I do, then I'm not the man I thought I was.'

'I know you love me, Julian. But the way you're talking now....I'm scared....'

'I know. But the contracts needs to be in place. Eva, it's important stuff. Legal shit that needs all the I's dotted and T's crossed.'

'Is this how you proposed to Meghan?'

Julian swallowed hard. His throat was dry, and he could murder a gin and tonic. His doctor's drinking in moderation advice was bollocks. He knew Eva's business head was not in the room.

'I'd appreciate it if you left Meghan out of this,' Julian said.

'Me?' Eva banged her chest with her clenched fist. 'Me leave her out of this! You're the one who keeps dragging her in. You and your rules, and paperwork, and crossed T's. I know about the other paperwork, Julian. I know you're hiding something from me, still. Something Meghan is involved in. God, do you know how that makes me feel? That even now, even when you're asking me to be your wife, you're still letting her in where you're pushing me out.'

Julian dropped his head back and groaned. He was trying not to lose his temper as he prepared for whatever odd conclusion Eva had come to based on some bullshit someone had told her.

'What the fuck are you talking about, Eva?' Julian asked dryly.

'A mountain of paperwork with my name all over it. Ring any bells?'

Julian ran his fingers across his eyes as he digested what Eva had just said. He'd been hoping to surprise her, but *damn, Pam had a big mouth.*

'It's a charity,' he said eventually.

'Okay? And what the hell does it have to do with me?'

'It's the Andrews Charity.'

Eva didn't reply and Julian couldn't tell if she wanted to slap him or kiss him. He braced himself knowing it could go either way.

'The Da Lucas don't get to win, Eva. They just fucking don't. Look at what they've done to us. I want everything they own. Even down to the goddamn stationery in their fucking office. And I want them to know who took it. I want them to suffer like we did.'

'Julian, what have you done?' Eva stuttered.

Julian smirked seeing the worry on Eva's face.

'It's all legal and legit, Eva. The Da Lucas are royally fucked over and the best part is I get a nice little tax break for the trouble.'

'What does that have to do with Meghan?'

238

Julian flicked his eyes to the machine behind him. 'I'm a little incapacitated at the moment. Meghan is a good businesswoman; I knew she'd get the best deal. She flew over to New York to negotiate the terms on my behalf. Her involvement is purely business, Eva.'

'Okay. Thank you for explaining.' Eva's cheeks flushed.

'You're welcome,' Julian said enjoying watching Eva's body language soften.

'Why the Andrews Charity? Not the Harte?' Eva asked.

'Because it's not mine. It's yours. Yours and Melissa's and your mother's too, if she wants to be a part of it.'

'I...I...I don't understand.'

'Da Luca had several properties; a little seedy but nothing some paint won't sort out. With the whole family behind bars, there are a lot of prostitutes out of work. If someone doesn't look after them, they'll end up in some other shite hole club selling themselves for whatever dirty bastard runs the place. It's a vicious world out there, Eva. These girls have nothing and no other choice. They are trapped.'

'You want to help them?' Eva said.

'I want you to help them. If you want to.'

'Yeah. I mean, of course I'd help them, if I could. No one should have to live that kind of life.'

Eva ran her finger up and down Julian's thigh. It tickled. He liked it.

'Good,' Julian said. 'So you agree; you'll take the role?'

'What role? You're going to have to spell it out for me, Julian. You've just told me a million different things tonight. I'm pretty confused right now.'

'I want you to head up the charity. It's all yours,' Julian grinned contently. 'Funding isn't an issue. You can take what you need to get things off the ground.'

'What? I don't know anything about all that stuff?'

Eva looked scared.

'You've a better business head on your shoulders than you think you have. Stop doubting yourself. I never doubt you. I know it'll be hard to start. I'll make sure Meghan gives you all the support you need. It's in her interest, too.'

'What? Is the charity hers, too? Like partners?' Eva asked.

'No. All yours. But it is part of the Ignite family of companies.'

'And she has a reputation to uphold,' Eva said, nodding.

'Yes, that. And she also has a share in the company,' Julian admitted.

'A share?' Eva's eyes widened.

Julian laughed. He laughed even more when he saw the frustration on Eva's face because he was laughing.

'You will receive a ninety percent stake of Ignite Technologies. The other ten percent is divided between Meghan and Daniel, at five percent each.'

'What? Julian, that's crazy. It's your company. You can't just give it away. You're scaring me, talking like this.'

Eva stood up and ran her hands down her body, like straightening out her clothes would straighten out her head. It was adorable and Julian desperately wanted to kiss her.

'Eva, I'm dying,' Julian said, the words cold and icy as he said them.

'No. No…you're getting treatment now. It's all going to be okay. I know it's scary, but this hospital has some of the best renal doctors in the world.'

'You've been doing your research.' Julian smiled. 'I told you, you have a good business head on your shoulders'

'Yes, well, thank you. And, anyway, there's loads they can do while they're waiting for a transplant donor. It's a bit of an inconvenience coming into the hospital twice a week for dialysis, but it's manageable.'

'Eva, look at me,' Julian said, reaching for Eva's face.

The tears glistening in Eva's eyes were breaking Julian's heart.

'It's not looking good, baby. I wasn't even supposed to start dialysis this soon. But my body couldn't hack it any longer. I'm not going down without a fight. But even I know you can't win 'em all.'

'You're talking like you're giving up. There are options to explore. Did you read the leaflet?' Eva was fidgeting with her nails.

'They're just words on a page, Eva. Guidelines and possibilities. It's not even very well written.'

'…but there's the donor option…' Eva said bending down to Julian's level.

'Why do you think I discharged myself from the hospital in Limerick?'

Eva shrugged her shoulders. 'Honestly?'

'Yes. You always want me to be honest with you. I want your honest opinion now.'

Eva pulled her body up until she was standing like an arrow with her head pointing towards the ceiling. 'I think you

241

discharged yourself because you're a stubborn bastard and you couldn't handle anyone telling you what to do. And that includes the doctors and nurses trying to save your life.'

'You really do know me, Miss Andrews. I am stubborn. Stubborn as hell. But I'm not a fucking idiot. If there were a fix to this, I'd have stayed there. I'd have put up with their shite food and the clinical stench. I like games, but one thing I'm never prepared to play with is life and death. They could run a hundred more tests and they would all have come back with the same answer. I have a rare blood and tissue type. I'm as good as fucked. It's almost impossible to find a donor. My only shot is a relative…and, you know how that story ends.'

'Daniel,' Eva said softly.

Julian expression darkened, and he shook his head.

'Have you asked Meghan; asked to have him tested? She was once your wife, Julian, and I know she loves you. She'd do anything she could to help. I know she would.'

'Eva, we've been over this. I told you that Meghan needed security. Marriage was a psychological thing with her. It was never emotional or anything to do with love. She needed to know I was committed to taking care of her…and Daniel. She couldn't just take my word for it. She needed proof. The marriage certificate was proof. I was all about business, Eva. And what's the most important thing in business? A contract! If I was prepared to tie myself into a lifelong contract, then she knew I had no intention of abandoning her like her family did.

'So it was a test. She needed a piece of paper, not a husband. And she was happy to screw you over to get what she wanted.'

'She didn't screw me over, Eva.'

'But she didn't want a husband. Did she even want you?'

'No. She didn't want me. Well, not like that, anyway. But she needed me. She wanted what that piece of paper represented. Permanency. The annulment of our marriage never changed that. I will always be there for her. Always. And she knows that.'

'Does she know about the annulment?

'Of course.'

'But at the hospital…she said…she told them she was your wife.'

'She was scared she was going to lose me.'

Eva threw her cup of coffee against the wall. The cup smashed and crumpled to the ground and the coffee rained down the wall leaving a milky, brown stain behind.

'I was fucking scared. I FUCKING thought I was going to lose you. But I couldn't see you. She made damn sure of that.'

'Eva, I've spoken to her about that. And she feels bad. In fact, it was Meghan who gave me a telling off for leaving the hospital without telling you. So don't judge her for something that happened ten years ago.'

243

'I'm not. I'm judging her for how big a bitch she's been to me for the past year.'

Julian shook his head and tossed Eva a cheeky grin.

'What?' Eva snapped, her hands on her hips and an I'm-done-with-games look on her face.

'You're shit hot when you're mad, do you know that?'

'Don't,' Eva warned.

'Don't what?'

'Don't look at me like that.'

'Like what?' Julian's salacious smirk was melting her.

'Like you want to fuck me.'

'How can I look at you any other way? I always want to fuck you.' Julian stood up and took a step forward.

'No. Stop. We're not doing this. Not here. You can wipe that look off your face, Julian. We're talking. That's all.'

Julian threw his hands to each side and tilted his head towards his shoulder. 'What I had in mind was a lot more fun than conversation but...'

'But nothing. Look, I'm never going to like Meghan. She's a witch. I know you don't see it, but your head is so far up your ass when it comes to her that you think her shit smells like roses. And it's fair enough. You've been through a lot together. But she's just so mean to me –'

'She's intimidated by you. And she's overcompensating. I'll ask her to be nicer.'

'Julian sit down, please?' Eva asked.

Julian sucked his lips between his teeth and inhaled sharply as he lowered himself back into the chair. He didn't need to sit, but he hated to see Eva looked so worried.

'I don't want Meghan to be nicer,' Eva admitted impressively certain. 'I've accepted that we're never going to be friends. I actually don't care. I think I hate her as much as she hates me. But there's a child messed up in all this. Daniel seems like a great kid. At least some good can come out of all this.'

'Eva –'

'Your son might be a match. C'mon, Julian. You must have at least thought about it?'

Julian stood again and was right in front of her in an instant, the needle in his arm pinched as it objected to the distance between him and the machine.

'What? Surely you've thought of that, Julian? Jesus, was it not the first thing the hospital suggested.'

'He's not getting tested,' Julian said, venom in his eyes.

'What? Why?'

'Don't be coy, Eva, it doesn't suit you. You heard me. My decision is made.'

'Julian, that's stupid. He needs to be tested. He could save your life.'

Julian pounded his fist against the table so hard that his coffee cup fell off and onto the floor. Eva jumped. The veins on the side of his neck bubbled under his skin and his chest flared.

'Please. Why won't you just consider it? I know you want to protect him but...' Eva continued, taking a step back.

'Eva, stop it,' Julian growled.

## 28

Eva had never seen Julian so angry. He was seething; every inch of him told her that he wanted to punch something or someone. She knew if she pushed much further, he'd lose his temper completely. But she also knew that no matter how angry he was, or how far she pushed his buttons, he would never hurt her. She had to push. If there was any chance she could make him see sense, she had to push.

'You put Daniel first once before, why won't you do it now?'

'EVA, DAMMIT. Just stop!' The veins in Julian's neck pulsed faster.

'It's not just me or Meghan who will lose you. Daniel will lose you, too. Why are you being so selfish?'

Julian's hand ran through his hair. His grip was so tight, his knuckles whitened. Maybe she was getting through to him.

'Will you talk to Meghan? Will you ask to have him tested? He's your son, for God's sake.'

Julian threw his arms in front of him and flipped the chair over. The loud bang of the metal legs clanking against the tiled floor sent Eva's heart flying into the back of her throat.

'He's not my FUCKING son.' Julian dropped to his knees.

Eva held her breath. '*What?*' What had she done? Maybe she'd finally pushed him too far. Broken him completely.

'He's not biologically mine.'

Eva's hands flew to cover her mouth. 'But I thought...'

'I know what you thought. It's what anyone would think. But Meghan and I have never been together like that. Ever.'

'You've never slept with her? But the ball. You always picked your one girl for the year. Meghan was the first? Shelly told me.'

'Shelly was right. Meghan was the example. But it was just a setup for the game. I've never touched her. She's like my sister, for fuck's sake.'

Eva dropped to her knees beside him and wrapped her arms around him. Taking care not to hurt him or pull his IV line she cradled him close.

*More twists.* Eva's head was spinning. But this time it was spinning in a good way. Julian and Meghan were never together. They really were the true definition of just friends. *Thank God!*

'I'm so sorry. I shouldn't have assumed. It's just I had so many different people telling me different things all the time, and I never really knew the truth. And you didn't make it any easier, Julian.'

'I always tell you the truth.'

'I know. I know. So all the girls. You fucking your way around the office. None of it was true. It was all just part of the game.'

'Eva. I like sex. All of *that* was true.'

'Oh.' Eva couldn't hide her disappointment.

'I *still* like sex. A lot. The only thing that's changed is the only woman I like sex with now is you.'

Eva laughed. Could she laugh about that now? It certainly felt like she could. All that shit seemed like a lifetime ago. A lifetime when she didn't know Julian. Or love him. A lifetime when she wasn't half the person she was now.

Eva stroked Julian's cheek. 'You told me once that I surprise the hell out of you, Julian.'

Julian smiled and Eva knew he remembered.

'Well, right back at you, baby. You never stop blowing me away.'

Eva and Julian sat on the floor for what felt like forever. Their limbs entwined together. Julian Harte had so many layers and Eva believed that she had just peeled off the last one. He'd protected Meghan and her son, loved the kid as if he was his own, and never once sought any credit for it. He just did it because it was the right thing to do. Eva loved him before, but she loved him even more now. Julian Harte was really just a big softy. *Who knew.*

Eva stood up, kissed Julian on the cheek, and then left the room. *Fuck.* He did not see that coming. She was up to something; he knew it. But he had no idea what her next move was; he should have been shocked or even upset that she'd walked out, but instead, he sat stroking his chin between his fingers and thumb and smiled. Evangeline Andrews had become the Queen of Games. And she would be okay. With or without him. God, how he wanted it to be with him. He wanted to share his life with her. Every bit. If someone had told him a year ago that he was dying, it would have been rather inconvenient. He'd have had acquisitions to tidy up and some general administrative stuff to double check, but that was all his life boiled down to. He was just a man in a suit, albeit an expensive one with some fine hand stitching. Julian Harte never needed anyone. But somehow, this girl had snuck into his heart, made herself comfortable, and changed him to the point where he didn't even recognise himself for the better. And the thoughts of leaving her behind was killing him more than his failing kidneys.

## 29

Julian was asleep when Eva came back into the area sectioned off by a hideous purple and orange floral curtain. She watched him for a long time. Every line of his beautiful face, his dark hair that matched his sallow skin so perfectly. His broad shoulders spanned the back of the chair and he looked deliciously casual in a pair of faded navy jeans and a white, rugby style jersey. She was almost afraid to blink. Every blink cost her a millisecond of watching him; of committing every bit of him to memory in case she ever forgot. Eva couldn't imagine the world without Julian Harte in it. She shook her head and exhaled deeply. She couldn't go there. She couldn't think about it. Vomit swirled in her stomach like some little creature was trying to blend up a smoothie with her insides. Her head was reeling and she couldn't remember the last time she ate. It didn't matter anyway, the last thing she felt was hungry. She felt horribly ill. But she couldn't feel sorry for herself, not compared to what Julian was going through. Every single thing he was suffering now was because of her. Because he loved her and saved her.

She'd asked one of the junior doctors for a pen and paper which she clenched tightly in her fist. She took a seat in the chair waiting opposite Julian and began writing, her fingers couldn't move as fast as the words tumbling out of her mind. She closed her eyes.

Eva was vaguely aware of a nurse or doctor coming in every so often to check on Julian, but she was too sleepy to open her eyes wide enough to pay full attention. She woke fully when Julian's hand shook her shoulder.

'C'mon, sleepyhead. Let's get going.'

Eva rubbed her eyes and sat up straight. There were no windows where they were so she couldn't tell if it was still night or if the day had snuck in while she was sleeping. 'Are you finished? Did they say you could go?'

Eva didn't really know why that was the first question that came into her head. Maybe because she worried Julian had become impatient and just decided to discharge himself again.

'Yes, Eva. I've been a good boy. I finished my run through the spin cycle,' Julian mocked and pointed back at the dialysis machine behind him.

'Okay, good. When do you have to come back?'

'…few days,' Julian said pulling an unimpressed face as he pulled on his coat. 'What's that?' he asked, his eyes dropping to the page in Eva's hand.

Eva looked down at the paper. She'd fallen asleep before she had a chance to finish writing. 'Nothing…I'll show you later.' She pulled her coat off the back of the chair and stuffed the paper into the pocket. 'C'mon. Let's get some decent coffee.'

'Eva, I saw my name on the paper. What were you writing?' Julian said, raising an eyebrow inquisitively.

'I told you I'd show you later…'

'Eva. Now. Please.'

Eva put her hand in her pocket but pulled it back out empty, shaking her head. 'It's a surprise.'

Julian's eyes narrowed. 'I don't like surprises.'

'Okay.' Eva shrugged.

'Excuse me?'

'Julian, it's your kidneys that have the problems, not your ears. You heard me. It's a surprise. And I'm not showing you.'

Julian's face reddened, but Eva couldn't help but notice that his lips pulled up at the sides. He was smiling. *Why was he smiling?* She'd expected an argument. *Was Julian Harte mellowing?* If she hadn't seen it with her own eyes, she wouldn't have believed it.

Damn, it was cold. Eva glanced at her watch. It was coming up on seven am but it was still pitch dark outside. Julian's phone was accosting his pocket with vibrations of emails and texts filtering through. Eva was standing close enough to Julian to feel it, too.

'Wow, someone is really trying to get a hold of you,' Eva said.

Julian shook his head. 'It's just work stuff, Eva. My day usually starts around now. No one knows I'm out of the office. All my calls and emails are automatically redirecting to my phone.'

'What? No one knows you're ill? Julian, you can't keep working now. That's crazy. You need some time to rest.'

Julian stopped walking and turned to face Eva. 'No one knows, Evangeline. And I am keeping it that way. Do you understand?'

Eva gulped down a lump of air far too large for her throat and tried to hide her discomfort. When it came to anything work related, Julian made it very clear that he was the boss. Nothing was ever open for discussion, and Eva didn't intend or want to overstep that mark. But it still hurt to be put in her box with the tone of his voice.

'Meghan text.'

'Oh,' Eva said almost choking on another oversized lump of air.

'She said thank you for looking after Daniel?' Julian's head turned to one side, and Eva knew that was his way of enquiring why in the hell Eva had been spending time with his son.

'Meghan asked me to bring him to the hospital, but he was sleeping and…'

'You don't have to explain.'

'I don't?' Eva's face scrunched.

'Thanks for watching him. But Meghan's home now. Anthony brought Daniel to the airport.'

'Oh.'

'I've asked Meghan to join us for lunch this afternoon.'

Eva's face fell. She thought of the note in her pocket. She'd hoped to have Julian all to herself all day.

'I want to get all the paperwork for the Da Luca properties sorted out as soon as possible. This afternoon, hopefully.'

Eva nodded. She wasn't as overwhelmed as she'd expected to be about the whole thing. 'Okay, sure.'

They reached the city centre in record time; they'd been walking faster than usual to keep warm. The conversation was sporadic but the silences were just as comfortable as the chitchat about both their childhoods. They talked openly about their demons and happy memories. It was therapeutic and Eva never dreamed she'd be recanting childhood memories and laughing and smiling at the same time.

Julian veered away from Eva and bent down slowly, but the man Julian approached barely looked up. Julian crouched a little lower until he was on his hunkers, his shoulders level with the shoulders of the man sitting in the doorway. Eva watched as Julian slipped some money out of his inside jacket pocket and handed the notes into the man's gloved hand. She didn't notice the amount. She was too distracted by the dirt and holes in the man's gloves; it was obvious that age and not design had them fingerless on every second finger.

'There's a hostel just down there,' Julian pointed. 'It's pretty damn cold out here and you look like you've been here an hour or two too long. Spend it wisely, my friend.'

Julian shook the man's hand and stood up.

'Aren't you worried that he'll spend it on drinking?' Eva whispered as they turned to walk away.

Julian sighed. 'Not my call. It's his money now.'

'He'll freeze if he spends any longer out here, though.'

Doubling back, Julian slid his arms out of his grey, wool crombie and placed it on the man's knees.

'What's this?' the man said, instantly pulling the coat up as far as his neck.

Eva followed Julian's glance to the money the man clenched in his first.

'It's just in case something sensible tastes a lot like a bottle of whiskey,' Julian said. 'The drink will warm your blood and this will warm your bones.'

'You're a good lad,' the man said as Julian and Eva walked away, hand in hand.

'I'm learning,' Julian whispered squeezing Eva's hand and shooting her a smile.

Eva's heart pinched. Julian was a good man. The best. She wished that she'd always trusted that and had never let the other people or office rumours shape her opinion of him. She was never going to make that mistake again.

## 30

Anne opened the door and wrapped her arms around Julian's neck. 'Sweet Jesus, ya little bollocks,' she said pulling back and eyeing Julian up and down. 'You had the heart crossways in me. I didn't have a clue where you were. My head was thinking all sorts.'

Julian apologised like a scolded schoolboy, and Eva was smiling as they stepped inside and savoured the warmth of Julian's house.

'You two must be famished. Why don't you get a couple of hours sleep? I'll fix some breakfast and call you later,' Anne said, taking Eva's coat and eyeing Julian up disapprovingly for not wearing one.

'Thank you, Anne,' Julian said turning towards Eva. 'You tired?'

Eva nodded. 'Very.'

Julian shot Eva a look that said you-better-not-be-too-tired, and Eva could feel her face redden standing beside Anne.

Julian led the way upstairs and Eva followed. His house was just as impressive as she remembered, but somehow, it felt warmer now, more inviting, and less intimidating. It felt like him. Julian stopped outside a closed door.

'This is my room,' Julian said reaching behind his back for the door handle.

'Oh,' Eva said, suddenly feeling uninvited.

'You can take your pick from the guest rooms.' Julian tilted his head to one side and Eva looked around at a landing laden with doors. 'I've taken the liberty of having my staff pick you up a few things. Toiletries and stuff. Anthony will take you to the hotel later and you can collect the rest of your things.'

Eva sighed. This wasn't what she had pictured when Julian asked her to stay with him. She thought they'd be sharing a bedroom at the very least. 'Okay, thank you,' she said, quashing any sign of emotion.

Julian leaned in and kissed Eva on the forehead. 'Get some sleep, baby.'

Eva nodded and opened the nearest door to her. 'Night.'

*** 

Julian changed into a clean t-shirt and some lounge pants. He sat on the edge of his bed and made some work-related calls. He checked in on the domain name for Andrewsharte.com. He'd made a last-minute change to the charity title. He hoped it would remind Eva of him in the future. It was a surprise. He'd show her later when she was signing all the documentation. Thinking of surprises sent

Julian's mind wandering towards Eva's coat pocket and the note inside she was hiding from him.

A few minutes later, he was standing outside her bedroom door with the note in one hand and he was knocking gently with the other hand. Eva came to the door wearing just a white t-shirt and a pair of silky crimson knickers. Julian cock immediately sprung to life. She was utterly fuckable. And he wanted nothing more than to scoop her into his arms, throw her back on the bed, and push deep inside her. But he hid his desire…for now.

Eva had snatched the note out of his hand before he had a chance to speak. 'Julian, Jesus. You know you're impossible. You shouldn't have read that. It was a surprise. It's not even finished…'

Julian's jaw twisted to one side and he pulled an unimpressed face. 'I didn't read it, Evangeline. That would be fucking rude.'

Eva blushed, scrunching the note. 'Sorry… I thought.'

'Well. You were wrong. But I do want to know what it says. Are you going to tell me or am I going to have to fuck it out of you?'

Eva slipped her hand up her t-shirt and slid the note into her bra. 'You'll have to come looking for it,' she said grinning like a loon.

Eva took a couple of steps back. Julian followed and closed the door with the back of his heel.

'I'm only going to ask you this one more time, Miss Andrews. What is on that piece of paper?'

For every step forward Julian took, Eva took one back. Julian hid his amusement and the enjoyment of the chase. In a matter of seconds, he had her backed up against the far wall. He pushed his body up against hers, his cock swelling even more as it brushed against her belly. He rested one hand at each side of her head and kissed her deeply. He'd been aching to taste her since she walked into the hospital last night. He couldn't hold out any longer. He dropped one hand and slid it behind her thigh, pulling her leg up to his waist. He did the same on the other side and lifted her clean off the floor. He spun around, his lips never leaving hers, and he walked over to the bed and dropped her onto her back against the soft cream cotton.

She scurried back until her head was on the pillows. Julian stood at the end of the bed watching her. She stared back at him with the same burning intensity. If he didn't fuck her soon, there was a very real possibility that he was going to come in his pants.

'What about the note?' Eva's lips pulled into a delicious smirk.

'Oh, I'll find that when I'm ready. Right now I'm more interested in finding my cock between those delicious lips.'

Eva flipped onto her belly and slowly made her way to the edge of the bed on her hands and knees, like a lioness stalking its prey. She was so fucking hot. And she damn well knew it, too. God, how she'd changed. She wasn't shy and timid anymore. She looked like she was getting ready to fuck his brains out. And he was more than happy to oblige.

Julian caught the bottom of her t-shirt as Eva kneeled up on the edge of the bed. She obediently lifted her hands over her head as he tugged her t-shirt up and threw it to the side.

'Mr. Harte,' she purred as she bent forward and dragged her teeth along his rock hard cock, his pants between the warmth of her lips and his skin. He thought about slipping his fingers inside her bra and pulling out the note, but as she slipped his pants down his hips and slurped his cock into her mouth, his arms were taut against his body and he didn't want to move. She was sucking him like his cock was a four-course meal and she hadn't eaten in weeks.

He dropped his head back, closed his eyes, and groaned as she had him close to the edge in seconds.

'Evangeline Andrews, you sexy bitch,' he said, putting his hands on her shoulders and breaking the seal of her lips around him with a slurping sounding pop.

Julian dragged her to her feet and spun her around to face the bed. Julian was way too horny for foreplay, but there was no way he was going to come without hearing the sweet sound of her orgasm first.

He placed his palm flat against the soft skin of her back and guided her to bend over, pulling her perky ass closer to his cock. He slipped a finger inside her knickers. She was soaking wet and so ready for him.

'Close your eyes, baby,' he whispered.

He reached for the electric toothbrush that was left on top of a cute, pink and purple striped shorts and t-shirt style pyjamas that Anne had picked up for Eva at his request. He hadn't tried this before, but in the absence of toys, it could be fun.

He pulled Eva's knickers to one side and placed the bristle head against her clit. She gasped and jerked upright. But he placed his hand firmly on the base of her spine and guided her back down again. She didn't protest.

His took his hand off her back, content that she wouldn't spring back up again and used it to guide his cock to her. She ground her hips around and around, and Julian knew she wanted him every bit as much as he wanted her.

He flicked the toothbrush on, thrust inside her with gentle force and enjoyed the sound of her shocked whimpers as the toothbrush buzzed against her.

'Oh my God, it's so good,' she panted.

Julian closed his eyes and exhaled slowly, savouring the warmth of her pussy around him as her body pulsed and gyrated with pleasure. He could feel her on the edge already. Her pussy gripped him tightly as her ass cheeks clenched, pulling him deeper inside her. He could feel the buzz from the toothbrush rippling around her. Her breath was rapid and even as she gave one huge, tight squeeze and called out his name over and over as she came, before collapsing on the bed, her ass was still in the air.

She took a moment to recover, purring like a kitten. 'Use me,' she whispered, still lying with her belly against the bed and her body offered up to him.

Her perky, round cheeks begged him to spill inside her. Teasing him.

Julian turned off the toothbrush and tossed it onto the bed. He palmed her hips. Gripping her tightly, he slammed into her. Hard and fast until he couldn't hold back any longer. He groaned with deep satisfaction as he reached his own release.

'I love you, Julian,' she said sliding him out of her and turning around to face him.

She leaned up on her tiptoes and kissed him. Julian kissed her back, slipping his tongue between her silky lips.

'I love you, too,' he whispered softly into her open mouth.

Eva pulled away, and Julian ran his eyes over every inch of her. Her elegant lilac underwear was perfect against her delicious hourglass figure. Julian's hand slapped her ass cheek, and he smiled with satisfaction as she squealed and giggled, tossing him a naughty grin. She slipped on the bed, turned down the sheet on the other side, and patted the mattress.

'Sleep beside me,' she whispered. 'I want to feel you close. Please?'

Julian climbed in beside her and pulled the folded piece of paper out of her bra all in one motion. 'I've some bedside reading to do.' He grinned.

Eva smiled back at him and nodded. He knew it was her approval to unfold the page and he had the oddest feeling as he did. Like some sort of fucking giddy excitement. *What in the hell was that shit?* He didn't do fuzzy. But something about Eva's smile, and the piece of paper with her secret scribbled on it, a secret she wanted to share with him, gave him the fuzzy. *Fuck!* Evangeline Andrews had changed him. She'd turned him into the type of man who climbed into bed with his girlfriend after sex and laughed and joked. She'd made him a *real* man…and now it was too goddamn late.

## 31

Julian read and reread the words on the page while Eva sat silently beside him.

'Is this some sort of bucket list?' he asked, finally turning his attention away from the paper and towards Eva.

Eva's face was wearing a thousand worries and he hated to see her like that.

'No. Not really. It's a list of stuff I want to see and do. I never really took on the tourist side of Ireland. I thought it would be fun. Stuff we could do together…'

'So it *is* a bucket list,' Julian said, looking back at the page.

Eva took the paper out of his hand. 'It's not finished. You went all Detective Harte on me before I could finish it. So maybe we can finish it together now?'

Julian called out the first point on the list from memory. 'Visit the Ailewee caves in County Clare? Nope. Big dark hole in the ground? Waste of time that could be spent doing something much more interesting.'

'Okay. Fine. Scrap the caves. What about point number two? Check out the Guinness Storehouse.' Eva smiled.

Julian grunted. The idea of visiting attractions overrun with tourists and rip-off prices was so far from his idea of enjoyment, but if it was Eva's way of coping then the least he could do was flitter away a few hours in one of the locations on her list. But he wasn't visiting them all. *Fuck no!*

'Is there anything you'd like to add?' Eva said, running her finger over the words on the page.

'I can think of a couple of things…'

Eva's face lit up. 'Great. Hang on.' Eva reached over the side of the bed and pulled a pen out of her handbag. 'Okay, go. What would you like to do?'

'Fuck you?'

'What?' Eva shook her head. 'Ah c'mon, Julian. I thought you were going to take this seriously.'

'I am.'

Eva's whole face scrunched and Julian had to restrain himself from flipping her onto her belly and fucking her right that second.

Julian looked outside at the tall oak trees and precision manicured grounds of his Ballsbridge home. 'I want to lean you up against that tree, push a butt plug in your ass, and fuck you so hard you lose your mind.'

Eva shook her head.

'I'm serious,' Julian smirked. 'Write it down.'

'Julian. No. C'mon.'

Julian snatched the pen from Eva's fingers and scribbled *'Fuck Eva senseless'* just under Picnic in the Phoenix Park.

'Okay, next point…you ready?' Julian asked, struggling to keep a straight face.

Eva rolled her eyes playfully. 'Yes. I'm ready.'

'Maybe we should make this point number one…'

'Okay.' Eva raised an eyebrow, clearly intrigued. She moved her hand to the top of the page and pointed the tip of the pen above the Ailwee Cave suggestion.

'Fuck Eva up against the wall.' Julian tossed his head towards the opposite wall of the bedroom. 'And against that wall.' He turned his head to the other side. 'And in this bed.'

Eva laughed. 'I see a pattern here.'

'Good. I knew you'd catch on quickly.'

'Yeah, but this isn't a bucket list anymore now. It's just a list of sex stuff.'

'Isn't a bucket list supposed to be a list of stuff you want to do?' Julian raised an eyebrow.

'Well, yeah…but…'

'I want to fuck you. This is my kind of list.'

Julian's cock sprung to attention as Eva ran her teeth across her bottom lip. She ticked off point one on the list, threw the pen and paper onto the ground before throwing a leg over Julian, sitting upright and straddling him.

'I like your list, too,' she whispered, guiding him inside her.

***

Eva had watched Julian sleep for a long time before she dragged herself out of the bed. She was exhausted and her pussy ached from Julian fucking her like he was going for a Rough World Record. She smiled thinking back on it. She'd never come so many times before, and her head was still spinning a little from it. But she had a lot she needed to sort out, and she wanted most of it done before he woke.

She slipped on the pyjamas waiting for her and closed the bedroom door gently behind her. The smell of Anne's signature pancakes wafted towards her as soon as she stepped into the hallway. They smelt like heaven and Eva's mouth was watering just thinking about them. But her stomach was objecting to the smell. Her eating habits were so messed up over the last few days, her body was convulsing every time she dared to think of food. She dashed into the bathroom and threw up what little was in her tummy.

She wiped her lips with some tissue and then it hit her. *Oh Christ. She couldn't be.* She'd completely lost track of her cycle. She couldn't remember when her last period was, but it was definitely before she left New York. *No. She couldn't be.* It had to be stress. She remembered reading in some trashing agony aunt column how stress fucks with your cycle. It had to be that. She couldn't tell Julian she was pregnant, not now. She couldn't tell him she was about to bring a child into the world that he might never get to meet. It would be his worst nightmare. It would destroy him to know he was abandoning his child. Fuck! This was the worst timing ever.

Eva thought about texting Shelly, but she deleted the text halfway through typing it. She needed to find out for certain before she started telling people. Julian was the first person she wanted to tell, but what if the news broke him completely?

## 32

**From:** eva135@mymail.com
**To:** pamelawinters@HTK&associates.com
**CC:** shelly.k.fox@ignitetech.com.
nathan.shileds@thepress.com,
meghan.s.sutton@ignitetech.com
**Subject:** I need your help
**Date:** Mon 7th Jan 11.15

Hi Everyone,

Sorry for the group email, but I don't have much time and I need to get in touch with all of you.

Firstly, what I'm about to say is a secret, please no one breathe a word of this to Julian. I know I can trust you all, right?'

So…I want to restore Julian's old family home in Dun Laoghaire. I want it to be perfect. And I need it done asap! I hope I can count on you all for this. It's VERY, VERY important.

Meghan, do you still have access to Ignite Technologies funds? We're going to need some cash.

Nathan, what contacts do you have through the paper in the building trade? Guys who advertise with you, maybe? We'll probably need every trade you can think of because the house is in a bad way. Can you please recommend names of guys who are the very best at what they do? This has to be one hundred percent perfect. It's not a re-decorate job. It's a re-create job. Everything has to be exactly as it was before the fire.

Pam, can you process the money through HTK accounts? I know Julian trusts the finances in New York office to Mr. Thompson. I'm pretty sure Julian would notice anything going on in the Dublin office within hours of a transaction, but I think running it through you guys should buy us a few weeks. What do you think? Can you and Meghan please work together on this?

Shelly, can you be at the house once work starts? I need someone checking in on the trades and making sure it's all running smoothly? I'd love to be there myself, but I don't want to take the risk of Julian suspecting something.

All my best,
Eva xx

_____

**From:** meghan.s.sutton@ignitetech.com
**To:** eva135@mymail.com
**CC:** shelly.k.fox@ignitetech.com.
nathan.shileds@thepress.com,
pamelawinters@HTK&associates.com
**Subject:** I need your help
**Date:** Mon 7ᵗʰ Jan 11.17

Yes, I have financial control, but I'm not comfortable going behind Julian's back. I don't think this is a good idea. Julian has never been back inside that house. He has a good reason. I doubt he wants to go back now. I think this would upset him more than anything else.

Meghan.

_____

**From:** shelly.k.fox@ignitetech.com
**To:** eva135@mymail.com
**CC:**. nathan.shileds@thepress.com, meghan.s.sutton@ignitetech.com
pamelawinters@HTK&associates.com
**Subject:** I need your help
**Date:** Mon 7<sup>th</sup> Jan 11.18

I'd be happy to help. But I do agree with Meghan, unfortunately. I don't think Julian would be very happy with us all going behind his back. It's a sweet idea, but I think it'll piss Julian off more than anything.

Shelly xx ☺

_____

**From:** nathan.shileds@thepress.com
**To:** eva135@mymail.com
**CC:** meghan.s.sutton@ignitetech.com,
pamelawinters@HTK&associates.com
shelly.k.fox@ignitetech.com
**Subject:** I need your help

**Date:** Mon 7th Jan 11.20

Hi Eva,

I'd be happy to help. It sounds like you have it all under control. I know a good builder. He should be able to take care of everything. I'll get in touch with him today and get back to you with details.

Best,

Nathan

---

**From:** pamelawinters@HTK&associates.com
**To:** eva135@mymail.com
**CC:** meghan.s.sutton@ignitetech.com,
nathan.shileds@thepress.com
shelly.k.fox@ignitetech.com,
**Subject:** I need your help
**Date:** Mon 7th Jan 11.21

Hi Eva,

The books are checked monthly here. They've just been done so that buys you some time. But not much. The accounts team here are eagle eyed and it's going to be tricky to hide a dime. Maybe I could pretend it's a personal loan? I'm pretty sure Mr. Thompson would lend me the money. Let me know if that helps? I really care about Julian, and I think this would be an awesome surprise for him. I so hope it works out. He's very lucky to have you, Eva. Even if he's keeping you in Ireland and I'm missing you like crazy.

Love,
Pam xx

-------------------

**From:** eva135@mymail.com
**To: CC:** meghan.s.sutton@ignitetech.com,
nathan.shileds@thepress.com
shelly.k.fox@ignitetech.com,
pamelawinters@HTK&associates.com
**Subject:** I need your help
**Date:** Mon 7th Jan 11.21

Thanks for the quick replies, everyone.

Nathan that sounds great. Let me know as soon as possible what the story is. Thanks

Pam, if you could pull that off, I'd be soooo grateful and love you even more than I already do. I'll make sure you get EVERY penny back. Thank you, hun.

Shelly, I appreciate your concern but I wasn't asking for your advice. LOL. I know Julian better than anyone does, and I know what I'm doing. For once, just trust me. Okay?

Meghan. WTF?! Just get over yourself and help! Everyone else is, and anyway, you damn well owe it to me after the shit you pulled at the hospital.

Eva.

Eva followed her group email up with a text message for Meghan's eyes only.

**I'll keep ur secrets if u keep mine.**

**Julian has told me EVERYTHING.**

**C u after lunch. Don't say a word!**

Eva switched her phone to silent, threw up a couple of more times, and headed back to the bedroom to wake Julian for brunch.

## 33

### Three Months later

'Miss Andrews, Miss Andrews,' someone called.

Eva smiled at the man in the one-size-too-big suit tapping on her shoulder.

'They'll be ready for you on stage in about five minutes,' he said.

'Thank you,' Eva replied. 'Could I get some water first, please?'

'Certainly. I'll just be a moment.' The event manager hurried away.

Eva craned her neck and tried to peer out from behind the black, floor-to-ceiling curtain temporarily erected in the function room of the five-star Dublin, City Centre hotel. It was Eva's first press conference. First of many perhaps, and she was so nervous she could pee in her pants. Then again, nervous or not, she'd need to pee. If she wasn't throwing up in the toilet bowl, she was peeing in it. This being pregnant business meant spending a ridiculous amount of time in the bathroom.

'Ladies and gentlemen. I'm so pleased to introduce my friend and founding member of the Andrews Harte Trust, Miss Evangeline Andrews.'

Eva's heart jumped into the back of her throat when she heard her name. Loud applauding erupted and Eva squinted as she stepped out from behind the curtain and onto a low stage at the top of the room. The flashes from hundreds of cameras blinded her. She took a deep breath and kissed Shelly on the cheek as she stepped away from the podium in the centre of the stage to allow Eva to take the spot.

Seeing Nathan in the front row giving her a huge thumbs-up helped to set her nerves at ease. The exclusive he'd written a few weeks ago had done them both a favour. The scoop on the newest Harte investment, and especially a charitable one, had finally gotten his editor off his back. And it had been great publicity for the foundation. Nathan had written in just enough detail about the Da Luca's and Eva's family to make for a juicy story, but he'd held back enough information so Eva could retain her privacy. She never asked who Nathan's source was, but she didn't have to. The article was perfect and tasteful. She knew Julian was behind it.

Eva cleared her throat, held her head high, and leaned towards the microphone that was waiting at just the right level. Eva spoke with confidence and excitement as she gave her rehearsed speech.

276

'Thank you all for attending today. It's a great honour to stand before you all and tell you proudly that the Andrews Harte Trust is delighted to announce the expansion of our charity outside the United States. The first European safe house will be here in Dublin, with many more soon to follow in London, Paris, and most large European cities. Andrews Harte is committed to providing support to vulnerable women who need our help. Ignite Technologies has kindly donated twenty-five million Euro to our fund this year and many more wonderful companies have expressed an interest in donating also.'

Loud whooping and cheering followed Eva's announcement of such a large donation of money and some reporters down in the back of the room even threw in a wolf whistle. Eva smiled brightly.

'I'd very much like to express my personal gratitude to every one of you for your attendance today; your support has meant the world to us and those who we help. Now, I would like to hand you over to the face of Andrews Harte, and a lady I am very proud to call my sister, Melissa Andrews. Melissa would like to share her story with you. Please hold all questions until the end. Thank you once again.'

Eva stepped away from the podium, but someone was shouting her name from somewhere in the middle of the room. She could just about hear the thick Dublin accent over the crowd cheering and she turned around, but it was impossible to see anything with so many cameras flashing at her.

'Is it true you and Mr. Harte are engaged and having a baby?' the voice asked.

Eva's eyes pinched and she made it very clear there wouldn't be an answer forthcoming to that question. She was disappointed that someone had tried to drag her private life into it, but of course, she wasn't surprised. Nathan had taught her that anything might be asked and to never let your distaste or surprise show. Nathan's coaching on how to deal with press attention and the media had been helpful, and she was making it look like she was a natural.

'It's rumoured Mr. Harte's health continues to fade. Can you please elaborate for us, Miss Andrews?' another journalist shouted across some mumbles that were starting to fill the room.

Eva leaned back, just close enough for the microphone to pick up her soft tone. 'You shouldn't believe everything you read in the papers,' she said with a satisfied toss of her head.

The loud applauding began again, mixed with some laughter and good humour.

'Please, as I asked, hold all questions until the end. Ladies and gentlemen, my sister, Melissa Andrews.'

Eva hugged Melissa tightly as they switched places behind the podium and, then, catching Anthony's eye behind the black curtain, she hurried off the stage.

'How is he?' Eva asked the words tumbling out her mouth.

Anthony was smiling and Eva breathed a sigh of relief.

'Julian is fine. Good even. He should be ready to leave the hospital in less than an hour.'

'Okay, great.'

Eva's fingers were twitching nervously. She so wanted this afternoon to go according to plan. There was so much involved that the slightest mistake would ruin everything.

The cheeky journalist had heard correctly. Julian's health was declining. The dialysis was working, but not as well as it had been. A donor really was imperative now, but Julian made it perfectly clear that even if a donor did become available, swapping body parts was not an idea he wished to entertain.

'I'll see you there, Anthony, yeah?' Eva said.

'Everything will be okay, Eva. Try to stop worrying. You worked so hard to make everything perfect. Julian will be blown away. Nothing more you can do now so just relax. Allow yourself to enjoy it.' Anthony smiled.

Eva smiled. Anthony was sweet, but there was no way she could relax. She might calm a little when Julian was by her side, but right now, her heart felt like it was in her stomach.

279

'Are you sure the Wi-Fi was disabled on Julian's phone? I had a message from him less than an hour ago,' Eva mumbled, pulling her phone out of her pocket to check again for messages and calls.

She was beginning to panic that they wouldn't be able to pull off the surprise without Julian figuring it out at the last minute. She was still counting her blessings that he hadn't already noticed something.

'The Wi-Fi is off. The guy from the phone company was a bit reluctant at first. I think he was afraid he'd lose his job or something. But when I explained the story, he was excited to help. The guy said the Wi-Fi would be off for a whole hour. Julian will have hundreds of work messages coming in as soon as he leaves the hospital. I promise he'll be so busy on the bloody phone, he won't take the time to look out the window of the car. I've told him you're meeting him for dinner so he's asked me to bring his best suit. I promise, Eva, I won't let anything mess this up on you. Julian doesn't suspect a thing.'

Eva kissed Anthony on the cheek. 'Thank you. What would I do without you?'

'Get the bus more.'

# 34

Anthony passed Julian a gin and tonic as soon as he sat in the backseat of the car.

'Thank you,' Julian said, relieved to be out of the goddamn hospital. Another afternoon spent confined in a small space, with God-awful décor and a fuck hideous lunch, was trying his patience. He was grateful to the doctors and nurses working so hard to keep him alive but this half-life shit wasn't his cup of tea. He'd have to talk to Eva about it. But he'd let her have her fun today first. She'd put a huge amount of work into today and he was proud of her, and he was actually excited about it. He'd put an equal amount of work into acting clueless. He'd be glad when tomorrow came and the pretence could end.

'Looking dapper as always, Mr. Harte,' Anthony said.

Julian smiled and straightened his tie. The hospital loos didn't offer the changing facilities he was accustomed to but that was the least on his mind today. 'Thank you. How did the press conference go?'

'Great. Miss Andrews was a natural,' Anthony said proudly.

'I didn't expect it to go any other way.' Julian smiled.

It was true. Eva was doing a stellar job at the forefront of Andrews Harte. Even surpassing Julian's expectations. But the success of the charity was just a pleasant bonus. Andrews Harte was serving its intended purpose nicely. Julian made damn sure the media would never get their hands on the real reason for setting up Andrews Harte…to bring two damaged sisters back together. Melissa dropped the giant chip on her shoulder and was more than happy to be a part of the organisation. Eva's family wasn't one hundred percent repaired, and Julian knew it may never reach that milestone, but it was damn well on its way. It made every sacrifice he'd made along the way worth it. *Every sacrifice.*

'Okay, Anthony. Now, can you please sort out whatever the fuck is going on with my phone? Have you any idea how bored I've been for the last hour?'

Julian caught Anthony's blushing face in the rearview mirror and didn't bother to hide his amusement.

'Me?' Anthony squeaked.

Julian pulled a face but didn't reply.

'I'm not sure if I would be able to help, Mr. Harte.'

'Oh. I'm very certain you would. And quickly please, Anthony. I've tolerated this little charade long enough. I'm expecting an important email from Singapore. I don't plan to miss it.'

Anthony's blushing cheeks grew to full-on puce, engulfing his nose and even his ears.

'How long have you known?' Anthony mumbled.

282

Julian smiled brightly. 'Who says I know anything about Eva's surprise and about how all my staff were happy to go behind my back to help? Hiding things from me; money and information. Attempting to keep me in the dark completely. A big web of lies. A. Web. Of. Lies.'

Anthony's eyes widened and Julian jaw twitched to one side.

'Mr. Harte, I'm so sorry. Everyone just wanted to do something nice for you. Especially Eva. No one meant any harm.' Anthony stumbled over his words.

'Anthony, just get my fucking phone working again, please. I can't miss that email.'

'Of course, of course.'

Julian could hear the level of urgency in Anthony's voice.

'As for the rest of it. The going behind my back and lying to me...' Julian paused, and he could practically hear Anthony holding his breath. 'Thank you. Today means a lot to Eva, and so it means a lot to me. So let's get back to pretending, shall we? You drive and I won't look out the window. I'll act none the wiser about where we're heading and it'll all go to plan.'

'Sounds good, Mr. Harte.'

'One more thing, Anthony.'

Anthony twisted around in the driver's seat and looked at Julian.

'How about another one of these?' Julian held up his empty glass.

'What happened to drinking in moderation?' Anthony asked, concerned.

Julian shot Anthony a look that said don't-go-there. 'For the day that's in it! I'm about to get a very big surprise. I could use a little something to calm the nerves.'

'Okay.' Anthony chuckled. 'But you can be the one to deal with the lecture from Eva when she finds out.'

Julian smiled, thinking of how fucking hot Eva was when she was angry and how bloody lucky he was to have the most amazing girl in the world ready to lecture him on his health because she cared so damn much.

'Okay, Anthony. I think I can just about handle the wrath of Miss Andrews.'

## 35

It was a beautiful afternoon. The sky was cloudy but every so often the sun broke through and the springtime feeling sat in the air. April was just around the corner; Eva couldn't believe how fast time was flying by. Her hand instinctively crept to her belly and a giant smile lit up her face. She couldn't wait to meet her baby, but she was conscious of wishing time away. Terrified that maybe that meant wishing Julian away, too. She quickly pulled herself together. She absolutely refused to allow anything to spoil today. Even the thoughts of her worst nightmare, life without Julian, that were always lurking in the back of her mind.

'You've done a fabulous job,' Shelly said, appearing out of nowhere, her voice cutting into Eva's daydreaming.

'I couldn't have done it without your help. Thank you, Shell. You look fan-tastic!'

Shelly caught the sides of her red, skater dress and pulled them out as she spun around. 'Thanks, hun. But I think you're stealing the show here. You're bloody glowing.'

Eva blushed, wondering if Shelly was secretly implying she knew about the baby. 'Thanks. New make-up.'

Eva wasn't telling anyone about her pregnancy until she told Julian first. But she was waiting for the right moment.

She'd been waiting for the right moment for three months and she was beginning to worry the time might never be right. She wasn't just telling Julian he was going to be a father, she was telling him that their child might have to grow up without a dad. Eva knew the thoughts of Julian abandoning his child would break his heart. It was outside his control but that wouldn't be any consolation to ease Julian's conscience. Eva hated to think that something as special as bringing a child into the world together could be the very thing that completely broke Julian.

'There you are, sweetheart,' Samantha said kissing Eva on each cheek as she reached her. 'This place is beautiful, isn't it?' Samantha added, stretching her arms out and looking all around the hall of Julian's Dun Laoghaire house. The black and white checked tiles were restored to perfection; any broken ones had been matched so closely that it was impossible to tell the difference. The freshly painted cream walls gave a sense of calm without losing any of the warmth of a family home. The dresser had simply needed a sanding and varnish and the mirror hanging over it was a beautiful antique Shelly had found on eBay.

Eva gave herself a brief once-over in the mirror. Shelly was right, her skin looked great. A little too great. She wondered how no one had noticed. She adjusted her loose fitting, royal blue shirtdress. Anything fitted was no longer an option.

'It's all been restored as close as possible to the original,' Eva said proudly, turning away from the mirror.

'Julian will be delighted, sweetheart. He's a very lucky man,' Samantha said.

Eva's heart warmed. Her mother had grown very fond of Julian despite her initial impression. Eva was glad Julian had been wrong about one thing. She didn't need to go back to New York to fix her family. She just needed Julian by her side. This was Samantha's third visit to Dublin in as many months. She seemed to have the same love affair with the city that Cameron had had. Eva was pretty sure that once she announced her pregnancy, her mother would suggest staying permanently. It was definitely a suggestion Eva would welcome. Today marked Melissa's first visit back to Ireland, and the first time Eva and Melissa had met again. But they'd spoken endlessly on the phone. Initially about business, but more recently about everything. If Eva was going to crack and tell anyone about the baby before she got a chance to tell Julian, then it would be to Melissa. In fact, she'd had to consciously cover her mouth a couple of times when they were on Skype.

'A car just pulled into the drive,' Nathan said, skidding into the hall from the kitchen.

'Julian?' Eva gasped and looked at her watch. 'Anthony is dead on time. Okay. Positions, everyone.'

Everyone scurried into the kitchen leaving Eva alone waiting at the bottom of the stairs. A huge shiver thundered down her spine and she held her breath as the handle turned and the front door creaked open.

***

Julian couldn't remember the last time his heart was beating this fast. Maybe it was the night of the fire. Maybe it was the first time Eva had walked into his office. Maybe it was the moment he realised that, despite his best efforts not to, he had fallen in love with a broken girl from New Jersey. Or maybe it was a combination of all of those things added together. Things that had shaped him and made him the man he was now. Julian put his palm flat against his chest and felt his heart racing against his fingertips. He knew it wasn't any of those things. Not today. His heart was racing because he was standing on the edge of his past, unsure if he had a future.

Being back at this house always did strange things to his head. But today was the strangest of all. He paused for a moment before putting his hand on the handle and pushing the door forty-five degrees open. The next step would be huge, but with Eva on the other side of the door, he knew he was ready.

The blue paint on the front door was just as damaged and depressing as always. Julian was impressed. It was a clever decoy. Eva clearly didn't want him to suspect anything and ruin the impact of stepping inside. Either that or the budget had run dry and couldn't stretch to a tin of paint. Eva had spent a small fortune on the project.

Julian took a deep breath and opened the door fully. He expected to feel apprehensive and reluctant. He didn't expect to feel overjoyed by the familiarity.

His jaw dropped slightly and his chest was heaving as he stood in the open doorway, but he didn't take a step forward. His eyes darted from one familiar wall to the next. From the floor to the ceiling and finally to Eva.

'Surprise,' she whispered, twirling a strand of her hair around her finger.

Julian could tell that she was nervous. Maybe she was worried about his reaction. She didn't have to be; this was the most beautiful gift anyone had ever given him.

Eva walked slowly towards him as his eyes continued to circle his surroundings. She stopped just in front of him and held out her hand. He took it, his fingers sliding over hers as he held her tight. He glanced back outside, back to the car. Anthony was gone – as he'd expected.

'You okay?' Eva said, leading him into the hallway.

'Really okay,' Julian replied pulling Eva back.

Eva spun around to face him. Julian looked her up and down. She looked utterly fuckable. Julian wished the house wasn't full of well-meaning friends hiding in the background ready to throw the house warming of the century.

'You look great,' Julian said, kissing the top of her head.

'New make-up,' Eva mumbled.

Julian smiled, but he didn't say anything. God, she was a terrible liar.

'Do you want to see more?' Eva asked, her bright smile illuminating her whole face.

Julian smiled back. Her enthusiasm was intoxicating.

Julian could feel her fingers twitching against his as she waited for his answer. He pulled her a little closer and into his arms, slipping one hand behind her head, his fingers working through her silky hair. His lips pressed to hers. Her mouth opened in response and he slid his tongue between her lips, enjoying the soft underside of her tongue against the rough top of his. He circled around and around, losing himself in her taste.

Eva pulled away after a few delicious moments. 'Do you like it?' she whispered.

Julian tossed his head to one side. 'The house or your mouth?'

'The house, silly.'

'I like both…very much.'

Eva giggled. 'Phew,' she joked wiping her brow for dramatic effect.

Julian tapped his foot against the shiny tiles. 'Wow. These are nice. It couldn't have been easy to get your hands on exact matches. I can't tell which the originals are and which have been repaired.'

'I had a little help,' Eva admitted, giddily.

Julian didn't reply. He didn't have to. He was glad Eva had built a circle of friends in Dublin. It would be important that she had that support when he was gone.

'C'mon,' Eva said, taking Julian by the hand. 'The best bit is back here.'

Julian followed Eva's lead into the kitchen at the back of the house. Bright spring daylight was peeking out from under the closed kitchen door and Julian was actually excited to look inside.

Eva paused outside the closed door for a moment, kissed Julian on the cheek, and whispered in his ear, 'I love you so much.'

'I love you, too,' Julian replied as he watched her fingers close around the door handle.

Eva walked into the kitchen first, and Julian followed waiting for everyone to jump out of their hiding places and yell, 'Surprise.' But there was no one there. It was just the familiar old kitchen, with its light coloured wooden cupboards and shiny white marble countertop. He let go of Eva's hand to walk around the familiar room. It was perfect, just like an old photograph had magically been brought to life. All it was missing was the smell of his mother's delicious home baking.

'Thank you, Eva.' Julian said, turning to face a very quiet Eva. 'You blow me away, Evangeline Andrews, you really do.'

'I'm so glad you like it. I was really nervous.'

'I know.' Julian took a step forward and ran his finger down the length of Eva's nose. 'I didn't think I'd ever be okay with coming back into this place.'

Eva sucked her lips between her teeth. 'And are you okay?'

'I'm more than okay, Eva. I'm happy.'

A tear ran down Eva's cheek and Julian caught it on his fingertip and pressed his finger to his lips.

'I wouldn't be here if it wasn't for you. I'd have never had the balls to step inside.'

'You would have eventually maybe? You've always wanted to come in, I think. The time just had to be right.'

'Yeah. The time did have to be right. And it's right now because you're here with me.'

'Julian…I…I've something to tell you,' Eva mumbled.

Julian pressed his finger against Eva's lips, 'Shh,' he whispered. He had a suspicion of exactly what she was going to say, and they'd have an epic amount to talk about once she said it. Now, with a house full of people lurking behind curtains and hiding in the loo under the stairs, was not the time to discuss it.

Julian took Eva by the hand and this time he was doing the leading. 'This way, baby.'

## 36

Eva's eyes were scanning every corner as she followed Julian back into the hallway. She couldn't figure out where everyone had gone. The plan was completely falling apart. They were supposed to all be waiting in the kitchen. But the house was silent and still.

Julian led Eva to the bottom of the stairs and stopped.

'There's something upstairs I'd really like you to have.' he said.

'What? Upstairs? Something for me? How did you get it there?'

Eva's eyes pinched as the realisation that Julian had been one step ahead of her the whole time dawned on her. She realised he knew about the surprise she'd been planning all along. *Why had he never said anything?*

'Julian?' Eva said, questioning his motive with the tone of her voice as she said his name.

'Go see,' Julian said tilting his head towards the stairs.

Eva caught the handrail reluctantly and looked back at Julian as she put her foot on the first step of the stairs.

'Go on,' Julian laughed. 'The stairs won't bite.'

Eva tossed her eyes up the steps and onto the landing, looked back at Julian again. His delicious smile sent hippos on roller skates rippling around her belly. She raced up the steps with an enthusiasm she couldn't hold in. She stopped at the top, not sure which room to search first. There was so many. It didn't really matter; she was delighted with another excuse to visit each freshly painted room with a delicate, new bed linen. All the bedroom doors were closed though, except for one. *It made sense to start there,* Eva thought, expecting her search to end there, too. She was right.

Eva gasped and her hands flew to cover her nose and mouth, as she stood starry-eyed in the doorway. An exquisite ivory dress lay on the bed. Eva raced to it, her jaw dropping as she took in the beauty of the sweetheart neckline. She traced her finger over the hand-stitched beading on the bodice, leading into a matte satin skirt that finished with a subtle kick out at the bottom. It was the most beautiful dress she'd ever seen. She moved closer, kicking a box she hadn't noticed lying next to the bed. She picked it up and opened it. Delicate peep toe, ivory stilettos waited, cradled in soft ivory tissue paper that smelt like a summer's breeze.

Eva raced back out to the landing with the shoebox in her hand. She was so excited she hadn't even taken the time to put it down. She leaned over the banister.

'I love it,' she shouted down to a waiting Julian. 'I really, really love it.'

'Put it on,' he called back.

'What. Now?'

Julian nodded.

Eva's fingers twitched against the box with giddy excitement. 'Okay.'

She raced back into the room and began to undress. He must be taking her somewhere, she thought as she fumbled with zippers and buttons. Her mind was racing so much she gave herself a headache.

She slipped into the beautiful, silky dress with ease, especially considering her expanding waistline. And she sighed with relief that the dress was a generous size around the middle. She slipped into the perfectly sized shoes and made her way back to the landing. Julian stepped forward as soon as he saw her. His waited on the ground, with one foot resting on the bottom step. Eva grasped the banister, feeling like a princess from an old fairy tale. And her prince charming was waiting at the bottom step. She glided carefully down each step, taking Julian's outreached hand as she reached the bottom.

'Wow,' Julian gasped. 'I knew you'd be beautiful. But I didn't know it was possible to be that beautiful.'

'You've changed,' Eva said, noticing Julian had swapped his suit for an impressive tuxedo.

'Couldn't have you showing me up, Miss Andrews.'

Eva's heart was pounding. The last time she'd seen Julian dressed like that was the night of the ball in his country mansion. He'd turned her world upside down that night and her head was spinning as she wondered what he had in store for her now. *Did the princess really get to keep her prince charming,* she thought, knowing whatever lay ahead, with Julian in control it was going to be spectacular.

Julian let go of Eva's hand and took a step away from her. He looked her up and down and she couldn't stop smiling. *What was he doing?*

Eva's breath caught in the back of her throat as Julian dropped one knee onto the ground, reached into his jacket pocket, and pulled out a little black box.

'Evangeline Andrews, will you marry me?'

Eva didn't speak. Her mouth was open but no words were coming out. She couldn't take her eyes off the little box, resting open now in Julian's hand. It was a smoky cream inside and waiting in the middle was the most sparkly, solitaire diamond ring she had ever seen. She had planned to surprise him. But instead, he had turned all the tables and taken her breath away.

'A contract?' Eva mumbled.

'No. Just two people who are madly in love and want to spend the rest of their lives together,' Julian said.

Eva's whole body smiled hearing her words leave Julian's mouth.

'I want you. I've always wanted you,' Julian continued. 'I want to wake up next to you every day. I want to introduce you as my wife. I want to know other men hate me because you're mine and they can't have you…and I want to be a great father to our child.'

Eva raced to him and pulled him to his feet, crying as she threw herself into his arms. 'You know about the baby?'

Julian bent down and kissed the material of her dress covering her belly. 'When were you going to tell me?'

'I wanted to for ages. But it was hard to find the right time.'

'Who else knows?' Julian said pulling himself upright again.

'No one.' Eva shook her head.

Julian raised an eyebrow suspiciously.

'Honestly, Julian. No one knows. I didn't want to tell anyone before you.'

Julian nodded, and Eva knew he believed her. What she didn't know was how he felt about it. She couldn't read him right now.

'Are you okay?' she mumbled, feeling like the question was pathetic and tired.

'I'm about to become a father, and I'm still waiting for an answer to my previous question, but I'm hopefully about to become a husband. I'm very okay, Miss Andrews.'

'Oh, my God. Yes. Julian. Yes. My answer is yes.'

Eva couldn't believe that she hadn't already answered. She didn't need any time to ponder over the answer. She wrapped her arms around Julian's neck and he kissed her deeply before lifting her off the ground and spinning her around.

'You're not upset?' Eva said as Julian put her back down.

'No. Why would I be?'

'It's just the baby…well, you married Meghan because you didn't want Daniel to grow up alone. But our baby might. You know, if things take a turn for the worst.'

Eva couldn't believe how awkward she was being. She'd rehearsed this conversation in her head over and over, but now that she was saying it out loud, she felt sick. Asking someone how they felt about dying was tough. Asking the most important person in the world to you about it was excruciatingly difficult.

Julian lifted the ring out of the box and took Eva's hand in his, slipping the platinum ring onto her finger. He placed the box back into his pocket, pulled out something else, and passed it to Eva.

'I don't get it?' she said looking at a photo Julian gave her.

It was a picture of a woman she didn't know, sitting on her front porch with two little boys. One sitting on each side of her. They were about four and six, maybe, and their bright smiles were so sweet they made Eva want to smile, too.

'Her name is Lilly Rose Henderson. She's a prostitute from Dallas,' Julian said.

'What?'

'She's thirty-six and a mother of two. And she swears if it wasn't for The Andrews Harte Foundation, she'd be high or dead, and her boys would be in state care,' Julian said looking down at the photo in Eva's trembling fingers.

Eva's heart fluttered. She loved that something that brought her family back together was saving other families, too. 'Andrews Harte is fantastic, Julian. I'm so grateful for it. But why did she send you this picture. Do you know her personally?'

Julian shook his head. 'We've never met. But she knows *of* me.'

'I suppose that makes sense. You're the money behind Andrews Harte, after all. Most of the girls probably Googled you. I know I would.' Eva didn't admit that her internet search history was full of articles on Julian. She'd Googled him more times than she could remember when she'd first returned to New York.

'Maybe some do, I suppose, out of curiosity.' Julian tossed his shoulders. 'But that's not why Lilly Rose got in touch. Apparently, a reporter visited most of the safe houses over the last couple of months. He filled them in on all the shit with the Da Lucas. Gave them a goddamn history lesson on how the charity came about, by all accounts.'

'Nathan?' Eva gasped, her hand flying to cover her mouth.

'Looks like your friend *can* do undercover after all. I had no idea about any of this,' Julian admitted.

'Looks like Nathan is better at surprises than I am, then.' Eva pulled a face.

Julian threw Eva a delicious smirk. 'He told them about the last night in Vertigo and about the unfortunate legacy it left me with.'

A large lump of air plummeted down Eva's throat. She suspected Julian wouldn't appreciate Nathan shooting his mouth off. Especially about something that painted Julian as weak or hurt.

'And…' Eva said stretching her eyebrows.

'And almost every girl volunteered to be tested. Nathan was determined to find a tissue type that matched mine.'

'Lilly Rose Henderson,' Eva said running her finger over the photograph.

'Bingo.' Julian smiled. 'Turns out, Nathan Shields might be the man who saves my life.'

'Oh. My. God. Julian really? This woman...' Eva turned the photo around to show Julian as if he hadn't seen it before. 'She is a match? Really? Is it confirmed?'

'Yes, Eva. She is a match.'

Eva actually wanted to jump up and down on the spot like a giddy schoolgirl. 'That's fantastic news, Julian. But you said you've never even met her? I think it's great that she's a match, but I just don't understand why anyone would give a kidney to a stranger. She's doing all this because Andrews Harte helped her?'

'Because Andrews Harte saved her life. Now, she wants to save mine.'

'She sounds amazing. But this is a huge deal. What if she changes her mind? Chickens out, or something.'

'She won't, Eva. I understand Lilly Rose. Some girls will take what they can from the charity and move on. That's great, and it's what the foundation is there for. Other girls, girls like Lilly Rose, will feel they owe something back.'

'Like a debt, you mean?' Eva said. 'She shouldn't have to feel that way. Andrews Harte is there to help, not take.'

'Exactly. But girls like Lilly Rose don't take handouts. I know what the feels like, Eva.' Julian leaned forward and kissed Eva on the forehead. 'And I know what it's like to do anything and everything you have to until that debt is repaid.'

A tiny shiver ran down Eva's spine. Repaying the debt Julian felt he owed to her family was what got him into this mess in the first place. She couldn't understand what that felt like, but she knew how strong willed and determined Julian was. He would have stopped at nothing; he'd have given his life if he had to, he almost did. If Lilly Rose was anything like Julian, then Eva didn't have to worry about her backing out or changing her mind at the last minute.

'And you'll do it? You'll really go ahead with the surgery?' Eva mumbled, knowing the last hurdle was Julian accepting help.

Julian placed his hand on Eva's tummy. 'I don't relish the thoughts of accepting a donor's kidney...'

'Julian, it doesn't make you weak, it makes you human.'

'I wasn't finished,' Julian said, his hand circling her tummy. 'I know what it's like to grow up without a father. I'm going to do everything I possibly can to make sure our child never has to know that feeling.'

Eva sighed. It was the deepest most relieved sighed she'd ever experienced. Like the weight of the world exhaled from inside her with that breath.

'Julian Harte. I fucking love you.'

Eva threw her arms around Julian's neck, the photo still in her hand. She kissed him all over, his neck, his lips, his cheeks. She couldn't get enough of him. Julian reached for her hands and forced them back to her sides. He slipped his fingers between hers and he didn't let go. The photo floated to the floor and landed with the faces smiling up at them. Eva was smiling just as much as the family in the photo but the look on Julian's face warned Eva to brace herself.

'I need to be in the hospital tomorrow,' Julian said barely above a whisper.

'Tomorrow,' Eva squeaked.

'There's no point in wasting any more time. I'll leave for Texas early in the morning.'

'Texas?'

'Yes, Eva. Lilly Rose lives in Dallas. So that's where the surgery will happen.'

'Okay. We're going to Dallas, then.' Eva nodded her head keeping up but her heart lagging behind.

'No! I'm going,' Julian corrected.

'NO, actually. We're both going.' Eva held up her left hand and wiggled her wedding finger. 'See this?' Eva pointed to her engagement ring with her other hand. 'This means we're in it together from here on out. Everything and anything. If it's important to you, then it's important to me. You go to Dallas for life-changing surgery, then I damn well go, too. Period.'

Julian shot Eva a coquettish grin and Eva's insides fluttered. She wanted to pull him to the floor and make love to him right there on that very spot. She blushed wondering if the house was still full of hiding guests or if Julian had sent them all home. She'd bring that up in a minute. This was a much more important conversation.

'Okay, baby. You win. If the doctor says you're okay to fly, then fine.' Julian softened.

'Julian, I'm pregnant not ill. I am coming and that *is* final.'

'Okay, okay.' Julian raised his hands over his head jokingly as he surrendered.

'Good, that's figured out, then,' Eva said tossing her head to one side, triumphant in battle.

A few silent moments passed as Eva and Julian stood, their fingers woven together, their bodies close enough to feel each other breathe. Eva's head was spinning. She was euphoric and terrified all at the same time.

'What are the risks?' Eva asked reluctantly, afraid to spoil the moment but desperate to know the answer. She knew the real battle was just around the corner. *Shit, this was sudden!*

'There are risks, Eva. But they're a lot better than the alternative.'

Eva winced. It hurt to hear Julian talk about the possibility of anything going wrong. Secretly, she wanted him to tell her there was a one hundred percent success rate and every patient left there with a bunch of roses and a pet, bright pink unicorn. But glitter and rainbow lies to take the edge off wasn't Julian's style. He was more likely to drink copious amounts of whiskey and head into surgery with a kick-ass attitude. This was one occasion where Eva would be reaching to help him crack open the bottle.

'Life and death, Eva. It's all just a big game,' Julian said assuredly. 'We have to play with the hand we're dealt.'

'Bring it.' Eva forced herself to smile, despite her jelly insides. 'Julian Harte, this is the final round. You better win this one. Do you hear me?'

'Count on it, baby.'

## 37

Julian walked toward the sitting room. Eva wasn't sure if she should follow. He looked deep in thought. *Maybe she should give him some space to take it all in,* she thought. His head must have been exploding with old memories. The sitting room door was closed and Julian stopped in front of it. He turned back to Eva and stretched out his hand. She hurried towards him and slipped her hand into his again, like their hands were two halves of a whole.

'Are you ready?' Julian asked.

'Me?' Eva tapped a finger against her chest. 'Shouldn't I be asking you that question?'

The corners of Julian's lips turned up into a subtle smile and Eva knew whatever was on the other side of that door wasn't anything of her planning. Whatever it was, it was making it hard for Julian to keep a straight face. Bubbles rushed around Eva's tummy like a Jacuzzi of excitement.

'I think we're both ready, Mr. Harte.' Eva smiled.

Julian turned the handle and stepped into the room. Eva shot a deep breath out through her lips pressed into an o shape and took the next step. Her forehead pinched as she stood centre floor in the sitting room. Everything was exactly as it been earlier when she'd given the house one last look over. The cream, marble fireplace housed a small, open fire. And perched proudly on top was a digitally remastered old photograph; the photo of Julian as a child in his mother's arms. It was Eva's favourite thing in the whole house. She knew how much that photo meant to Julian and she couldn't wait to see his reaction when he noticed it.

She didn't have to wait long. Julian picked up the silver frame and ran his finger over the glass.

'Wow,' he said.

Eva waited but he didn't say more. He didn't need to; his face said it all. The stress of sneaking behind Julian's back, Meghan's control freak tantrums, Shelly's meltdown every time she had an argument with a builder, Nathan's odd dodgy contact, and Pam's inability to keep a secret and almost giving the surprise away a couple of times; it was all worth it just to see that look on Julian's face.

'This is beautiful. Thank you,' Julian said putting the picture back down, 'but it's missing something.'

'Oh, really?' Eva said, unimpressed with Julian's choice of words. She'd tried so hard to get it perfect. One photo was all she had and Julian guarded the damn thing with his life. It was next to impossible to get her hands on it to make a copy, but she'd succeeded.

Julian lifted Eva's hand to his lips and kissed it softly. He was grinning like a Cheshire cat, and Eva knew he was messing with her head, but she couldn't help grinning back.

'What?' she sang.

'It needs another photo. Something just as special,' Julian explained.

Eva's hand instinctively reached for her belly.

'It's a bit early for a photo of that,' Julian joked. 'Gorgeous as you are, I don't think a photograph of your belly button is the look we want on our mantel.'

'Our mantel?'

'Welcome home, baby,' Julian whispered. 'This place is all yours. All ours. If you want it.'

Eva nodded, excitedly. She couldn't think of anywhere she'd want to raise her child more.

'And the photo?' Eva said not letting the subject change.

Julian pulled out his phone and held it up in front of Eva. 'Say cheese.'

Eva smiled. 'Me?'

'Yes, you. You in that dress on our wedding day?'

'You want me to wear this to our wedding?' Eva shook her head, confused.

Julian nodded.

'I love this dress,' Eva said, running her hands down the soft satin, 'but the groom isn't supposed to see the dress before the big day.'

'I didn't,' Julian smiled.

'What?'

'Surprise. Surprise. Surprise.' The double doors between the sitting room and dining room burst open and Eva's family and friends spilled through. 'Surprise.'

'Will you marry me, Eva?' Julian asked once more.

Happy tears were glistening in Eva's eyes.

'Oh, don't cry, hun. You'll ruin your make-up,' Shelly said running up to hug Eva.

'Evangeline,' Julian said, gaining her attention again.

'You mean right now, don't you?' Eva said.

'I mean right now.'

Eva caught a priest out of the corner of her eye. She turned around and smiled recognising Father O'Malley straight away.

'It's lovely to see you again, Eva,' Father O'Malley said. 'And under such happy circumstances today.'

'It's lovely to see you too, Father,' Eva said. 'A little bit of shock, but lovely.'

Eva turned back to Julian. 'Oh. My. God. I can't believe this. Wow. How did you...did you know about the restoration of the house all along…who helped you organise this? Oh, my God.'

'You worked so hard on a surprise for me because you wanted me to be happy. Well, that's all I ever want for you. I want to make you happy, every day for the rest of my life.'

'I am happy, Julian. I'm so, so happy.'

'Were you all in on this?' Eva said turning to face everyone. 'Meghan, did you know? He tells you everything, you must have known.'

'He didn't tell me *this*, Eva. We were all as surprised as you.'

'How then?' Eva said

'I did have a little help,' Julian smirked.

Anne and Samantha stepped forward.

'Sorry, sweetheart. We weren't going behind your back or anything. You deserve the best day of your life and when Julian asked us to help, well, we just couldn't refuse,' Samantha said, knocking shoulders with a conspiring Anne.

Eva smiled brightly. The two elderly ladies were like a pair of old friends and their body language, happy faces, and blossoming friendship confirmed to Eva that Samantha wasn't going anywhere. She fit in in Dublin. Just like Eva did.

## 38

Eva stood in the master bedroom staring at her beautiful dress in the freestanding mirror. If anyone had told her last week when she was picking the mirror out in the furniture store that next time she looked into it would be on her wedding day, she would have laughed and told them they were crazy.

Shelly passed Eva a bouquet of beautiful, cream orchids as Meghan clipped a long, floor-length veil in Eva's hair.

'There,' Meghan said, stepping back. 'You look amazing.'

Eva could see the sincerity in Meghan's reflection as she spoke.

'Eva. I'm sorry. I'm so sorry for everything I put you through. I was so afraid of losing Julian. I didn't think I had any choice but to push you away.'

Eva shook her head. 'Now's not the time, Meghan.'

'Please, Eva. Let me say this. Now is the perfect time.'

Eva turned around to face Meghan. 'I never wanted to steal Julian from you, Meghan. But you decided from day one that I was the enemy. It wasn't fair. I never deserved that.'

'I know. I know,' Meghan said. 'But Julian is different around you. And I thought that would mean he would be different around me. I thought that if he loved you then he'd stop caring about me.'

'That would never happen. You're too important to Julian. And Daniel. You will always be friends.'

'Maybe we could be friends, too?' Meghan said, slightly stumbling over her words.

Eva tossed her shoulders. 'Yeah. Maybe. Someday.'

'Okay. I'll take that,' Meghan said.

'Meghan, I don't hate you, if that's what you think. I actually understand – kind of. I know what it's like to lose everything and I get that you were afraid of losing your life as you know it. It doesn't excuse your behaviour, but it does kind of explain it.'

'Thank you, Eva. I'm not sure I would be as understanding if it was the other way around.'

'You wouldn't be,' Eva assured.

Meghan laughed. So did Eva and Shelly. It was a joke, but it was even more funny because all three women knew it was also true.

'C'mon,' Shelly said, linking her arm around Meghan. 'My best friend is marrying your best friend today. Don't know about you, but I'm bloody excited.'

Eva was a little shocked as Meghan broke away from Shelly and grabbed Eva tightly for a huge hug.

'I *am* excited,' Meghan said releasing Eva, and Eva actually believed her.

There was a gentle knock on the already open door and Eva spun around without hesitation to smile at the man who was going to walk her down the aisle.

'Holy shit, you're a stunner,' Nathan said, stepping into the room.

'Thank you,' Shelly chirped in, 'but Eva looks nice too, doesn't she?' Shelly joked.

Nathan shot his girlfriend a playful look. Eva wouldn't be surprised if Shelly and Nathan were announcing an engagement of their own soon.

'Are you ready, Eva?' Nathan asked.

Eve turned to catch her reflection in the mirror one last time. *So this is what normal looked like,* she thought, beaming brightly. Normal girls got married to the man they loved. Normal girls shared that special day with the most important people in their lives. And normal girls knew what it felt like to be so happy you just might burst. Evangeline Andrews, soon to be Harte, was just a *normal* girl – at last.

'I am most definitely ready,' Eva replied. 'Game on.'

Nathan stuck out his elbow and Eva slipped her arm around.

'Thank you,' Eva whispered. 'All of you. Julian and I are very lucky to have such great friends.' Eva specifically looked at Meghan as she spoke. Normal girls could even allow old enemies to become new friends.

## 39

The garden was a little chillier than Eva was expecting and the cool spring breeze caught in her throat as she stood just behind the open patio doors leading from the house into the garden. Today had taken such a huge turn in direction that Eva was still reeling as she tried to take it all in. Julian was never done surprising her. Her mind wandered to thoughts of Julian's pending surgery, the risk and the fear. She knew everything Julian had been doing over the last few months was his way of preparing her for life without him. The charity, healing her family, and now this. Julian was saying with actions what he didn't say with words. He was saying good-bye. This was the most important and amazing day of Eva's life and she was so excited to become Julian's wife, but her heart was aching with a fear of the future.

'Can you give me a minute?' Eva said turning to Nathan who was standing beside her, smiling with pride and ready to walk her down the aisle.

Nathan nodded understandingly. 'Sure. I need to pee anyway.'

Eva giggled. 'Really? That's the best excuse you could think of?'

Nathan laughed, too. 'Well, you did kind of put me on the spot. I'll be in the kitchen. Call me when you're ready, okay?'

'I'll just be a sec. You know, I just need a moment to get my head around all this.'

'Eva...' Nathan's toned changed as he said her name. 'Are you okay? Are you sure you want to do this?'

'I'm really, really sure, Nathan. I want my happily ever after. I just want it to last forever...not maybe just twenty-four hours.'

'Oh, don't you dare think like that. I can't believe I'm going to say this but...' Nathan pulled a face like the words tasted funny in his mouth. 'Julian Harte doesn't do losing, Eva. He will show this new kidney who's boss. Just wait. It's all going to be okay. Actually no, it's all going to be great. You deserve great, Eva. You really do. And Julian deserves to be the man to make sure you get it. He's not going anywhere. I know it.'

*I wish I knew it,* Eva thought, her hand rubbing her tummy and the little part of Julian growing inside her.

Eva watched as Nathan walked slowly away. She looked up at the sky. A duvet of thick white clouds was broken up by scattered splashes of sunlight streaked across like a messy water painting. If ever there was a time heaven was looking down on her, this was it.

'Dad,' Eva whispered still staring up. She ran her hands down her sides, over the silky material of her dress. 'It's my wedding day,' she said struggling to hold back tears. 'I wish you could be here. Every girl needs her father to give her away. I forgive you, Dad. I'm so sorry it's too late, but I forgive you. Please, I've never asked you for anything, but today I'm asking you for something huge. Please help Julian. I can't lose him. I just can't.'

Eva dabbed at her eyes with her fingertips, hoping she wasn't sporting some very unflattering panda eyes as she heard Nathan come back.

'You ready now?' Nathan asked softly, not noticing she'd been crying.

*Phew.*

'Yes.' Eva took a deep breath in through her nostrils, pulled her body up as tall as it went, and shot the air back out roughly through her mouth. *So ready.*

Julian was waiting with his back to her at the end of the garden aisle under a silver, iron arch laced with stunning white roses. Father O'Malley waited facing Julian. Eva could see they were chatting and laughing. Samantha stood next to and a little further back than Julian. Melissa, Shelly, and Pam were next, all standing side-by-side as if waiting on an invisible line. Waiting on the other side of Julian was Daniel. He was dressed smartly in a miniature replica of Julian's suit and he looked so adorable that Eva just wanted to squishy hug him. Eva smiled realising that Julian's son was also his Best Man. Meghan was next, then Anne, Anthony, and Mr. Thompson. And that was everyone. It was a small group, and only people who were very important in both Julian and Eva's lives were invited. It was perfect.

Shelly kept turning around every few seconds. She finally stepped forward and sang Beyoncé's "Halo" as Eva and Nathan began to walk out into the garden. Tone deaf and a cappella as Shelly was, Eva couldn't help but love it. It was fun, just like Shelly.

Julian turned around just as Eva and Nathan reached him. Julian shook Nathan's hand, they exchanged mutual head nods, and Nathan patted Julian on the shoulder. Eva was smiling so hard her cheeks actually hurt. Somehow, a friendship had formed there, and she loved it.

'Libertas supra omnia,' Julian leaned in to whisper in Eva's ear as Nathan left to take his place between Shelly and Pam.

'Freedom above all,' Eva mouthed back, surprised by Julian's choice of phrase at the moment.

'Are we ready to begin?' Father O'Malley asked bright-eyed.

Julian looked at Eva, letting her lead on this.

'Yes. We're very ready,' Eva replied.

'Dearly beloved, we are gathered here today…' Father O'Malley began.

Julian held both of Eva's hands in his as he stood facing her. Eva's whole body felt warm inside. She couldn't take her eyes off Julian. He looked delicious. Every so often, her mind would wander to thoughts of his tight abs hiding under his suit, or her eyes would drop to his pants and she'd feel a warm hue light up her cheeks as she imagined him inside her.

'And now the vows,' Father O'Malley said, pulling Eva out of her fantasy.

'What?' She gasped. 'But I don't have any prepared. I didn't know.'

'You don't need anything written here,' Father O'Malley said turning around the paper he'd been reading from. 'They're all written here.' He placed his hand over his heart. 'Julian. Would you like to go first?'

Julian's delicious smirk told Eva that maybe his mind had been wandering to the same places as hers and she couldn't wait for later.

Julian took a deep breath and his dark, delectable eyes locked on hers.

'Libertas supra omnia. It means freedom above all.' Julian paused, and Eva's heart was racing so loudly she was actually worried it would be heard.

Julian scratched his head, and he actually looked awkward. It was adorable and Eva loved him even more for it.

'I very rarely have trouble with words. But right now, finding a way to say how much I love you, Evangeline…words fail me. Libertas. Supra. Omnia,' he repeated, saying the words slowly and clearly.

'I used to think freedom was the most important thing in life. I'd spent my childhood desperately trying to be free. Free from this place as it burned to the ground.' Julian glanced back at the restored house.

'Free from the orphanage that took me in and destroyed my innocence.' Julian looked at Meghan now, and she nodded back at him. 'Free from memories and pain. Just free. But what I learned is that I was never really free at all. I was actually trapped. Trapped in this little world I had created for myself. It was cold and lonely in there. I had built walls so high that no one could climb them. Almost no one. Somehow you, Eva, you made it. You climbed right over. I was supposed to be saving you. Fixing you. But I can see now that you were never broken. It was me. I was in pieces. You found the pieces and you slowly put them back together. Even when I gave you so many reasons not to. You even found the one last piece, the most important piece of all. That piece was you. You make me whole. I love you more than life itself.'

Happy tears streamed down Eva's cheeks and this time she didn't care about what they did to her make-up. It was her turn.

'Julian. You're right. I do make you better.'

Everyone erupted in laughter and applause. It took quite a while for everyone to pull themselves back together and for silence to fall back over them.

'Anything else you'd like to add, Eva, or are you a woman of few words?' Father O'Malley joked.

Eva looked at Father O'Malley and then back to Julian. Anything she could say Julian already knew.

'You're wrong about one thing,' Eva said softly. 'I didn't find all the pieces, Julian. Just half. The other half are right here.' Eva pointed to herself. 'We're two halves of a whole, baby, right?'

Julian slid his fingers between Eva's and pulled her hand to his lips, kissing her skin softly. 'We haven't even gotten to the I do's yet and already you're putting me in my place.'

'Well, let's skip to the good bit then, shall we?' Eva said. 'Father, if you'd be so kind.'

Father O'Malley nodded and grinned. 'Repeat after me... I, Julian Harte...'

'I, Julian Harte.'

'Take thee, Evangeline Andrews, to be my lawfully wedded wife in good times and bad, in sickness and in health, as long as we both shall live,' Father O'Malley finished.

'Take thee, Evangeline Andrews, to be my lawfully wedded wife in good times and bad, in sickness and in health, as long as we both shall live,' Julian said, his eyes sizzling into Eva's soul.

Father O'Malley turned from Julian to Eva. 'I, Evangeline Andrews...'

'I, Evangeline Andrews.'

'Take thee, Julian Harte, to be my lawfully wedded husband in good times and bad, in sickness and in health, as long as we both shall live.'

'Take thee, Julian Harte, to be my lawful wedded husband in good times and bad, in...' Eva hesitated, the next words hurt her throat. She looked into Julian's eyes. They were so bright and full of happiness, encouraging her to continue.

'In...in...sickness and in health, as long as we both shall live,' Eva finished unable to choke back her tears.

Julian pulled her into his arms, and Father O'Malley barely had time to say, 'Kiss the bride,' before Julian's warms lips were pressed against hers, assuring her that everything would be all right.

'I love you, Mrs. Harte,' Julian whispered from his open mouth into hers and the words sent a shiver down Eva's spine.

*\*\*\**

They spent the rest of afternoon enjoying the ambience of the house. Julian watched with pride as his beautiful wife mingled with friends and family. Caterers had arrived with more food and drink than they could possibly eat and the afternoon had passed in a blur of chat and laughter. Every so often, Eva would leave whomever she was chatting with and come to check on Julian. She'd throw a soft kiss on his cheek and whisper that she loved him in his ear, then he'd watch her glide gracefully in her elegant dress back to mingle some more. All evening he watched her. Of course, he chatted with friends, too. He even discussed a little casual business with Mr. Thompson, but his eyes were never far from Eva's delectable body.

## 40

Julian closed the front door after Melissa and Samantha, and sighed. 'Gah, I thought they'd never leave.'

'They were just as excited,' Eva said.

'Not as excited as I am right now. Get your sexy little ass upstairs, Mrs. Harte,' Julian smirked.

Eva raced up the stairs but Julian caught up with her halfway and spun her around.

'Too slow, baby,' he said. 'I'll just have to take you right here.'

Eva arched her back, easing herself against Julian's chest and away from the edge of the step grazing her back. 'Here,' she mumbled, kissing him.

Julian dragged her bottom lips between his teeth. Eva could feel his cock throbbing in his pants against her thigh. She knew he wasn't waiting for them to get to the top of the stairs. He slipped off her shoes one at a time, and cupped the back of her calf, his fingers slowly creeping up her leg. He pushed her dress out of the way and she lifted her ass in response so he could guide it over her hips. Julian groaned with appreciation as he eyed up her silky, white thong.

'Fuck! I knew that would look hot on you,' he said, catching the elastic at the top between his teeth, pulling his head back, and letting go. The elastic pinged against her skin with a sharp sting, and just as she was about to protest, she felt his fingers glide the lacy silk out of the way, serving her pussy up to him. He lowered his head and his tongue swirled against her. She dropped her head back in pleasure and repeated his name over and over.

'Tell me I own this,' Julian said, his hot breath rushing against her.

Eva gasped. Words were hard to form.

'Tell me,' he insisted. 'Tell me I own my wife's pussy. I need to hear you say it.'

'You own it, baby,' Eva whispered. 'You own every inch of me.'

Julian pushed Eva's dress higher and she lifted her arms so he could pull the dress off over her head. He tossed the beautiful dress over the banister, followed by her thong and bra that he ripped off roughly.

She was laying back against the stairs completely naked, and he was still fully dressed. She had to even things up a little. She slipped her hands under his jacket and slipped it off his shoulders, but he reached for her wrists and dragged her hands over her head. His tossed his shoulders and his jacket slipped back into place. 'I want to hear you scream my name as you come first...'

Eva didn't argue. She closed her eyes, laid back, and let her husband's soft tongue against her pussy tip her over the edge.

Her fingers gripped his hair, and she screamed his name as her hips bucked uncontrollably against his face.

'Fuck baby, where did that come from?' Julian said, pushing himself up to lean his chest over hers and wiping her wet from his mouth with the back of his hand.

'I dunno,' Eva mumbled. 'I read somewhere that orgasms are more intense when you're pregnant.'

'We are doing that again,' Julian said, tossing Eva a yee-fucking-haw look.

Julian scooped Eva into his arms and walked up the stairs. He kicked open the bedroom door gently with one foot and tossed Eva onto the bed.

She helped him out of his suit, grasping as his cock sprung free from his pants. She was married to a man whose body took her breath away. And right now she couldn't be any happier.

Julian flipped Eva onto her belly and pushed her ass cheeks apart with his hands, serving her glistening pussy up to him. 'I want to make the most of taking you from behind before your bump grows.'

'Then we can just try this,' Eva said, pulling herself up onto all fours.

Julian groaned with appreciation and Eva ground her hips to sweeten the deal.

He palmed her cheeks again, this time slipping his cock inside her. Slowly pushing all the way until his balls rested on her.

Eva ground her hips around, and around, each twist driving more and more pleasure circling around her inside.

Julian slapped her ass as he pounded into her, giving it to her rough as he whispered two words that made her want to let her orgasm go just hearing them. 'My wife.'

Eva met him thrust for thrust, clasping the sheet in her clenched fists. Just as she was on the edge, Julian's hand reached around her and tortured her clit with the tip of his fingers. She felt the tightness before her explosion, but he denied her once again.

'Ah, Julian no,' Eva called out, frustrated as hell.

Julian flipped her onto her back, a look of pure lust and hunger splashed across his face. 'I want to watch you come.'

He rammed into her again, harder and faster than she'd ever remembered. He throbbed hard and Eva felt her muscles clench around him sucking every last drop out as they came together.

Julian fell forward. His weight hovered just above her for a moment as he leaned down to kiss her. He rolled to the side and flopped onto his back. Eva turned towards him and threw one leg over his. 'Julian, I…'

Julian cut her off with another kiss. 'I love you, too,' he said.

Eva lay content beside her husband for what felt like a blissful forever. They drifted in and out of sleep. Waking every so often wrapped around each other in all sorts of different ways. And all too soon, the morning light peeked in through the gap in the curtain and Eva could hear the rattle of Julian's phone as it vibrated with a call against the bedside table.

'That'll be Anthony,' Julian said, sliding his arm out from under Eva's head as he reached for his phone. 'We need to leave for the airport in about an hour.'

Eva swung her legs out of bed and stood up.

'You okay?' Julian asked, ignoring his still ringing phone.

'Yeah. Of course, I'm fine. It's you I'm worried about.'

'Don't be,' Julian said. Standing up and walking around the bed to stand in front of Eva. 'Come for a shower with me.'

\*\*\*

Julian watched as Eva sat in the back of the car before he pulled the front door closed behind him. He took a couple of steps back, just enough to take in a view of the house in one blink. Eva would be okay no matter what. And so would his child. His little boy or girl would grow up in the place he once called home. Even if Julian couldn't be there for his child, he knew Eva would make damn sure the little kiddo grew up with all the memories. Julian had been too scared to allow himself memories, but his child would never experience that. Eva would make sure the memories were there to be cherished, never to hurt.

Julian sat in the backseat of the car and placed his hand reassuringly on his wife's knee. 'To the airport please, Anthony,' Julian said far more confidently than he felt. *Game over.*

# Epilogue

## Five and a half months later

Eva sat in the dark behind the large, solid walnut desk. Her elbows rested on the table and her chin rested on her clasped hands. She glanced around the room making out the shadows of the office she knew by heart. When the time came, Julian made it very clear he wanted Eva, and only Eva, to take over the running of the entire Harte empire in his absence. It had been hard, sometimes too hard. Every inch of the place reminded her of him. Even more so in the dark, and she smiled now as she thought of him. The office just wasn't the same without Julian. The company still ran smoothly, Eva made damn sure of it. Investments were made, deals were struck, apps were created. But the atmosphere was missing something. It was missing an arrogant Irish man with chocolate eyes that burnt into her soul, a huge heart covered up with a mask of sophistication, and most of all, it was missing the man she loved most in the world by her side.

Ignite Technologies had changed considerably since the first time Eva had stood in that office. For one thing, a name, everyone from the security guards at the main door to the suited fat cats on the board of directors knew and respected

330

was Evangeline Harte. Ignite Technologies was world recognised for its advances in computer software and programming. But it was also one of the largest donators to charity in the world. Andrews Harte was growing from strength to strength as was Melissa at the helm of it all.

Shelly was no longer an employee of the company, but far from being upset about it, Eva was thrilled to see her friend doing so well. It had been a long, hard road for Shelly and Nathan. The Irish media was a tough market. But their online paper, *The Whisper*, was gaining readers faster than Eva could blink and she had no doubt the silent investment Ignite Tech had made to help them get off the ground was money very well spent.

A gentle knock pulled Eva out of her daydream. She didn't answer. Another knock followed. Eva lifted her head and sat up straight. After the third knock, the door creaked open a fraction and a sliver of light crept into the room like someone had taken a slice out of a dark chocolate cake.

'Are you going to lurk in the shadows all day?' Eva said, cutting into the silence.

The door opened a little wider.

'Shut it behind you,' Eva added, her voice clear and her request concise.

The door closed and the corners of Eva's lips curled. *Good.*

'Come here,' Eva commanded.

Her stomach twitched as the footsteps crept slowly across the floor. 'That's far enough, thank you.'

Eva allowed a silence to fill the air for just long enough to edge on intimidating.

'Sit. There's a chair waiting for you.'

Eva waited a moment until the shadow of a body crouched.

'So. Do you have what it takes to join us here in Ignite Technologies?'

'I think so,' he said.

'You think so,' Eva echoed dryly. 'Well, unless you know so, you may as well get your ass the hell out of my office right now.'

'Your office?' he questioned.

Eva's eyes pinched hearing his tone.

'Have you heard otherwise?'

'I know this company was started by Julian Harte.'

'Yes. It was. Is there some point to this history lesson?' Eva questioned sternly.

He didn't reply.

'You have the audacity to question my authority?' Eva continued.

'I apologise.'

'Don't apologise. It makes you weak. You're not weak, are you? This company has no room for weakness.'

'One thing I have never been, Mrs. Harte, is weak,' he said, the confidence in his tone was giving Eva a hot flush.

'Good,' she said, hiding her attraction to his voice. 'I have your resume. It makes for impressive reading.'

'Thank you.'

'One thing it neglects to mention is your ability to make the boss come three times before breakfast.'

'Mrs. Harte, I believed we proved that already this morning, didn't we?'

Eva stood up slowly from behind the desk, her back yielding a little to the weight of her expanding belly. She flicked on the light and smiled at the beautiful man waiting for her in the centre of the room.

'How's my baby today?' Julian asked walking towards his wife.

'She's fine,' Eva said rubbing her belly.

'I meant you,' Julian replied turning his wife around to gently massage her neck with the tips of his thumbs.

Eva groaned gently, enjoying Julian gently work the knots out of her neck. 'Oh. Oops. I'm fine, too. Except your daughter thinks my ribs are a pillow and she's definitely taking some Irish dancing lessons in there.'

'Well, I hope she's not too comfortable in there. I can't wait to meet her.'

'Me, too. And I can't wait to see my feet again. The doctor did say labour could start any day now.'

'He did, didn't he? I like that doctor.'

'You just like him because he said the best way to bring on labour is sex.'

Julian gently spun his wife back around and shot her his signature coquettish smile. 'Who am I to argue with a medical genius?'

'Are you sure you're ready for this? Eva said concerned.

'We've had nine months to prepare. We're ready,' Julian replied.

'You know that's not what I meant. I meant are you ready to come back to work?'

'Fuck, Eva. You'd wrap me up in cotton fucking wool if you could. Yes, I'm ready. I've been working from home for months now. I'm sure the little extra effort of getting my arse into the office every day won't kill me.'

'I know, I know. Sorry. I just worry.'

'Well. Let's put it this way. If I had the energy to fuck you doggy style on the kitchen table last night, I'm sure I can manage sitting behind that desk for a few hours every day.' Julian's coquettish grin sent a wave of lust rushing down Eva's spine.

'Lock the door,' Eva said meeting Julian's smile head on with a sultry twinkle in her eyes as he did as she asked.

'I love you, Mrs. Harte,' Julian said scooping Eva into his arms and laying her back against the office couch.

Eva glanced at the hard bulge in Julian's trousers. She wrapped her fingers around his tie and pulled him close to her. He placed a hand at each side of her shoulders and held his weight just above her, careful not to lean on her bump. Her pregnancy was driving his sex drive through the roof, but he was gentle and tentative and his throbbing cock and deep groan were the only signs of his urgency. She ran her tongue over his bottom lip and exhaled with a soft moan.

'I love you too, Mr. Harte. Let's play.'

End of Round Three.

Game over.

# The End

## About The Author

USA Today bestselling author Brooke Harris is a self-diagnosed romance addict. Realising at the age of seven that being a real person and not a cartoon character may prove a hindrance when applying for a role as a Disney Princess, she decided to create her own stories. As a grown up Brooke tried swapping the heels and tiaras in her stories for sex and revenge and published her first book, Rules of Harte in 2014. The Harte Series went on to become a #1 international bestseller.

Brooke lives in Kildare, Ireland with her young family. She daydreams about a climate where it doesn't rain every day, but secretly she loves the green fields and heritage of Ireland.

Brooke also writes Psych-thriller as her alter ego Janelle Harris.

Made in the USA
Las Vegas, NV
15 September 2021